HE KISSED HER.

It wasn't a conscious act. Maybe it was just another delaying tactic, since everything she said was dead-center right. If he distracted her with a kiss, maybe she wouldn't realize what she'd figured out. Or maybe he just wanted to taste that too-smart mouth and get up close and personal with her ski slope of a nose. Maybe he just wanted to press her against the tree trunk and possess the woman who saw things too clearly.

She was startled. Of course she was. He'd moved with shifter speed because it had been the act of his grizzly. But she didn't fight him. After a split second of frozen surprise, she softened against him. Her gasp opened her mouth, and he wasted no time tasting her. And now was when he expected her to bite his tongue off or shove him away. Instead, she pushed at him with her tongue. Hot and fierce, they dueled while her hands gripped his upper arms, squeezing them enough to make him growl with hunger.

Then she did it. A little whimper of a sound that came from deep within her. He felt it pass through her lips and knew it for what it was: *yes*.

BOUND BY SHADOWS

ALSO BY KATHY LYONS

BOUND BY SHADOWS

KATHY LYONS

FOREVER
New York   Boston

Copyright © 2016 by Katherine Grill

Cover design by Daniela Medina.
Cover copyright © 2020 by Hachette Book Group, Inc.

Forever
Hachette Book Group
1290 Avenue of the Americas, New York, NY 10104
read-forever.com
twitter.com/readforeverpub

Originally published as *The Bear Who Loved Me* by Forever in September 2016

Mass market reissue edition: July 2020

Forever is an imprint of Grand Central Publishing. The Forever name and logo are trademarks of Hachette Book Group, Inc.

The publisher is not responsible for websites (or their content) that are not owned by the publisher.

The Hachette Speakers Bureau provides a wide range of authors for speaking events. To find out more, go to www.hachettespeakersbureau.com or call (866) 376-6591.

ISBNs: 978-1-5387-3619-7 (mass market), 978-1-4555-4091-4 (ebook)

Printed in the United States of America

OPM

10 9 8 7 6 5 4 3 2 1

BOUND BY SHADOWS

CHAPTER 1

M ore. Power.

Thoughts came slowly to Carl Carman, but each word reverberated with power. That was the best part of being a grizzly bear. Simple words meant simple, strong deeds. Human complexities were nonexistent in this state, though they echoed in the back of his mind. He was on a mission, had come to this Christmas tree field on a clan purpose. That he took joy in what he did was a trivial detail.

Now.

He braced his legs, shoved his claws deep, and then he thought it. One word, and the power crashed through every cell in his body.

Destroy.

He did.

What he held, he uprooted.

What he gripped, he crushed.

Whatever he touched, he tore apart.

Joy.

He grinned, though he grunted with effort. He tasted blood—his own—and the coppery tang was sweet. Human language tried to intrude in this moment, but the grizzly had no interest in it. His language was action, power delivered with thrilling ease. And he liked to rip things apart. So he continued and was content.

Until something else disturbed him. Red and blue flashes across his retinas. At first he flinched away from the lights, but they roused the rational part of him. Red. Blue.

Police.

With a roar of fury, he began to tuck the animal away. His bear fought the shift, holding on to his shape with every ounce of his determination. But in this, the man was stronger, the mind crueler. With steadfast will, he folded the grizzly into an envelope in his mind. It had taken him years to master it. A thing that large doesn't origami into a tiny flat rectangle easily.

His bones shifted and most of the fur thinned and disappeared, though some fell to the ground. His face tightened, and the strength in his arms and claws pulled inside, shrinking as it was tucked away. He straightened, the grizzly hump now gone as the energy coiled tight inside. His eyes burned. Damn, how they burned. But in time that last vestige of dark power would fade and his normal cool green color would return. Quiet control and long, complex sentences would be his norm. Though his first words as a human were always the last snarl of his bear.

"Shit."

"And Merry Christmas to you, too," said a familiar female voice, though that particular holiday had passed months ago. His vision settled, and he saw

Tonya dressed in her patrol uniform as she leaned against her squad car. The lights were still flashing, and at dawn, those colors would be seen far and wide.

"Flip off those lights," he growled as he started searching for his pants. He was out here swinging in the breeze for all to see, and though that rarely bothered him, naked and vulnerable was not a good idea around her.

She opened the door of the squad car and used one hand to flip off the lights while the other aimed her phone at him. Jesus, she was taking pictures.

"I'll tear that thing out of your hand," he snarled, "and I won't be gentle."

"Promises, promises," she said with a sigh. But she did drop the phone. "Doesn't matter. I already got my holiday screensaver." She pushed off the car and sauntered over, her hips swinging in a tantalizing rhythm. Tonya Kappes had short honey-blond hair, modest curves on her tall, muscular frame, and a dangerous look in her eyes that had once tantalized his grizzly like honey. Now it just made him tired. "See?"

She was hard to miss. He might not want to marry her, but that didn't stop him from appreciating her feminine charms. But then a moment later, he realized she was talking about the image on her phone, flipped around for him to see.

Hell. "Give me that."

She tried to pull away, but he was faster and stronger. He caught her wrist and squeezed until the cell dropped into his other hand. She might have fought him more, but a glare from him had her quieting, her head tilted to the side in submission. Then he looked down. There, full screen on the phone, was a video of him as a grizzly bear methodically destroying a field of Christmas trees. The telltale silver streak down his back flashed clear in the dawn light.

"Why would you record this?" he asked.

She flashed him a coy look that only pissed him off. "I like watching you work."

Bullshit. She liked collecting blackmail material on people. She'd never used it, as far as he knew, but that didn't stop her from gathering intel on everyone. It was just part of her character and probably helped her be a good cop. But that didn't mean he had to like it. With a quick flick of his thumb, he initiated a factory reset of her phone.

"Hey!" she cried when she saw what he'd done. "That's evidence!"

"You here to arrest me?"

"You did just destroy Nick Merkel's best tree field."

"It had to be done, and you know it."

Her lips compressed into a flat line. "The Merkels' farm brings a boatload to the local economy. Hurting this field damages everyone."

"He refused a direct order to fix his pesticide platform." Pesticides were a fact of modern agriculture, and most farmers were extra careful about the area where the chemicals were mixed and stored. Not Nick Merkel. Spills were common, and his platform leaked like a sieve. But he didn't seem to care because the runoff went off his property. Too bad for him that Carl cared. A lot. "He's leaking poison into the groundwater."

She nodded, grim anger on her features. "So kill him and be done with it."

"You'd rather I murder him than destroy his prize field." It wasn't a question. He knew that shifter law gave him the right to kill anyone in his clan who openly disobeyed him. But the man in him kept looking for a more civilized punishment. Not so for Tonya.

"He's got a wife and two sons to carry on the farm. They'll fix the platform and still bring in money to the area."

Carl didn't answer. Tonya was a cop through and through. That meant black-and-white law and swift justice. If kids vandalized a building, they went to jail. If a man poisoned the land, he got killed. For the most part, shifter law bowed to human law, but there were two unbreakables. Don't hurt the land. Don't disobey the alpha. Nick Merkel had done both.

Something in the Merkel bloodline was just ornery. The man had been a thorn in Carl's side since Carl had stepped into his position as the alpha of the Gladwin grizzly shifters eight years ago. But Carl had seen firsthand what happened when a leader took the law into his own hands. He had sworn his tenure as Maximus of their mid-Michigan clan would not be one of terror and vigilante justice. So he'd done one step short of murder. He'd destroyed a field of Merkel's Christmas trees, cutting the bastard's pocketbook instead of his jugular.

"It won't work," Tonya said. "You'll have to kill him eventually."

"And then they'll crucify me for killing one of our own." He knew because that's what had happened when he'd taken control of the clan. Another idiot had challenged him, and he'd let his grizzly out. One bloody death later, and Carl was the acknowledged alpha. But then the widow had started grumbling. And before long, others had agreed that an alpha should never kill one of his own.

"It's an endless cycle," Tonya agreed. "You can't stop it. So get on with the next step and kill him. Deal with the next step when it happens."

"Just help me find my damn pants," he grumbled, unwilling to admit that there wasn't a way out.

Her lips curled into a slow smile. "They're locked in my trunk."

Carl's head whipped back to her. "Why?"

She shrugged, a roll of her shoulders that set her breasts to bouncing. "Evidence."

"Blackmail, you mean."

She chuckled, a low throaty sound. "Or just a way to keep you naked for a little bit longer."

She took a step back, her gaze rolling slowly down his torso. Jesus, she was bold. She had a way of making even the most exhibitionist of his set feel dirty in a completely teenage, horny, fuck-'em-fast-and-furious kind of way. But he'd left those hormones behind years ago.

Then he caught her scent. "You're in heat."

Damn it, if he hadn't been so absorbed in dealing with Nick Merkel, he would have noticed it right off the bat. No wonder he was keyed up around her.

She arched a brow. "Ticktock goes the biological clock."

"Give me my clothes. I am not fucking you. And

especially not in the middle of a destroyed Christmas tree field."

She chuckled. "I don't care where we do it, Carl, but we gotta do it."

"No, we really don't."

He watched hurt flicker in her eyes. It didn't even touch her face, but her eyes flinched, and it was more telling on her than a scream on anyone else.

He didn't want to insult her. He had some warm feelings for her. They'd known each other all their lives, but cuddling up to her was like snuggling with a live hand grenade. He could control her. She always submitted to him eventually, but who wanted to spend his off hours in a constant game of dominance and submission? He wanted someone he could relax and have a beer with. Around Tonya, he'd be on duty as the Gladwin Max 24/7.

"All right," she said as she folded her arms across her chest. Her breasts plumped nicely, and his bear took notice. The rest of him was seeing that despite her words, Tonya had not given in. "Let's look at this logically." She almost sneered the last word. Grizzly clans were not known to be deep thinkers. Something he daily tried to change.

"Not until I'm dressed."

She didn't move. "Our bears are compatible. We established that as teenagers."

"Everyone's compatible at sixteen." And back then, they had "compatted" as much as possible for a hot, horny month. But even at sixteen, he had grown tired of the constant power play.

"You're Maximus now, but you need a strong wife at your side to hold the position. Merkel openly defied you. Unless you do a massive show of strength, more will follow. The last thing we need is a civil war inside the clan."

He knew this. It had been burning through his brain ever since Merkel had refused to fix his platform. Carl had tried to sic the EPA on the man, hoping that human justice would help him out, but the organization was overloaded and undermanned. The earliest they could get someone out to check on violations was three weeks away. Hence his morning rampage.

"We're short on numbers as it is," he growled. "I'm not going to murder my own people."

"You don't have to," she said. "I will."

"Tonya!"

"I'm a cop and the strongest she-bear in a hundred miles. Get me pregnant and my brothers will line up to support you."

"They could line up without me knocking you up."

She shook her head. "That's not how it works and you know it."

True. Family loyalty trumped clan groupings all the time. It was the reason Merkel's wife and sons hadn't taken care of Nick themselves. That kind of betrayal was nonexistent within shifter communities. Tonya's family was large and powerful, and there were rumblings of them splitting off to establish their own clan. Or of them taking over his. That would all end the moment he impregnated Tonya. If she became his Maxima, then that would fold her family into his, locking up the leadership for generations to come.

But he just couldn't do it. They'd drive each other

insane inside a year. Besides, he had a better idea, but first he had to end any romantic ideas between the two of them.

"I think of you like a sister," he began, and it was the God's honest truth.

She didn't argue. Instead, her gaze drifted down. The shift was slow and deliberate, and he forced himself to let his hands go lax, opening up his entire body for her perusal.

Flat. Flaccid. And absolutely uninterested despite the fuck-me pheromones she gave off.

She didn't speak. There was no need to. She simply lifted up the car key fob and pressed a button. The trunk popped open, and he finally got his hands on his clothes.

They didn't speak as he dressed. He didn't even want to look at her. He'd hurt her, and the guilt weighed heavily on him. Maybe the others were right. Maybe there just wasn't enough bear in him to effectively lead the clan. His uncle had been so much bear he was almost feral. When he'd been Max, he'd killed with impunity, destroyed at random, and taken the most powerful she-bear by force. It had been human cops who had killed him—with Carl's father's help—opening up their clan to another way to rule. Logic and law—human concepts that the Gladwin shifters desperately needed.

Ten years later, Carl had stepped into power, but everyone seemed to think he was more man than bear. He couldn't kill without exhausting all other possibilities. And he couldn't fuck the most power-ful she-bear around just because she was in heat. Which left him with a fracturing clan and his best ally hurting as she answered a call on her radio. Some drunk teens were cow-tipping a few miles to the east.

"I have to go," she said as she climbed into her cruiser and shut the door. But the window was still open, so he leaned in.

"Tonya, you're still a valuable member of the clan. Maybe my most—"

"Save it. I've heard it all." They'd had this argument in one form or another since they were old enough to marry. The only sop to his guilt was that she wanted the power of Maxima way more than she wanted him.

"I have a better idea," he said. "Be my beta."

She froze, her eyes widening in shock. "Alan's your beta."

His brother, Alan, had served as his second from the very beginning. It kept the power in the family, but Alan had never shifted. The grizzly DNA had missed him, and the man couldn't hold the position for much longer. Privately, Carl believed that's what had sparked Merkel's latest round of disobedience. The idiot hoped to force Carl into making a compromise and giving him the beta honor.

Never going to happen. He needed someone he could trust as his second.

"I know it's unorthodox," he continued, "but I can't think of anyone better."

"Unorthodox? A female beta is unheard of! You think you have problems with Merkel now? Every shifter in the state will be calling you a pansy-assed *human*."

A big insult in the shifter community. Everyone

seemed to believe that the animal side was the power center. The *male* animal. But if any female could change their minds, it was Tonya.

"A female beta makes the clan look weak. Those Detroit bastards will be on us in a split second."

"The Detroit clan has their own problems. They're not looking to start a war with us." He hoped.

"You should ask one of my brothers."

He'd thought of that, but he didn't trust them like he trusted Tonya. He'd known her since they were children. Everyone expected them to marry, so they'd been shoved together from their earliest moments. He knew the way she thought and which way she would jump. In most things, their opinions aligned, though she tended to more of a black-and-white rule of the jungle, while he tried to think a problem through. All of that added up to her being an excellent beta.

"I choose you. Swear unwavering loyalty to me, and we can hold the clan together without marriage. That's what you really want, anyway."

She arched a brow. "You underestimate your attraction as a mate."

"Bullshit. You want the power."

"And the hot sex."

Carl rolled his eyes. "So get a gigolo and be my beta."

She shook her head slowly, not in denial but in stunned amazement. "You're trying to drag the shifter community into a modern mind-set. It's going to backfire on you. We're just not as logical as you." To her credit, she didn't sneer the word "logical" like most shifters would.

"Will you do it? I can announce it at the next clan meeting." He needed time to tell Alan, and that was not going to be a comfortable discussion.

"Yes," Tonya said, being typically decisive. Then she pushed the car into drive, but she didn't move. "One more thing. You had a message. That's why I came out here to find you."

He frowned. Damn it, she should have told him that first thing instead of trying to trap him into mating. "What?"

"There's trouble in Kalamazoo."

"What?" The word exploded out of him, but Tonya didn't hear it. She'd already hit the gas and was roaring away.

Just as well, he thought as he sprinted for his truck. Even clothed, there was no way to hide his reaction at the mention of that place where *she* lived. He hit the freeway with his erection lying hard and heavy against his thigh.

CHAPTER 2

Becca Weitz's hands worked so fast they were almost a blur. Fortunately, she could be blind-folded and still make fondant turrets for Cinderella's castle. After five espresso drinks, she could sculpt walls and lay in a moat, too, if the princess wanted extra protection on her specialty birthday cake. And if the little girl was prone to horror, Becca could add in flying monkeys without breaking a sweat.

What she couldn't do was force one fifteen-year-old boy to call her to say he was home safe from track practice.

The jangle of the bakery's doorbell sounded, and Becca froze in place. She was in the back, so she couldn't see who entered, but her mind's eye conjured her nephew as he sheepishly thudded into her place of business. He'd apologize for not calling, then show her an A+ biology test. She'd curse his forgetfulness, then they'd hug out last night's fight, and all would be well.

Except instead of Theo's voice, she heard the low rumble of an adult male. A customer, then, and she was glad that she had Stacy to handle the sales. Until Theo called, all she'd be good for was making cake castles. So she turned her attention back to the cake's battlements. Maybe add some crenellation?

"You can't go back there!" Stacy's annoyed words were buried under a man's deep voice.

"Miss Weitz? Do you have a moment?"

Both voices startled her enough that she jumped, knocking her elbow into the newly decorated battlements. On a normal day, she could have caught the unstable walls, but today she was jacked up on caffeine and worried about Theo. What she didn't ruin in her fumbling fell to the floor with a dull splat.

"Fudge!" she cursed, more furious with herself than her intruder. Caffeine and delicate cake structures never mixed. But that didn't stop her from glaring at the man who…oh shit, he was big.

She took a deep breath as she placed him in her memory. Carl Carman, or Mr. Max as the kids called him, was the head of Theo's summer camp program. But since they'd met only outdoors, she'd never seen how the man could fill a doorway—not just with his height but with shoulders that stretched on forever. To his credit, he wasn't trying to be intimidating. If anything, he looked horrified as he stared at the cake remains. She, on the other hand, had ample nervous energy to burn off.

"Stay back!" she ordered. He hadn't moved, but she barked the order as if he were crashing into her battlements.

He froze, blocking the doorway as Stacy peered around his shoulder. "Oh hell," the girl said. "Is that the Smithsons' cake?"

"No," Becca answered as she waved at a whole line of princess castles and assorted cupcakes. "That's over there."

Stacy whistled. "You've been busy."

"Yeah." When she got stressed, she made castles. And thanks to the arguments with her moody teenage ward, she now had eight princess homes. Well, seven, given that one was on the floor.

Meanwhile, Mr. Big and Apologetic gestured to a broom in the corner. "Can I help clean up?"

Becca took a breath and forced herself to be rational. It wasn't Mr. Max's fault that she was überjumpy, but she didn't like big men. They tended to throw their weight around, both physically and metaphorically. And in her experience, handsome big men were the worst.

"I've got it," she said as she grabbed the broom. She also glanced at Stacy, silently letting her know that everything was okay. "You can stay there and tell me why you're in my kitchen."

He twitched, his shoulders hunching slightly. He obviously wasn't used to being given orders, but his tone remained polite. Almost friendly. "I'm not sure if you remember me—"

Of course she remembered him. How many huge, handsome men wandered through her life? Exactly two, and the first one was her home again/gone again father. "You're Mr. Max, but summer camp is months away."

"Call me Carl. Max is just what the kids call me."

She'd be calling him Mr. Max because...well, because he was big and handsome and she couldn't think straight around that. "Theo wants to stay the whole summer this year," she said, wondering again how she was going to afford that. "He's hoping that he could be a junior counselor or something."

"I got his application already. And, yes, we'd be happy to have him, but that's not—"

"That's great news," she said with false cheer. The doorbell jangled, and Stacy disappeared to handle the customer. That left Becca alone with Mr. Max, who seemed to be sniffing the room. Well, lots of people liked the smell of sugar, so she shouldn't find that weird. "I'll tell Theo as soon as I see him. He can call you for details." She looked again at her cell phone, hoping she'd missed a text during the cake disaster, but no luck. The screen remained stubbornly dark.

"That's great," he said, not sounding like it was great at all. Then he stepped farther into the room, his muscles rippling beneath his tee and his body dwarfing the remains of Cinderella's castle. "Do you know where he is right now? I need to talk to him face-to-face."

She swallowed. Trust the man to barrel right into her personal crisis. "Theo's still at track practice." She hoped. "Leave your card. I'll have him call you." She carefully turned her back on him. It was the only way to deal with obnoxious men.

"I'm sorry, Miss Weitz. I've been to the track field. Theo never showed up for practice."

She whipped around, her hands curled into fists. How dare he approach her adopted son without her permission.

Then the rest of his words penetrated.

Theo didn't show up for practice? But he lived for

track and field. Even as a freshman, he was headed toward being the school champion at the discus. But that didn't explain why this man had been looking for Theo. "You better start talking, Mr. Max, before I call the cops."

He held up his hands, doing everything he could to appear nonthreatening. She wasn't fooled. Just because he was big didn't mean he was slow. "I just wanted to talk to Theo. About the job and…some other things." Then he took another step into the room, his eyes tracking her closely. There was an intensity to the way he watched her that she found unnerving. "I'm friends with Amy. She told me that Theo has been difficult lately."

"Amy Baum, my next-door neighbor?"

He nodded as he moved even closer. She'd back up, but there wasn't a lot of maneuverability in her kitchen. "The walls are thin, and she's heard stuff."

This was getting way too personal. He was too close, literally and figuratively. So she poked the man straight in the chest. "He's a teenager who lost his mother. Of course he's moody." And argumentative. And forgetful. And *missing*.

He took hold of her hand, firmly pulling it down and curling her finger into his palm. His hands were large and warm, but what she noticed most was that his completely enveloped hers, and he didn't let her go. "I know. Look, Theo and I have a good relationship. I was in town and I thought I'd stop by. Maybe talk to him."

"Because you're such good friends."

"Because I'm an older male who has been through…puberty."

There was a hitch in his voice right before the word "puberty." She had no idea what it meant, but it didn't settle her nerves any. What did she know about hormonal boys? She'd grown up in an all-female household since she was eight, when her dad skipped. And damn it, Mr. Max still had hold of her hand.

"Come on, Miss Weitz. You've known me for years. I'm just trying to help."

That was true. Theo had been going to Camp Max since elementary school. She wasn't even sure how her sister had first heard of the place tucked next to Gladwin State Park. But Theo had loved it, and so first Nancy, then Becca, had saved every year to afford the place. She'd never heard one bad word about Mr. Max from anyone, including Theo, who lately hadn't had a good word to say about anything. Which meant that the man probably was here just trying to help out.

But damn it, he was *crowding* her, and she couldn't think with him so close.

"Why don't you sit down? Tell me what's been going on?"

His words were mesmerizing and had a tone of command that she resented. And yet, she did exactly what he suggested. Her shoulders slumped, and she dropped onto a stool and stared at Mr. Max's boots. They were workman's boots, hard, scuffed, and dirty. Normally, it would drive her insane to have those things in her kitchen, but for some reason, she found them reassuring. Normal guys had dirty boots. And Mr. Max had the most normal boots she'd ever seen, even if they were massively huge.

But she wasn't going to just sit there and let him tower over her. "You sit, too," she said, indicating another stool. "Here. Fill your hands with these." She passed him a daisy cupcake and a tulip cookie. "Somehow big guys aren't so threatening with their hands filled with baked goods. But before you eat, tell me what you found out at school."

He didn't like moving away from her. She could tell by the way his eyes narrowed and his shoulders twitched. But he didn't argue with her either as he sat down. The stool didn't creak under his weight, which she counted as a good sign. Then he picked up the cookie, sniffed it, and neatly bit through the entire flower.

"Theo was in classes all day, according to his friends," he said after he'd chewed and swallowed. "But he never made it to practice."

"Which friends?"

"Tommy, Willy, and...um...Bruce?"

"Bruno." They were Theo's best friends, all on the track team with him. "They usually go to track together."

Mr. Max nodded. "They said he was being pissy and wanted to be alone. Their words, not mine."

"They're right. He has been pissy." She sighed. "We got into a huge fight last night about his English grade."

"Did he storm off?"

"If slamming his bedroom door and blasting his music at a hundred and ten decibels counts as storming off, then yes. That's what he did."

"But he didn't leave?"

She shook her head. "He knows I'd freak. He

might be angry, but he's not cruel." She picked up the knife and started absently cutting a sheet of fondant. It was the only thing she could do to keep herself from breaking down. "You think he ran off?"

"We shouldn't jump to conclusions. Where might he go?"

She swallowed. "I already called the parents of his friends. They're all on the lookout for him, so if he stopped by, they'd call me." Still, she grabbed her cell phone just in case. And then, because it had been at least ten minutes, she dialed Theo's number.

"Voice mail," she said as she thumbed it off. No point in leaving another message after the last five. She sighed, willing Theo to call. To her surprise, a ring tone did sound, but it wasn't hers. It was Mr. Max's. He whipped his phone out with practiced ease.

"What have you found?" he said, his voice more brusque than she'd ever heard before.

She waited, watching his face as his expression tightened. When he noticed her watching him, he flashed her a quick smile. It wasn't reassuring. Especially with his next words.

"You're sure? Definitely Theo?"

Hope sparked blindingly fierce, but his expression wasn't happy. If anything, it was grimmer.

She couldn't keep quiet. "Have they found him? Is he okay?"

He didn't answer her. "Any point in sticking around there longer?" Pause. "Okay. I'll meet you at the boy's home. We'll regroup there." He snapped the phone shut and then turned to her. But he didn't speak. Instead, he just tightened his mouth into a frown.

"What?" she demanded after five long seconds of nothing.

He pushed up from his stool and seemed to prowl closer. It was a weird thing to think, especially for a man his size, but his movements were so smooth and fluid, she straightened up in instinctive alarm.

"What do you know?" she said, her voice low and angry.

His gaze sharpened at her tone, and he stopped moving. Stilled like an animal caught in the glare of a flashlight. And then he straightened. His shoulders rolled back, his jaw tightened, and his expression flattened. He'd obviously come to some sort of conclusion, but what kind, she had no clue. So she held her breath and waited for whatever he needed to say.

"I'm not just someone who runs a camp for kids."

Her gut cramped tight, but she kept breathing. Her voice even came out in some semblance of normal. "What else do you do?"

"I run a private investigation company. We're small potatoes, mostly. Just me and sometimes a few others."

"What do you investigate?" If he said missing or abducted children, she was going to lose it right here next to a fondant castle wall.

"Nothing all that exciting. But when I heard that Theo was having troubles, I called a friend of mine. He was in the area, anyway, and he's the best tracker I know."

"Tracker? Like a moose or bear hunter?"

He made a choking sound, quickly recovered, then he shook his head. "Well, he can track animals, but…Look, I just asked him to poke around the school, okay? He knows Theo's scent."

"I beg your pardon?"

He grimaced. "It's a figure of speech. He helps out at the camp and he knows Theo."

"So what did he find out?"

Mr. Max rubbed his trimmed beard, scratching at his jaw as if something bothered him. Then he rounded the table and gently pulled her up from her stool. "Theo was afraid."

She gripped his arm. She didn't even know she'd reached out, but suddenly she was pulling on his muscular forearm, squeezing his solid strength. "Afraid? Why? And how would he know that?"

"He smelled—I mean, he talked to some kids. They said he seemed spooked or something."

"Which kids?"

He reached for her coat and handed it to her. His expression had tightened down, telling her that he didn't want to say more. "It's not something to get alarmed about." He spoke with a calm assurance that she wanted desperately to believe. "Boys his age get scared all the time. I know a guy who used to completely freak every time a girl talked to him."

"That's not Theo."

"I know. I know." He pressed his hand over hers where she was still clutching his arm. One hand and it covered her two with gentle ease. "My friend is going to meet us at your apartment. He'll tell us everything there."

She swallowed. "Maybe I should call the police."

"No." One word, barked more than spoken. Then he huffed out a breath when she stared at him in alarm. "They won't do anything for twenty-four hours."

"But he's a kid. They can put out an amber alert—"

"Let's just go talk to Bryn, okay? It's too early to panic."

Easy for him to say. She'd been panicking for hours now. "Okay," she finally said. She wanted to see this investigator for herself.

Bryn turned out to be a long, lean man with narrow eyes and a habit of sniffing things. He was subtle about it, but she could see his nose twitch in an animalistic kind of way. It was creepy as hell and she wouldn't have let him in her apartment if Mr. Max hadn't already swung the door wide for him.

"Hey, Bryn. This is Rebecca Weitz, Theo's aunt and guardian."

"Nice to meet you, Ms. Weitz. Don't you worry about Theo. He's got a good head on his shoulders, and he'll come through this just fine."

At least he was a polite weirdo. Then his words penetrated her mind and she spoke a little more sharply than she intended. "Come through what, exactly? What do you think happened?"

Mr. Max answered quickly, clearly trying to calm her frazzled nerves. "He didn't mean anything by it. Just that you shouldn't worry."

Oh no. No way was he playing big protector now, telling her not to worry like she was Ma Kettle in the wild frontier. "I'll decide when I worry, thank you very much. And I would really like to hear what Mr. Bryn meant. Exactly." Nothing like pulling out a guy's full name to make him respond.

"It's Bryn Walsh, ma'am, and, um, Theo's fifteen, right?"

"Yes."

"Well, that's a little young to be...uh, wandering off, but it's not that unusual. Shows he's mature for his age."

"Make sense, Mr. Walsh."

"Look...," he said as he stepped farther into the apartment. Then his eyes darted to a sweatshirt dumped casually onto the back of the couch. Picking it up, he brought it to his nose and spoke through the muffling fabric. "This his?"

"What the hell are you—"

Mr. Max interrupted. "He's tracking, Becca. I know it's...odd...but it's what he does."

Bryn shot Mr. Max a dark look, but he didn't stop sniffing the sweatshirt while wandering the living room. By the time he eased open Theo's bedroom door, Becca had her cell out to call the cops.

Mr. Max was there before her, grabbing her wrist and lifting the phone from her hand. "Just give him a moment. Please." He was clearly giving her an order despite his polite phrasing. She agreed, mostly because she didn't have much of a choice. Though when Bryn stuck his sniffer into her bedroom, she just about exploded. Fortunately, he didn't stay there long. He stepped back out and eyed Mr. Max.

"She's Theo's guardian?"

"And only living relative," Mr. Max answered.

"Then you better bring her into the fold because Theo's definitely about to pop."

"What?" Becca jerked her hand out of Mr. Max's

grip. Well, she tried to anyway. There was no escaping him.

"So you think he changed?" asked Mr. Max, his voice tight.

Bryn shook his head. "Not here. And not at the school. But it's coming. Soon."

Which is when Becca lost it. They were talking like they knew something about Theo. Something important that she didn't know. And damn it, she was his aunt and his only family. "Somebody better start explaining things to me now or I'm going to start screaming."

"I will, Becca, I swear," said Mr. Max, but his eyes were on Bryn. "What about that other thing? The reason you were here, in Kalamazoo, to begin with."

Bryn shrugged. "Don't know." Then he flashed Becca a rueful smile. "It'll be okay, Miss Weitz. Theo will be fine." Then he pulled up the hood on his jacket and headed for the door. "And, Max…"

"Yeah?"

"You'll get my bill in the morning."

She heard him grumble, deep in his chest. "You're all heart," he said, his tone wry.

"Someone's gotta feed the pack. Might as well be you." Then he was gone with a jaunty wave that was oddly graceful, given his general loose-limbed gait.

As soon as the door shut, Becca was ready. She tried to jerk her wrist out of Mr. Max's hand, yanking hard, but she was too slow. He'd already released her, which meant she stumbled from the force of her movement. He caught her by the elbow, steadying her with a firm grip, but she glared him away.

"Start talking. Why was he in Kalamazoo? What does it have to do with Theo?"

"Other business and nothing. He was just nearby, so I called on his talents."

"As a sniffing tracker."

"Yes."

"That's insane."

He scratched at his beard again, looking the most awkward she'd ever seen anyone appear. "Yeah," he said, drawing the word out. "Buckle up 'cause it's about to get weirder." Then he gestured to the couch. "Do you think we could sit down?"

She didn't want to sit. She was too keyed up, but she nodded because she figured arguing about this would delay things further. So she perched on the edge of a cushion while he sank into the sofa like an anchor into the seabed. And he still sat taller than she.

"What did he mean about Theo about to change?"

He leaned forward, setting his elbows on his knees. His gaze was steady—weirdly so—and there was no softness in him anywhere. "Surely you've noticed a difference in Theo. He's gotten surly, eats a ton, sleeps like the dead, then rouses like an...an angry bear."

"He's a teenage boy. Isn't that all of them?"

"Not like this. I heard he got into a fight at school. For no reason."

How the hell did he...? Amy, her next-door neighbor and confidante. "That's it. I'm never talking to Amy again."

"Don't blame her. She was keeping an eye on Theo for me."

An icy fist slid through her body. He'd been spying on her and Theo? "Just what kind of stalker creep are you?"

Mr. Max shrugged. The gesture would have been endearing if she wasn't so freaked. "One that has known about Theo since he was a boy and wanted to look out for him. In case this happened."

"What's 'this'?" she almost screamed.

"Theo's entering the First Change. He's a little young for it. It doesn't usually hit before sixteen, but with steroids in foods nowadays, kids are maturing faster."

"What the hell are you talking about?"

"I'm talking about Theo. Your nephew is a grizzly bear shifter."

Becca stared at him. She opened her mouth to ask him to repeat himself. To explain. To something, but nothing came out.

"I know. Werewolves get all the press. But there's all sorts of shifters in the world."

"Werewolves?"

"Yeah. Bryn's one. That's why he was sniffing everything."

"A werewolf?" He couldn't possibly have said what she thought she'd heard. Or be looking at her as if she should understand.

"Yes." He was getting frustrated. The one word came out clipped and a bit angry. "He's a werewolf. Theo's a were-bear, though we prefer being a little more specific. Were-grizzly, to be exact. And he's about to shift for the first time."

And then it all made sense. Normally, she would have caught on faster. If this were a usual day, her sense of sane and insane would have kicked in well before now. But she'd had that fight with Theo, so she'd been off her game. She didn't realize until now that Mr. Max was a stark raving lunatic. Fortunately, he'd set down her cell phone when he'd joined her on the couch. It was within reach if she was fast. And if she failed at that, then it was just another step to the front door.

"Becca? You're not saying anything."

"I'm just trying to process it, that's all."

"Look, I know you must think I'm insane, but it's all true."

"Sure. Werewolves. Bear shifters."

"Grizzly bears. He comes from a long, proud line of them."

She pushed to her feet. Let him think she was just pacing off her agitation. "I'm sure they're very proud."

"We're all through Michigan, but mostly around Gladwin because of the park. We like forests."

"That makes sense." It was a lie. Nothing made sense, but she'd managed to get within reaching distance of her phone. "I'm just...I'm gonna..." She pointed to the kitchen. "Maybe some more coffee."

He arched a brow. "Are you sure you need more caffeine? If I were you, I'd be reaching for a beer." He flashed her a lopsided smile. "Or a bottle. Or a keg."

Charming. The lunatic was being *charming*. She tried to smile back but didn't manage to pull it off. Which meant it was time to bolt.

She did it in one smooth move. She snatched up her cell phone and ran straight for the front door.

She wasn't an Olympic runner or anything, but she could be quick when she wanted to. She was highly motivated to be fast.

He was faster.

She barely got the door open when he was on her, pulling the cell from her hand and catching her about the waist. She started kicking him, but if it bothered him, she couldn't tell. Certainly not when he was lifting her off her feet and carrying her back into her apartment.

"Becca, listen to me!"

No way. No how.

She drew breath to scream.

She got half a breath in before he dropped a hand over her mouth. She tried to scream anyway, but it came out more as a muffled exclamation. And then every survival instinct she had kicked in. Every dirty fighting trick she ever knew. Every animalistic gouge through his skin, bite through his meaty palm, kick in the gonads, and scream tore through her system as if her life depended on them. She fought like she was a demon possessed.

And she still lost.

He was just too big.

Then he was pressing on her throat, cutting off her air.

Oh hell. Oh shit.

She couldn't breathe.

"I'm not going to hurt you, Becca. I swear!"

And that was one big fat lie because within seconds, there were dots in her vision. A few moments later, it all went black.

CHAPTER 3

Carl twisted in his desk chair at the quiet knock on his bedroom door.

"Come in," he said, keeping his voice low.

He wasn't sure he wanted to have the conversation with his brother here, but he was reluctant to leave Becca alone in his massive bed. He didn't want her to wake and jump to all the wrong conclusions. In the end, his need to stay with her was stronger than his brother's possible embarrassment.

Alan pushed open the door. His head was tilted to the side, exposing his neck, as was appropriate when entering an alpha's bedroom. His lanky frame was stooped as well, though his gaze missed nothing. Not Carl killing time at his desk or the unconscious Becca tucked neatly into his sheets.

"Did Nick go home or into town?" Carl asked, not because he really cared but as a way to distract Alan's attention away from Becca.

"Town," Alan answered. "Did you really destroy an entire acre by yourself?"

Carl smirked. Nick Merkel had shown up an hour

earlier, screaming about the destruction of his field. He'd stopped short of accusing Carl—which showed the man had some brains—but he had not held back about his opinion of such wanton destruction. On a different day, Carl would have had it out with the man, but the last thing he needed was a grizzly confrontation while a kidnapped woman snoozed in his bed. Both situations required finesse, and he didn't want to deal with two at once.

Meanwhile, he kept his tone deadpan as he answered his brother. "I have no idea what you're talking about."

"Of course you don't," Alan said. He leaned against the doorframe, his gaze traveling unerringly to Becca, sleeping in Carl's massive bed. But he didn't speak about her. He knew better. His thoughts were still on the Nick Merkel annoyance. "Why don't you just kill the bastard?"

"Why is everyone pushing me to murder?" Carl grumbled, even though he knew the answer. He also knew that out of everyone, Alan would give him the most logical answer. That's because his brother had gotten shorted in the shifter DNA pool. As far as anyone could tell, the man was completely human, even if his eyes were Gladwin grizzly golden brown.

"He's outright defied you. And now he's going around telling everyone that destroying an acre of Christmas trees is the act of a coward."

Carl knew it wasn't his brother defying him. Don't shoot the messenger, and all that. But even so, his shoulders hitched, the grizzly hump thickening between his blades. Externally, nothing showed beyond a slight lift to his tee, but inside, the bear was roaring in fury and tearing at the restraints in Carl's mind. It wanted to rip through Alan on the way to eviscerating Nick. Moron grizzly. Why the hell didn't it ever understand that leading anyone—especially a clan of bear shifters—required deft handling, not brute strength?

So he carefully blew out his breath, letting his gaze land long and hard on Alan's exposed neck. His brother was submitting and that should mollify the alpha grizzly inside Carl. Meanwhile, he let his human mind grouse out loud, just to blow off steam. "Does the idiot want to die? Jesus, the man is almost sixty. I'd kill him with the first blow."

"He doesn't believe that. And he's talking so loudly, other people are starting to think the same." Alan straightened off the doorframe but didn't dare take a single step into the bedroom. Entering a grizzly's den was never safe, even for brothers. "I know you're trying to give a measured response, and in normal times that might work."

Carl snorted. Normal? When had life ever been normal for any shifter clan?

"But things are getting ugly in Detroit. It's the shifter Wild West over there, and people here are getting nervous. They think a powerful leader is the only way we'll survive."

"The last thing we need is a leader who will kill just because he can. Don't they remember what it was like under Uncle Winston?"

Alan shrugged. "People have short memories when they're scared."

"Tell me something I don't know."

His brother's eyes turned mischievous. "I rather think that's your job right now." His gaze traveled over Carl's shoulder to where Becca lay curled on her side. "That was quite a spectacle you created, carrying her in here like that. Very Neanderthal of you."

"I had to knock her out. She thinks I'm insane."

"So do we all, but you're usually more subtle with women."

"Har, har." He swiveled in his chair, unable to stop himself from tracing the outline of her body with his gaze. She was curvy in a lush kind of way, and her strawberry-blond hair was cut short to emphasize her sass. "Don't let her size fool you. She can fight." There'd never been any question that he would overpower her, but he'd been trying to go easy on her. His restraint had cost him in the form of inch-long gashes in his arms, not to mention the bruises near his groin.

"I wouldn't go around telling people that."

Carl nodded. Wouldn't Nick have a field day with that information? If people found out that a petite blond woman marked him in a fight, he'd have challenges from every direction.

Meanwhile, Alan's mind was still sorting through angles and possibilities. "You're sure Theo has changed? Just because a boy gets into fights doesn't mean he's about to shift."

"I'm not sure of anything, but Bryn was and he's got the better nose."

At the mention of Theo's name, Becca's fingers twitched. It wasn't a big movement, but it was enough to signal that she was awake and playing possum. Smart of her, but it wasn't going to work. Especially since he could smell the increased fear coming off her skin. Alan noticed, too, even without shifter senses. His next words were a repeat of what Carl already knew, but it would be reassuring for Becca to hear.

"We've got everyone on the lookout, including the friendly police. We'll find him and Justin."

Justin was a local from a strong shifter family. He'd gone missing late this afternoon. "God, I hate spring," Carl muttered. No matter what they did to make it easier, a bear's first shift was an incredibly dangerous time. The kids had no control as their bears ran amok and people tended to shoot wild grizzlies.

"You need to marry Tonya," Alan said in all seriousness. "It'll quiet the grumbling in the clan and you'll get laid every spring."

And right there was the opening he'd been waiting for. And yet, now that it came to it, Carl hated every word he had to say. "Actually, I wanted to talk to you about that." It was, after all, why he'd summoned Alan in the first place.

"Time for wedding announcements?" his brother said with a grin.

"I'm making her my beta."

Alan didn't respond at first beyond a quick snap of his chin. He was completely human, but he'd learned some grizzly habits, including the angry jut of his jaw and the tensing in his shoulders. And that submissive tilt to his head was completely gone.

Even that small act of defiance had Carl's grizzly in an uproar. Carl had to grip the sides of his chair to keep himself from responding to the visual challenge. Alan was a good fighter for a human, but he'd be mincemeat against Carl's bear. And, anyway, all the man needed was time to process the statement. To realize that it was the best solution all around.

He didn't.

"I have served well as your beta," he said, his voice tight and hard. "You handle the bear part, I've got the paperwork. It's not glorious, but it's damned necessary, and you know it."

"I do." Alan was a lawyer, and a damned fine one. He also had an organized mind and had kept the clan running when no one else could.

"But you think Tonya can do better." It wasn't a question.

Carl snorted. "Not a chance." He leaned forward, straining to keep the gesture nonthreatening. His grizzly did not like anyone questioning something he'd already decided. But the man knew he had to be diplomatic. "The beta position is about appearing powerful—"

"And I don't shift, so I'm out of the clan?"

"Like hell!" he snapped. It was all he could do to keep it from a roar. As it was, he jerked out of his chair. Out of the corner of his eye, he saw Becca twitch in fear, but that was more reaction than he got from Alan. The man hadn't even flinched. Fortunately, that meant he kept his neck exposed in a submissive gesture. "You are a Gladwin, and I'll kill anyone who says anything different."

Carl let the statement hang in the air. The man in him was terrified at that statement, but the grizzly wouldn't let him take it back. He would indeed kill anyone who dared suggest his brother wasn't a Gladwin, and Alan's expression softened when he realized that truth. But he wasn't completely mollified as he knotted his hands into fists.

"Tonya won't do the work of keeping the clan assets together. She's got a job, and even if she didn't, that isn't in her wheelhouse."

"Which is why I'd like to offer you a job. You'd be a well-paid employee of the Gladwins."

"You're a shifter clan, not a corporation."

"*We're* a shifter clan," he emphasized. "And your first task will be to create a legal entity for us. It's long past time for that to happen." He pushed a piece of paper into Alan's hand. It was the job offer, complete with a generous salary.

Alan didn't even look at it. Instead, his gaze went out the window in the direction of Chicago. Carl knew he had opportunities there, ones that had nothing to do with shifters or clan politics. Once, his brother had wanted to practice law in the big city, handling clients worth millions of dollars. But he'd turned those offers down to stay in Gladwin and help Carl as Max. Now would be the time for Alan to spread his wings and explore what he could do in the human world. But Carl didn't want to lose his brother. And the grizzly in him would not release an asset as valuable as the only trustworthy lawyer for miles.

"Don't leave. Not yet." The man in him wanted to soften the statement. He didn't want to order his brother to accept the job, but his grizzly issued commands and would not politely ask clan members to stay loyal. But Alan deserved all the respect he could give, which is why he forced himself to add one more sentence through clenched teeth. "Think about it."

Alan didn't answer. His golden brown eyes churned with emotions he wouldn't express, and Carl's grizzly wouldn't let him reach out in any way that would make him less dominant. Which left the brothers exactly nowhere. So it was just as well that Alan dipped his chin in a nod before backing out of the doorway.

One problem down, Carl thought as his bedroom door slid shut. Next? His gaze went back to Becca and the thick layer of guilt suffocating him since he'd knocked her out. He hated fighting women in general, but taking down Becca had been extra disastrous.

She was everything he valued in a woman. It wasn't just her body, which was lush enough to make his mouth water. No, it was the way she protected Theo. He'd been watching her since the first day she'd brought Theo to camp after her sister died. She'd been matter-of-fact as she settled him in the dorm. And once she'd gotten him squared away, she'd handed him a big box of homemade cookies to share and had kissed him good-bye. No muss, no fuss. Almost brusque. But he'd seen the way she'd teared up at her car. He'd noticed that she sent a letter daily and new baked goods often enough to make Theo the most popular kid at camp. And best of all, she'd overnighted him sweatpants when the weather had turned unexpectedly cold.

In short, she thought about the kid without smothering him. A nurturing woman who fought harder than most animals when threatened. Both bear and man in him had wanted to bend her over the minute he'd seen her in her kitchen surrounded by Cinderella castles. And none of that assuaged his guilt at knocking her out and carrying her to his bed in full view of everyone. Damn it, this was not how to ease a woman into the shifter community.

And while he tortured himself with guilt and lust, she slitted open her pale blue eyes, probably trying to sneak a peek. He'd been waiting, and so their gazes locked immediately.

"Take it slowly," he told her, his voice as soothing as he could make it. "That tranquilizer dart was meant for someone twice your size, but it was all I had on hand."

Her eyes widened at that and the fear scent spiked, but she kept her voice calm. Pretty damn impressive. "Where am I?" she asked.

"My bedroom." She abruptly paled, and he rushed to explain. "It's spring, so the whole community comes together to watch for the new shifters. That means we're packed to the gills and there isn't an extra bedroom. I'm planning to sleep in the cabin with the kids, so you'll have privacy, but I didn't want you to wake up alone."

"Quite a bit of consideration from the man who attacked me."

And there was that feisty side that made him harder than granite. Best not to show her that, though, so he adjusted the angle of his chair to keep his horniness hidden.

"I couldn't let you get the police involved. Not when Theo's on his way up here."

She lifted off the pillow, her eyes wide. "You've found him?"

God, he'd give anything to reassure her, but he couldn't lie to her. "Not yet. But we're pretty sure he's coming."

She dropped back on the bed with her eyes closed, the scent of despair filling the room. But a moment later, it was over. She was back in control, her eyes flashing blue fire as she pushed herself upright.

"You're right," she said, false cheer in her voice. "I'm sure Theo's going to show up here any moment. But in the meantime, how about I go back to my apartment just in case he goes home?"

"Amy's there. She'll call if he shows up."

"Right. Of course, but I'm his aunt and guardian. He—"

"He's coming here. It's a bear thing, Becca. After the First Change, we always come here."

She looked around. "To Camp Max?"

"To Gladwin State Park. Not all bear shifters, of course. Just my clan." He leaned forward. "But don't worry. We've got spotters out looking for him."

"Theo's in Kalamazoo. That's where we live. Two hundred miles south of here."

More like 180, but he knew she wouldn't appreciate the correction. "I know it sounds like a lot."

"Because it is a lot."

"But bears in their First Change do that kind of thing. They just do."

She dug her fists into her eyes. "Do you hear yourself? God, do you understand how insane you sound?"

He took a deep breath. "Yes, I do. Which is why I want to show you a video—"

She bolted. One second she was rubbing her eyes with her fists, the next she was inches short of the door. He caught her. Even startled, he was fast and she had no weight to drag him out of his seat. And this time he was prepared as she began to fight him.

Jesus, she was wiry.

He stood up out of his chair, carrying her as she kicked. Bright flashes of pain on his arms told him he'd have more bruises there. And then she reared back to head butt him.

That was the last straw. He could handle bruises, but her head was hard enough to give them both concussions. So he tossed her on the bed. She landed on her backside with an "oomph," and he hoped she'd stay down.

She didn't. Even before she'd finished bouncing, she was scrambling up. So he did the only thing he could think of that would keep her from getting hurt. He spread-eagled and dropped right on top of her. It took about two minutes of heavy scrabbling to pin her. She reached up and to the right to grab the lamp, so he nailed that arm first. The second fist came at his head, but he was prepared, and he slammed that down until both of her arms were trapped above and to either side of her head. As for her legs, nothing would do but for him to drop his knees between hers and spread them. She fought every second, but she had no leverage. And all through it, Little Carl got happier and hornier. By the time she stilled, they were both breathing heavily, their faces were inches apart, and his erection was a hot, stone pillar between them. No way to hide it.

"Get off me," she hissed.

"I'm going to hand you your phone," he said calmly, though it was damned hard given how her every breath pushed those soft, rounded breasts against his chest. "You can call 911. Tell them who you are and where you are. Will you listen to their answer, please? Will you trust me that much at least?"

She swallowed. It took her two tries to answer, but eventually she got the word out. "Okay."

"If you run, I'll have to stop you again. It's almost dark and it'd be dangerous for you to be out there by yourself. Not to mention how it'll scare the kids."

"I can't believe I brought Theo here every summer."

"It probably saved his life, Becca. Otherwise he'd be completely lost out there. We teach them survival skills and make sure they learn the safe places in the park. It's for exactly this reason. In case one of them shifts. Even in bear form they'll head for safety. They'll head where we taught them to go."

She didn't believe him. God, how stubbornly ordinary people clung to their beliefs. But in her defense, she hadn't seen anything to suggest he was telling the truth. She hadn't been quiet enough that he could give her any proof. So first he would have to show her that she was completely safe.

He had to get off her. Little Carl was beyond pissed at that, but he was not a man to be ruled by his dick. Or his bear, for that matter, which took long moments for him to slam back into its mental cage. It wanted to flip her onto her stomach, lift her ass up to him, and plunge in for the next week until she was pregnant. He rolled off her instead, pulled her cell phone out of his desk drawer, and tossed it to her.

She grabbed it eagerly and he watched as disappointment flashed through her expression. No call from Theo. Even now she was more worried about the boy than she was for herself. She then thumbed on the phone and hit 911.

"Hello?" she said when the dispatcher answered. It was a female voice—probably Dot—and thanks to his shifter hearing, he could make out both sides of the conversation. "Hello? I'm Becca Weitz, and I've been kidnapped."

"Hello, Miss Weitz. Thank you for calling. Are you there at Camp Max?"

"I'm... I don't know. I'm in Mr. Max's bedroom."

"Really?" Dot was obviously intrigued by that. Fortunately, she returned to a professional tone a moment later. "Officer Kappes is on her way there now to give you an update. We've notified Kalamazoo police as well with a full description of Theo, but we had to keep it low-key for obvious reasons. Don't worry, though. We'll find him right and tight. And welcome to the Gladwin clan. I always thought you'd be joining us one day. Glad to see it finally happened."

"Um. Yeah. Okay. Is, um, is there someone else I could speak to?"

"Sure there is. Here's Sergeant Mummert. Say something reassuring to the scared mom, will you, Hal?"

A moment later, Hal's deep voice came on the line. He said all the right things, an echo of everything Dot had said. None of it helped. He could see the despair grow on Becca's face the longer they went on. In the end, she thanked them politely and thumbed off her phone. Then she looked him hard in the eyes.

"You've convinced them all."

"Didn't have to convince them. Dot's got three shifter kids and has been right where you are now waiting for them to come through the First Change. Hal's not a shifter, but he was born and raised here. He's seen it enough to know." He leaned forward. "You're not alone, Becca. We're not here to hurt you. In fact, it's the opposite. We're trying to help."

"By knocking me out and dragging me—"

"To where Theo is going to come. I promise, Becca, it's a natural part of being a shifter."

She swallowed and looked away. He knew she was fighting tears but was too terrified to let them fall. He sat there looking at her, desperately searching for a way to make this better. He came up empty, so he decided that retreat was the better part of valor.

"Tonya's going to be here in a moment. That's Officer Kappes. You'll probably want to get a little more together before then. I'll be right out here."

"Am I a prisoner?"

He sighed. "The bathroom's through there." She looked toward the bathroom and he took the opportunity to lift the phone out of her hand. "And, yes, I suppose you're trapped here for the night. We're too shorthanded waiting for Theo and Justin. No one can drive you back to Kalamazoo."

"I'll take a cab."

His grizzly growled at her stubbornness. According to it, she was here in his den and that made her his. He even felt his shoulder blades tingle as the shift started to gather. Damn it, she had no idea what defying him did to his sanity. In the end, he managed to force out a curt sentence. "You can't leave yet."

Her chin rose an inch at that, and he could tell she was about to challenge him. Normally, he could control his reaction to defiance, but after their wrestling match, he was on the edge. One more challenge from her, and his grizzly was going to dominate her completely and damn the consequences.

"Listen carefully, Becca. This is real. We're grizzly bear shifters. We'll show you, but you have to calm down."

She frowned. "You're going to change into a bear? Right in front of me?" Thankfully her tone was less of a challenge and more like confused questions.

"Yes."

"And you think that's going to reassure me?"

Well, okay, she had a point. "It's not my job to reassure you. It's my job to keep Theo safe."

"Because you're his father."

"Because I'm— What?" Jesus, she was keeping him on his toes. Throwing things at him left and right, trying to catch him off guard.

"I'm not stupid, though I should have seen it earlier." She climbed slowly off the bed. His grizzly tracked every nuance of her movement, ready to take her down at the first show of disobedience. "Your frame and his are similar. The eyes are different, but not the jaw. You've got the same belief that you're right and the rest of the world is wrong."

"I don't think—"

"And that would explain your obsession with him. To the point that you planted Amy next door to us."

A logical train of thought, though completely incorrect. "Amy was a lucky coincidence. And I'm not his father." He frowned. "Though I think we're third cousins or something. Once removed."

"No wonder Nancy didn't want you involved in Theo's life. She said you were insane."

He growled, deep and low in his throat. It wasn't a sound he liked making, but he couldn't stop it, either. It just happened and it drew her up short. "I'm not Theo's father. Frank died ten years ago." Probably not the best time to mention that Carl was directly responsible for that death. The man had gone feral and there'd been no choice.

Her eyes narrowed. "I don't know what kind of sick game you're playing, but it's not going to work on me."

"I don't see this as any kind of game." *Don't challenge me. Don't challenge me.* The man in him was all but begging her to stay back. The grizzly was busily envisioning all the ways he'd force her to submit.

"Then believe this." She dropped her voice to a low growl and advanced menacingly on him. "If you hurt Theo in any way, I will see you dead." And with that, she spun on her heel and stomped into the bathroom, shutting the door with a solid thud.

Carl gripped the desk rather than pursue her. In his mind, his grizzly roared the demand to possess her, while the man held him back with every ounce of sanity he possessed. And all the while, he kept replaying her words in his mind, seeing the fire that had burned through her pale blue eyes. No shifter could be fiercer. No she-bear could be more protective of her young. And no woman—shifter or not—could have hit him so clearly between the eyes.

She was magnificent. And she was his Maxima. It didn't seem to matter that she wasn't a shifter and didn't even believe in them. Logic didn't hold sway here. He was the Gladwin Max, and she was his mate. And she'd just threatened to kill him, which—now that he thought about it—was a grizzly bear mating ritual.

CHAPTER 4

Becca stared at her reflection in the mirror, desperately trying to think things through. Sadly, it wasn't her strong suit. She was great in a crisis. If you needed someone to remain calm and react with precision during a disaster, then she was your girl. The more panic there was around her, the better she did.

Except this time, she was the only one panicking. She was trapped in a town full of lunatics and hadn't a clue how to maneuver her way out.

But were they really lunatics? Part of her laughed at the question. Werewolves and were-bears were the stuff of bad horror movies. The most obvious answer was that the town was a victim of some chemical spill and the people were suffering from a mass hallucination. That made it all the more important for her to escape as soon as possible before she too succumbed to the vapors or got infected from the water or whatever.

Two things kept her from hightailing it out of Camp Max. First, she couldn't figure out how to escape. Not with the whole town invested in keeping her here. And second, there was something her sister had said about Theo's father.

The kindest thing she could say about her sister was that Nancy was troubled. Their father's abandonment hit her sister the hardest, and Nancy had found escape in the nearest bar. She hadn't even been thirteen, but she and her friends had found a way to get what they wanted, and from there it was a downward spiral. Not all at once. There were better years and worse years. Nancy managed to get through high school and even hold a job for a while. But alcoholics dotted their family tree, and she eventually lost the battle against her addiction.

She conceived Theo in one of those bad times but then made a valiant effort to get clean for the baby. Becca had helped all she could, but money had been beyond tight. They had squeezed every last dime to get by, which is when Becca had pushed hard for Theo's father to help out. Nancy had refused. She'd said the man was an animal. Not ugly or violent. Just a freaking animal most of the time, becoming human only when it suited him. Only she hadn't said animal. Her exact words were "grizzly bear." Becca had dismissed it as an alcohol-induced nightmare.

Until now.

It couldn't be true, and yet, everyone seemed so committed to the delusion, her own sister included. Fortunately, no one appeared violent except for the whole kidnapping thing. Which meant Becca was somewhat safe for the moment. Her best plan was to keep her eyes and ears open for an opportunity to escape. Until then, she just had to pretend to go along.

She'd keep everyone calm—herself included—until she could get the hell out of Gladwin.

That decided, she washed her face, brushed out her hair, and did her best to look like she was completely cowed. Next step: search the bedroom for any weapons. She'd barely gotten started poking through the desk when Mr. Max knocked on the door.

"Tonya's here," he said through the wood.

"Coming!" she called as she pushed a drawer of files closed. There were names there—neat little folders of people that included lineage, medical history, and lists of incidents. Many ended with phrases like "shot in the heart" or "lost challenge." She had no idea what that meant, but she sure as hell didn't want to see a folder with her name on it. Or worse, one with Theo's name.

But she didn't have time to think about that as she straightened her clothes—dressy jeans and a now-wrinkled blouse—and headed out the door. Mr. Max was waiting for her, a big hulking presence by the door. He didn't move as she stepped out, unless she counted the way his nostrils flared and his hands twitched in her direction. And she had to pass within a half inch of his body as she stepped into the main room of a very large house. But beyond the way his scent seemed to invade her senses at his nearness, everything else seemed eerily normal.

He didn't speak as he gestured for her to cross to the center of the main living room. The decor was male hunting cabin, complete with an extra-large refrigerator-freezer and a big-screen TV. No deer heads hung on the wood-paneled walls, thank God, but she saw a couple very old quilts on the over-stuffed couch and one of the three huge recliners.

There in the middle stood two women. The first was a police detective, her uniform crisp and her posture excruciatingly correct except for the way her head tilted slightly to the side whenever she looked at Mr. Max. Given that she was stunningly beautiful, Becca guessed that the stiffness was her only way to keep things professional in a male-dominated field. She'd been talking to a woman who looked to be in her mid-fifties with dark hair going gray. The older woman wore Crocs on her feet and a loosely tied dress that looked more like a sack with flowers printed on it. An odd pair of women, to be sure.

And when Becca crossed into the center space, the detective's cool gaze assessed her in every way. It was all Becca could do to keep from smoothing down her hair.

"Good evening, Miss Weitz," the woman said. "I hope you're feeling recovered."

"From my kidnapping, you mean?" So much for pretending to go along.

The detective's lips twitched. "Yes. From that."

"I'd like to be taken home, if you please."

"I could do that, ma'am," she answered. "But that would be one less pair of friendly eyes looking for your nephew."

The older woman spoke up, her tone tart. "She still doesn't believe." Her gaze landed heavily on Becca. "Don't pick stupidity over the evidence of your own eyes."

"She hasn't seen anything yet," Mr. Max said, his voice all but booming from above her shoulder.

He was standing much too close, but there wasn't room for Becca to move away. Meanwhile, the other women looked surprised, and he raised his hands in a frustrated gesture. "And when was I supposed to do that? When she was unconscious?"

The detective sighed. "We're not getting anywhere until she believes. So go on," she said with her brows arched at Mr. Max. "Show her."

Mr. Max crossed his arms and glowered. "I've got my turn at the second checkpoint in just a few hours. I'm not shifting. It'd cost me too much, and I won't put those boys at risk."

Tonya folded her arms. "I'm not stripping for you."

"Shut up, children," the older woman interrupted, her tone the sound of a mother at the end of her patience. Then she turned to Becca. "I'm Marty Dawson, Justin's mom. He's a few years older than Theo, but I think they know each other."

Becca didn't know. Theo talked more about his school friends than the ones at camp. "It's nice to meet you," she said as she reached out to shake the woman's hand. But she ended up with her fingers hanging there in midair as the woman untied the sash around her dress.

"I've been through this before. Got two older kids who went through their First Change a few years back. It's nerve-racking, and my Sarah came back with her legs torn to shreds from some fence. She's fine now, but it doesn't stop a mom from worrying."

How to respond to that? "Of course you worry."

"And you think we're all cracked." Marty kicked off her big Crocs. "I wore this just because sometimes

I get protective when my kids are running wild. No sense in ripping my clothes." She looked at Becca. "Pay attention. I'm only doing this once." Then she looked back at Mr. Max. And she waited. He just stared at her, clearly confused.

"Marty?"

"You know I have to be angry. Say something to get my dander up."

"Uh...I don't know anything."

The detective snorted. "Tell her about the dog when you were twelve."

He rolled his eyes. "I was *ten*."

"And old enough to know better, I expect," said Marty. "Come on. Out with it. What did you do to that dog?"

Mr. Max rubbed the back of his neck, looking for all the world like a man about to confess something terrible. "You know those tarts you made that kept going missing? That was me. I let the dog in and staged the scene so he'd take the blame."

"You let me cage that poor defenseless animal? Just so you could stuff yourself with my tarts!" She took an angry step forward. "Those were for Sarah's birthday party! Those are damned hard to make and— Grrrroar!"

Becca was watching Marty, her amusement kicking in at seeing big, bad Max put on the defensive by a middle-aged woman. But then the change happened.

She noticed the face first, though Marty's shoulders had grown disproportionately large as she advanced on Mr. Max. Then suddenly there was dark brown hair with white tips and a long muzzle.

Her arms were raised as she pointed a finger at him, but it wasn't a finger. It was a huge paw with a claw extended toward Mr. Max. The sacklike dress pulled tight across her torso, now doubled in size, and hair—fur—sprouted everywhere.

She was a freaking bear, standing there in a dress while roaring at Mr. Max.

It happened so quickly, and yet every split second seemed imprinted on Becca's memory.

Becca stumbled over her own feet, her entire body feeling cold as she scrambled backward. The detective was there, holding on to her with an incredibly strong grip, keeping her from falling but also keeping her from running. Meanwhile, Mr. Max stood his ground, wincing as the bear kept roaring right in his face. And most frightening of all? The big man no longer looked so big.

And then the bear turned to stare at her.

"Oh, shit...," murmured Becca.

"Stay strong," said the detective. "They respect strength."

What the hell was she supposed to do? Break a chair? Bench-press a Volvo? Nothing was going to stop that creature from attacking. It was still roaring! Or maybe it was more like a growl.

The beast took a step forward. Then another.

Mr. Max slid along with it, keeping himself between the grizzly and Becca. And he kept talking as if she could still understand him.

"It was wrong of me. Dead wrong. But you know I made up for it later. I rescued that dog when he got trapped in Bennet's fence. You know I fed him my food all the time under the table. He forgave me and loved me. You know he did. And I bought you flowers and new tarts when I could afford them. They weren't as good as yours, but you know I meant well…"

On and on he went, diverting the grizzly's attention. The thing didn't walk any closer to Becca. In fact, the more Mr. Max talked, the more the bear growled at him and not her. And then something strange happened. The creature started to shrink and the air in the room seemed to heat. Hair fell off or disappeared. The grizzly hump went down and the shoulders retracted. Pretty soon the grizzly's face became human, displaying a self-satisfied smirk.

"Well, now," Marty said as she dropped her paws—now hands—onto her hips. "Don't you feel better for getting that off your chest? You been carrying the guilt of a bunch of tarts around since you were ten years old."

Mr. Max snorted and folded his arms across his chest. "You knew from the beginning."

"Might be the case. Might be I was waiting for the guilt to eat you alive and make you confess. Didn't think it would take twenty years."

He snorted. "I was just a boy."

"And full of mischief. But you got enough to think about in your life without feeling guilty for a bunch of undercooked tarts."

"Undercooked? Is that why they were sitting out?"

Marty grinned. "They were a bad batch. Those weren't for the party. I was just practicing."

Max's jaw dropped. "And you let me feel guilty all these years?"

"Well, I figured if you didn't confess, I didn't have to, either."

They stared at each other, Marty with a lifted chin and a laugh bubbling on her lips. Mr. Max was indignant, but his expression soon shifted to amused. A moment later, he pulled her into a big hug—hell, it was a bear hug—and they chuckled together. And all the while, Becca just stared, her mind reeling from what she'd seen.

Were-grizzlies? No way. It couldn't be.

"I've been infected," she murmured. Whatever the chemical spill or hallucinatory poison in the water— she'd somehow gotten it. She was insane now, just like everyone else.

Then Marty turned to her, her hands on her hips. "You're not one of those stubborn people who won't believe no matter what, are you? I thought you had more sense than that."

Becca swallowed. Were-bears? It couldn't be possible. But then her gaze landed on the hair on the floor. Tufts of dark brown with white tips. Without fully realizing what she was doing, she knelt down and picked some of it up. She rubbed the coarse hairs between her fingers, even sniffed them. They were real. Not a hallucination, but real hairs from a real creature.

"Where'd the rest go?" she murmured, looking up at Marty. The grizzly had been almost double her size and weight, and now she was back to being an average middle-aged woman in an oversize sack of a dress. "The hair here doesn't account for all that size."

Standing behind her, the detective snorted. "You

can buy were-grizzly but get hung up on the fur."
The woman shifted to look her in the eye. "It's
an energy exchange. Did you notice the change in
temperature? Or it's magic. Or maybe it's some
sort of special biological DNA that draws from
the Force. Who the hell knows? Can't you just
accept this and move on so we can talk about your
nephew?"

The tone was irritated and the words downright
rude, but it was exactly what Becca needed to jolt
her out of her shock. Which meant she had a simple
choice. She could either cling stubbornly to the mass
hysteria idea or leap straight into were-creature land.
Given that crisis mode forced her to boil life down
to the raw facts, she had to go with the evidence of
her five senses. The fur was real. The change was
real. Ergo, bear shifters were real.

Maybe if she wished real hard, she could find a
knight in shining armor, too.

"Okay," she finally said. "Tell me why you think
Theo is one of you."

"Good," approved the detective. "You're rational.
There's hope for you."

Becca wasn't so sure, but she let the comment go.
Meanwhile, Mr. Max answered her question.

"Theo's father was a shifter like us. He was kind
of wild—"

"Feral," inserted Marty.

Mr. Max winced. "He fathered a few children on
different women before he died." Marty opened her
mouth at that, but the man shot her a quelling look.
She pressed her mouth closed and tilted her head
completely to the side. It was a strange reaction that

Becca didn't have the brainpower to process. "Theo was one of his children. Not every child shifts, so we stayed away. But just in case..."

"You bring them to camp," Becca said, remembering that her sister had never had to pay full price for the weeks away. She'd said it was a scholarship for special kids. Translation: potential shifter kids. "And once here, you teach them how to navigate Gladwin State Park if it's needed."

"Yes."

"But why do you think Theo's shifted now?"

"Because he's been fighting at school. His temperature has been running hot, which is normal before First Change."

"No it hasn't—"

"Remember all those fevers that got him out of his French tests?"

She swallowed. She'd suspected that he'd been faking his illness, but had stood over him and taken his temperature herself. It had never occurred to her that he was just normally hot. Or that it was part of some freaky biological shift into a bear. She took a deep breath, trying to think. This just wasn't possible, and yet... apparently it was.

"Also," continued Mr. Max, "he told Amy that he felt like there was a creature just underneath his skin and it was making him crazy." His expression turned sympathetic. "Sure, a lot of this could be passed off as normal adolescence, but put together, there are plenty of signs for those who know what to look for."

She hated that Theo had confided in Amy and not her, but the girl was closer to his age, and some things just weren't expressed to a parent. That was a natural part of growing up.

"And there's one more thing," he added. "All of Frank's children have become shifters."

She frowned. "Just how many are there?"

"At last count, seven. Four of them have turned old enough to shift."

Seven? Holy shit, Theo had six half brothers and sisters out there. She didn't know if the kid would be happy or freaked out by that. And wasn't that the most irrelevant thing for her to focus on?

"So now it's Theo's turn. And you think he did it and is headed up here."

"Yes." That was the detective answering, her tone dry. "This is a normal part of a grizzly shifter's life. That makes it a regular spring ritual, and Gladwin PD is well used to handling it. That's fine for the local kids." She glanced at Marty. "But the minute they start traveling from outside the county, things get dicey. We've got friendly eyes all over Michigan, but that's not always enough."

Of course not. Because if she were the Kalamazoo PD, she'd shoot a wandering bear on sight. They didn't belong in a populated area.

"Are there usual trails that they take?" she asked. "Someplace you watch?"

"Sure there are," said Marty. "And we got people watching them." She patted Becca's arm, and it was so comforting she wasn't even bothered by the woman's unnaturally warm touch.

Oh, hell. She finally understood now about Theo's fevers because his skin had felt just as hot as Marty's.

She swallowed and did her best to focus. "But Theo was in Kalamazoo. And you're just watching locally. Places in the park and in Gladwin."

"Yes," said Mr. Max as he once again stepped much too close. For all that his tone was conciliatory, his presence all but beat her into submission. "You need to trust us. We've been through this every spring since the Gladwins first settled here hundreds of years ago. People don't mess with bears, and there are natural instincts, too."

"Our boys will be just fine," said Marty.

Becca nodded, trying to feel reassured. Mostly she just felt unsteady. "So what's next? What do I do?"

"You? Nothing," said the detective. "You let us do our jobs."

"I know it's hard," Mr. Max said soothingly.

"Hard nothing," huffed Marty. "It's a nightmare only a mother can understand." She looked harshly at the other two, then she turned back to Becca. "Here's what we do, honey. We cook. It's hard, cold work sitting out there watching for our boys. The kitchen's set up, and I've made stew, but it's not going to last all night. Plus coffee and cookies—"

"Beef stew?" interrupted Mr. Max. "Thank God! I'm—"

"Hungry as a bear?" quipped Becca before she could stop her mouth. Gallows humor was something she excelled at.

"Look at you!" Mr. Max said with a grin. "Making shifter jokes and everything. You're going to fit in just fine."

Tonya rolled her eyes. "Yeah, yeah, she's a regular

comedian. I'm spelling the sheriff at the first checkpoint. You know how to reach me." Then she spun on her heel before heading out. All crisp, clean efficiency.

"She doesn't like me much," Becca said, once again proving that she was completely off her game. She didn't normally comment on stuff like that. Or let it bother her.

"She doesn't like anyone new," Mr. Max drawled. "They're unknowns, and she likes to keep things safe and contained."

Becca couldn't fault her for that. That was her usual choice as well. But there was nothing contained about bear shifters. Meanwhile, Marty headed for the door. "Come on," she said over her shoulder. "If you want something in your belly before you go out, you gotta get it now."

"I'm right behind you," returned Mr. Max, though he didn't leave. Instead, he stood by Becca's side, a large, overwhelming presence that didn't understand the words "personal space." He waited until Marty was out the door before he spoke. "You okay?"

"Nope," she answered honestly. "But I'm dealing."

"You're doing better than anyone else I've seen. The last two outsiders had to be sedated."

"Great. So you make a habit of kidnapping people."

He chuckled. "Only distraught mothers. But both their kids came through like champions. You'll see. Theo will, too."

She took a breath, holding on to that thought with everything she had. Not the idea that he'd already abducted two other women. Just that their children were fine. "So we just wait now."

"And watch."

"And eat stew."

"If we're lucky," Mr. Max said with a grin. His expression had turned wolfish and Becca started at her own thought. Could a were-bear look like a wolf?

Becca shook off her glib thought. Mr. Max was working extra hard to be charming, even if he did stand almost possessively close, but she needed to learn more about this world before she started trusting anyone or anything. So she kept silent as they headed out the front door, down the walk to the main circle. Camp Max was built on the edge of the state park and a couple miles from Gladwin village. It sat on an oval road a quarter mile long. At the top sat Mr. Max's big home and the access road to the main highway. At the base was a cafeteria where everyone ate their meals. To the east were the usual camp fun buildings: swimming pool, basketball court, baseball field. To the west were two small dorms and the parking lot. And in the center of it all sat seven beautiful apple trees barely showing their spring foliage.

As they moved, Becca started thinking, doing what she always did when she felt unsettled. She walked herself step by step through everything that had brought her to this moment. It was too far to go all the way back to when Nancy had gotten pregnant. Instead, she stepped herself through last night's fight with Theo, through today's worry-baking, and all the way up to the present.

"Tell me about the other guy who was at my

apartment." She felt Mr. Max stiffen, and his answer came out more as a grumble than a name.

"Bryn?"

She turned to face him for the next question. She wanted to see his face when he answered. "He's really a werewolf?"

"Yeah." He didn't evade her eyes when he spoke, but she got the sense that he didn't like talking about the man. His body seemed to bulk and his hands shifted restlessly where he'd shoved them in his pockets.

"And he was checking up on Theo?"

"No, he was just in the neighborhood."

She looked at him steadily, trying to notice every detail of his face and body. Something about his ears fascinated her. His hair was short enough to show her the curve of each lobe where they tucked tight to his head. But as she watched, they seemed to move slightly. Maybe she was imagining things, but they seemed to perk up, and he lifted his nose higher, as if scenting the wind.

"You're not afraid anymore," he said, satisfaction in his tone.

True, but how did he know that? "I'm grappling with reality. There's no room for fear."

His lips curved, as if he were pleased. "Nothing is going to hurt you here."

She was more worried about Theo than herself, but that was good to know. Meanwhile, she didn't like that he'd distracted her from her earlier question. "Why was Bryn in my neighborhood?"

"You're like a dog with a bone, aren't you?"

"Is that a werewolf joke?"

He snorted. "More like an insult." Then he touched her arm, gently but firmly pushing her to keep walking. She went along. Honestly, she had little choice given his strength. But that didn't mean she would give up her quest for information. "I don't distract easily," she said. "So why was he in the neighborhood?"

"It has nothing to do with Theo."

"Are you sure? Absolutely one hundred percent certain?"

He wasn't. In just a few hours, she'd made a study of his expressions. She was starting to see that when his gaze shifted away and his shoulders bulked by a tiny fraction that he was being evasive.

"Just tell me. I'll go insane worrying."

He shook his head and gestured to the cafeteria door. "Not now." And with that, he pulled the door open, calling out to the couple dozen of people milling around there. "Hey, everybody!" he bellowed. "Help me give a warm welcome to the newest member of our family. Becca Weitz, meet the Gladwin shifters. Or at least half of them."

And just like that, she joined the ranks of the crazies.

CHAPTER 5

Holding maneuver: successful. At least for the moment.

Carl watched Becca swallow and force a smile. Then she stepped forward to greet the core of the Gladwin shifters like a queen, no trace of fear anywhere. Good for her. Especially since the room was the size of an average high school gymnasium and every person in there turned to look at her. The man in him admired the way she faced them all without appearing to break a sweat. His bear was so pleased, he puffed up as large as he could and silently proclaimed ownership of the woman. Shifters weren't psychic, so it was all in body language. The way he stood beside her and met every man's gaze. And he held that position until they all deferred to him by a subtle sideways tilt of the head or downcast gaze.

Very Neanderthal of him, but some things couldn't be stopped. It was all about allowing his grizzly latitude without letting it take control. And right now, his grizzly had decided on owning Becca, so Carl allowed it the belief while his mind went about trying to *not* think about her. After all, he had a shifter clan to run.

So he pushed Becca toward Marty and the kitchen, then went for some food. He never made it. Instead, what felt like every man, woman, and child came to talk to him. He listened to their concerns, and did his best to not be aware of Becca. He laughed as people reminisced about other springs, he diminished Nick Merkel's poison by calling it the ranting of an old man, and he pretended not to notice when three different men in the food line flirted with Becca. And if he was excruciatingly aware of every person's reaction to her—mostly good, thank God— it was merely because his grizzly was uncomfortably obsessed with the woman.

And so it went for two long hours. The whole thing irritated his grizzly to no end. It was a creature of simple action, but his mind knew that sometimes delaying tactics were the only way to go. So he'd destroyed Nick's field rather than challenge—and kill—a man nearly twice his age. He'd made Tonya his beta and hoped another more palatable Maxima would appear. Then he'd shoved Becca—the only woman to attract his brain and his bear—into a room full of shifters rather than tell her news that would likely sour her on his kind forever. He wanted her to feel accepted in a new possible home here for her and Theo. The last thing he wanted to reveal was that the shifter community was a delicate balance of constantly shifting loyalties between extremely dangerous people. His closest friend today could be the man he had to kill tomorrow.

And speaking of best friends who might have

gone bad, Carl finally snagged a bowl of stew while
he scanned the crowd for Mark. The guy might
be slowly going feral, but no way would he miss
a spring hunt for the new shifters. First off, he
excelled at smelling out the young. Second, he was
obsessively protective of all kids. Probably had to do
with growing up knowing he wouldn't live to see his
thirtieth birthday. Mark had known since one fateful
night when he was sixteen that he had too much
shifter DNA. That meant he was slowly going feral.
Eventually the grizzly would take over and make
the man dangerously crazy. Given how much Carl
struggled to control his own grizzly, he couldn't even
fathom how Mark fought day after day to stay sane.
But Carl was working night and day to solve that
problem, too. So when he didn't see his best friend,
Carl caught Alan's eye and gestured him over.

"You seen Mark?" he asked when Alan joined
him on the bench.

"He went in search as soon as we heard." His
brother's voice was respectful, but his body language
was tight and angry. Not surprising since he was
probably still stinging from losing his position as
beta, but Carl couldn't let hurt feelings get in the
way of business.

"That was hours ago," Carl said, his grizzly making
his voice snap. Alan deserved some time to nurse
his wounds, but the alpha in Carl would not let even
subliminal dissent pass. "He shouldn't be alone. It'll
encourage him to the grizzly too much."

Alan's eyes narrowed at Carl's tone. "Sometimes
people just need space."

"Mark isn't just some person," he retorted. The

longer Mark wandered around using his bear senses, the more likely the beast would take over and he'd go feral. And once that happened, there was no hope for him. Carl would have to kill him for everyone's safety. And that, of course, was Carl's most critical delaying tactic. His every spare moment was devoted to finding a way to keep the wilder members of the community from giving in to the beast inside. Because when a shifter went feral, people died.

Meanwhile, Alan looked up, his expression shifting into wry amusement. "She looks like a woman on a mission."

Carl didn't need to look to know he was talking about Becca. He'd been aware of exactly where she was all evening. Worse, she'd tried to get his attention at least six times, but he'd managed to escape before she forced a discussion she wasn't ready for. He didn't think she'd let him get away with it again. Which meant it was time to bring out the big guns.

He pushed up from his seat, pitching his voice for her to hear. "Hey, would you like to meet Theo's grandfather?"

His brother snorted. "Subtle...not."

"Whatever works," he said with a hard glare. There was a message in that for his brother. It said quite clearly that Carl would do whatever it took to maintain the safety of the clan. Even if it meant unfairly demoting his brother. Or refusing to talk to a determined Becca.

He saw the message land as his brother flushed red, his head tilted, and his body shifted into a submissive pose. Carl the man wanted to follow up with a brotherly comment. Something to soothe the sting, but he didn't have time. Becca had arrived, her body tense, her eyes startled by his comment.

"Theo's grandfather?" she said, her eyes panicked as she scanned the crowd.

"This way," he said as he grabbed hold of her elbow and pulled her intimately close. That was his bear again, disrupting Carl's calm by breathing her scent deep into his lungs while her body heated every part of him.

Hell, this was torture. He had to get away from her quickly, before he lost control. So he was a little too rushed as he steered her to a corner, where Isaac was telling stories to a circle of shifter kids. "I'm sure he'd love to get to know you better right after story time. Besides," he said when she turned back to him, "you can hear *our* version of the fairy tales."

"I'd rather talk to you—" she began, but he cut her off.

"It's important for you to hear our stories told our way." Little Red Riding Hood's grandmother was a feral werewolf, as was the huffing and puffing wolf from "The Three Little Pigs." Grendel from *Beowulf* was a bear shifter, though obviously that wasn't a happy tale. More of an instructional lesson about not revealing yourself to ordinary people who then declared you a monster and decided to kill you. "And, besides, I've got to talk to Alan." He dropped her off at the edge of the group, then ducked away.

He was being a rampant coward, but he needed to gain some space from the woman. She stirred up things in him best ignored during the current crisis. Hot, erotic things that had no place in the clan while children were wandering lost in the wild. So he took the excuse and was grateful that those three tales bought him another hour to interact quietly with his clan. Plus, Marty had added a great deal of brandy to dinner, so he got a little mellower after his third bowl of stew.

And right when Isaac was deep into the "Three Billy Goats Gruff"—ram shifters vs. bear shifters— Carl slipped outside. It was time for his shift at the southern border of the park, and he was looking forward to some quiet time under the stars to think. It took him ten minutes to gather the supplies he needed, and then he climbed into his truck. He hadn't even touched the ignition when she hopped into the cab.

He didn't look at her—too distracting. Besides, he could smell her determination filling the cab. Right along with his sexual pheromones. Lord, he hated it when he smelled like a randy teenager, but apparently she ramped up his lust without even doing more than pointing that stubborn chin at him.

"Becca, you can't come," he said, already knowing it was futile to argue.

"You promised me answers."

"It's going to be a long, cold night of waiting. We can talk in the morning."

"When another dozen people fight for your time? I know you were fobbing me off tonight, but you were also cornered by every adult there at one point or another. You're their leader, aren't you?"

He nodded. "Every shifter group has an alpha. For us, we call that man Maximus."

"Mr. Max."

"The kids named me that and it kind of stuck. My father was Maxim. My uncle was Maximus Prime."

She tilted her head at him. "How very Roman of him."

"He enjoyed power." And that was the under-statement of the century.

She must have keyed into his tone because she twisted to look at him. "There's a story there."

Dozens, more like. All of them brutal and bloody. His uncle was a perfect example of what happens when the grizzly rules and the man obeys.

"Fine," she huffed. "Don't talk. But I'm going to pester you all night long, Mr. Max. So either get used to getting harassed or start talking."

"Please call me Carl. The Gladwin Maximus won't give you anything. He can't. It's too big a risk for someone who hasn't fully adopted our ways. But Carl might be convinced to share more." And why the hell had he just told her that? He needed more formality between them, not less.

"Does it make it easier to split yourself into two people, Carl?"

Two? He was at least three—his human self, the Maximus, and his bear—all trying to rip each other apart. And every time he thought he'd negotiated a peace with himself, something happened to upset the balance. Or someone.

He looked at her in the dark cab, using his bear's night vision to trace the contours of her face. She had beautiful eyes, but that's not what drew him. It was something about the curve to her nose. A little ski slope that ended in a pert tip that lifted into the air when she was feeling aggressive. His bear loved that. The rest of him adored the smooth skin that he knew was softer than down. He'd caressed her cheek often enough when she was unconscious. He hadn't been able to stop himself.

And then there were her lips. Plump and red from when she chewed on them because of nerves. Her mouth was always moving, not talking, necessarily, just expressing her emotions, even when she pressed her lips firmly together and refused to speak. The man in him watched that mouth obsessively and had fantasies about what she could do with it. There was the window to her soul, and that was what he wanted to touch, taste, and possess.

He was out of control.

"You can't come, Becca. It'll be hours just sitting." They'd be right next to each other within touching distance. He'd be able to smell her every shifting mood while he created elaborate fantasies around her. Hell, he was already hard. "We'll talk tomorrow. I promise."

"Tomorrow happens in about ten minutes," she said firmly. Then she finished him off: she touched his hand in the barest of tentative caresses. She didn't know how rare it was for someone to touch him softly. Bears, as a rule, were forceful creatures, shifters even more so. She touched the back of his hand as if she were nervous but unable to stop herself. The lightest of touches that felt like a whisper against his skin and sent reverberation everywhere through his body. "Please, Carl. I'm crawling out of my skin with worry. And being here with everyone makes it worse."

He sighed. He knew that feeling. Understood it

to the depths of his bones. "It's going to be really cold," he warned.

"You've got my blanket back there. I'll use that."

It was what he'd planned to use. He'd wrapped her in it when they'd taken her from her apartment. It smelled like her and Theo, and he'd wanted to bury himself in it all night long. Now he'd sit beside her and smell so much more.

"This is not a good idea," he growled.

"I'll risk it," she shot back, proving she knew absolutely nothing about what she was doing.

But rather than point out the obvious, he turned the ignition and headed out to the watch point.

He worried that she'd start to push her advantage the moment he put the truck in drive. That's what Tonya would have done. It was an animal thing. The minute predators sensed softness, they went in for the kill. Humans knew to take their time. To ease in patiently by degrees until everything was exposed.

Becca was all human and a woman as well. She touched him again—this time in gratitude—then settled back into silence to let him get comfortable with her presence. Both actions were guaranteed to intrigue him. His bear liked that she hadn't attacked, feeling intrigued by the atypical reaction. And the man in him...well, he had a boner the size of Detroit. He was pulsing with hunger after those two brief touches.

It took fifteen minutes to get to the lonely watch point: a huge weeping willow draped at the edge of a stream. A platform had been built around the lowest branches. The perch was high enough to see the distance, but low enough for a bear to jump down without problem, and the other trees had been cut back to give a good 360-degree view. And, best of all, a cell tower stood near enough to keep all five bars of his phone happy.

He parked the truck at the side of the road, then grabbed the picnic basket Marty had packed for him. Becca took hold of the blanket and thermos of coffee, then hopped out, peering all around her. He waited, wondering if she could see the perch with her human senses. She did, proving that she had spent at least some time out in the wild.

"You ever hunt as a kid?"

"Deer with my dad. It was about the only time I spent with him growing up. He went with his brother and let me tag along if I promised not to tell Mom what they did."

"What did they do?"

"Drink and talk shit."

"Ah. My favorite kind of hunter. Noisy and with lousy aim."

She chuckled. "We never caught anything but colds."

He narrowed his eyes as he studied her face. It was a mixture of emotions both bad and good. "What happened?"

She'd started walking to the tree, but stopped at his question. "What?"

"Something bad happened or you'd be glowing with nostalgia."

She snorted. "Drunk middle-aged men are not the most considerate people. I learned to shoot and drink beer. I learned that men are gross and think a lot about sex. I also learned that my father loved my mother even if he couldn't stand to hang around her for long."

Ah. Abandonment issues. "So Mom was the stable one."

"Nurses are there when you need them in the best possible way. Unless they're at work earning rent money because Dad has wandered off again."

"What did he do?"

"He was an electrician by trade. Get-rich-quick schemer by action. And..." She shrugged. "He had a big personality. Drunk, sober, at home or away, he was big in my life."

"And now?"

"Gone. Bad flu that he ignored. It was too late by the time he thought to see a doctor. We didn't even make it to the hospital in time to say good-bye."

"Tough break."

She was silent a moment, looking out at the dark horizon. "It's how he would have chosen to go. Quick, dramatic, and without hurting anyone else." Then she shrugged. "I was always terrified we'd lose him in an electrical fire or a drunk-driving accident."

"How old were you when he passed?"

"Seventeen. Old enough to process it and perfect timing to quit hoping that Dad would help out with my college tuition."

There was a wealth of disappointment in those words. Along with anger and all those things that come with an unreliable parent. "So you got your business degree on your own."

She snorted. "Hardly. Mom paid, I worked at

my aunt's bakery. And then when it was time, I took over."

"So which is your true love? The business or the baking?"

She frowned at him as if she hadn't ever considered the question. "They're both me. And neither. I'm also a single parent, a bad jazzercise dancer, and someone who likes to eat candy and read slutty romance novels. How do you separate one part from another?"

Good question. He'd been trying—and failing—to keep areas of his life partitioned from one another. But he couldn't imagine being a harmonious whole person either. It just wasn't in his nature. Good thing he was saved from answering by arriving at the tree.

Henry was already coming down, his nimble form dropping from the branches like a monkey. He might be small for a shifter, but the young father had always been deceptively quick. "Evening, Max," he said, his tone neutral, his head tilted to the side in submission.

"Hello, Henry. This is Becca, Theo's guardian."

The man flashed his teeth in a warm grin. "My mom had to keep watch for me, too. But don't worry. Instinct runs deep and keeps us safe."

Becca flashed a grateful smile, but Carl couldn't stop himself from correcting the young man. "It's not instinct. It's his good head that will save the day. Don't ignore the man in favor of the animal."

Henry's eyes narrowed. "Seems to me the animal is what counts in situations like this." He gestured around the dark land. "Open field, reacting

on a dime, heading by feel to your home—
that's something that will confuse a man. Never
a bear."

Becca blew out a breath. "Why do I get the feeling
that this is an old argument?"

"Because it's all chicken and egg," Carl answered.
"Which is more important? Who rules what?"

"Max here is a thinker. His uncle was a doer,"
Henry responded. And it was obvious Henry pre-
ferred action. But that's because he was too young
to remember Maximus Prime.

"But wouldn't you want brain behind the brawn?"
Becca asked.

The man's eyes grew flinty at that. "'Course you
do. But there's a point where there's only brain and
no brawn, and that's disaster."

Carl barely restrained a growl. "You've been waiting a long time to say that to me, haven't you?"

The man nodded with a quick slash of his chin. "I
got children and I don't want them Detroit assholes
getting—"

"I don't, either," Carl interrupted, trying not to
air all the political dissent in front of Becca. "But
before you start talking about brawn, ask your
grandfather what he thinks. Oh wait. You can't because he was disemboweled by my uncle. And do
you know why? Because your grandfather gave his
best pumpkin to his pregnant wife for her craving."
His uncle's clan tax had declared that the best crop
always went to Maximus Prime. "Brutality is never
the answer."

"You don't have to go that far," Henry countered.
Then before Carl's grizzly took over completely and

disemboweled the young father, Henry raised his hands in surrender. "I'm worried. People are saying you can't even keep Nick in line."

Carl growled low in his throat, scary enough to silence Henry and make Becca shy away. He hadn't meant to frighten her, but he was holding on to his position by the barest thread, and he couldn't afford to let a low man on the totem pole challenge him. Not even verbally. "You ought to be grateful that I don't maim people whenever they smart mouth off to me."

A deliberate reminder. Ages ago, Maximus Prime had permanently lamed Henry's father. Even if Henry couldn't remember the horror of those many years ago, he would remember his father's permanent limp. Henry's hard gaze flickered for a moment, then dropped.

Submission. Good.

But then the kid had to add an extra dig. "We're just damned scared, is all. Them Detroit—"

"I know!" Carl barked. "Everybody's scared and acting out. When the fuck are people going to *think first* before they do something stupid?"

Henry's chin shot up. "That's the problem. We're not *people.* We're *more.*"

"All the more reason not to go off half-cocked. Only a feral lets his grizzly run amok."

Henry didn't answer. He just stood there with his eyes downcast in submission, but his mouth and chin firmed into a hard sullen frown. He would bow to his alpha now, but the resentment was building, and Carl didn't know what to do about it. Especially since if he challenged Nick like everyone wanted, he would then be crucified for killing one of their own. That's what had happened when he first took control of the Gladwin clan.

And into that taut silence, Becca decided to intrude, her question completely out of the blue. "So you have children? They must be really young. Are you worried about what happens when they grow up and shift?"

Henry turned slightly, his mouth softening as he looked at her. "Can't help but think about that when sitting out here for hours. I got two little girls and they're feisty as hell."

"How old?" she asked.

"Eleven months and four years. It'll be a long time until we face a night like tonight."

"But you still worry. I thought I'd go insane when Theo started teething. But now he's out there alone somewhere." Her gaze slid across the landscape. "There's always something to freak out about. I don't know how we get through it."

"One day at a time, is how," Henry returned, his words gentle. "That's what I tell Donna. Just one day at a time."

Becca smiled, gratitude in her eyes. "Thank you so much for keeping watch. I cannot tell you how reassuring it is that someone who cares is helping him. A stranger."

"Aw." The man ducked his head. "Theo's one of us now. That means you are, too, and we Gladwins protect our own."

"I can see that," she said, then she reached forward and squeezed his arm. "Thank you again."

Henry patted her hand in response, all aggression

gone from his body. And then Becca gasped as if she'd just remembered something.

"I nearly forgot. We brought stew for you." She reached over and pulled the basket from Carl's hand. "I'll bet you're hungry."

"Sure am, if it's Marty's special stew?" he asked, looking at Carl.

Becca answered for him. "If by special you mean with a half bottle of brandy in it, then, yes, she made it overly special."

"Not possible," Henry said with a grin as he took the basket. "Welcome to the clan, ma'am," he said. Then he nodded briefly to Carl. "Mr. Max."

"Stay safe, Henry."

And with that, the man trotted back to his truck with Carl's breakfast. Carl watched the man go, seeing that his movements were casual, almost jaunty. Which, given that he'd been a half breath away from challenging the Max, was beyond startling. "How'd you do that?" he asked, his voice too low for even shifter ears to hear.

"What?"

He didn't have the words to answer. In just a few sentences, she'd defused Henry's resentment into nothing. "If I'd known all he wanted was my stew, I'd have sent someone hours ago."

She brushed away one of the weeping willow branches as she moved to the ladder. "It's not the stew he wanted. Just someone to understand his fears."

He looked at her. "We've all got fears." She more than most, given that Theo was out there somewhere.

"And that's what people think about when sitting out here alone in the dark for hours on end. He wasn't really criticizing you. He was just scared for his girls. All that fear has to go somewhere, so he chose to attack you as the nearest target."

He touched her arm to support her up the ladder, but didn't follow through with the motion. Instead he turned her around to face him so he could study the minute shifts of her mouth.

"How did you know what to say to him?"

She chuckled. "I served for years on the PTA."

He frowned. "I don't understand."

"What do you think the PTA is? It's a group of neurotic, sleep-deprived parents who are terrified they're screwing up their kids. Just about every ridiculous argument we had could be defused by simple support and understanding."

He stared at her. It couldn't be that easy, and yet the evidence told him she was right. "Scared doesn't give you the right to challenge your alpha. That's just begging for more trouble."

She tilted her chin up at him. It was a function of how close he'd stepped up to her, but he still saw it as an adorably impertinent gesture. "Did you miss the words 'terrified' and 'sleep-deprived'? No one's rational like that."

He shook his head, his mind replaying her words and fitting them to half the arguments he had with people. What if half the times he thought people were challenging his authority, they were merely blowing off steam and fear? It boggled his mind. And in that moment of confusion, she pressed her advantage in a very bearlike fashion.

"And don't think I missed the suggestion that shifters are *more* than people. Just how deep does that bigotry run?"

He shrugged, uncomfortable with the question. "You're part of the clan. You heard him. He welcomed you."

"Not the point. Plus, he was frightened about Detroit and Nick. What's going on there?"

He gestured with his hand as if he could push the fears aside. "I'm handling it," he said, praying that he was making smart choices.

"You do know that I'm not stupid, right? There're signs of problems all over the place. Plus kidnapping frightened mothers can't be your usual mode of operation. More like an act of desperation. I figure you're holding the clan together by sheer willpower and nothing else. That's impressive, but it can't last." She leaned back against the tree trunk, her eyes reflecting the moonlight and her pert little nose all but poking him in the eye. "How am I doing, Mr. Max? How close to the mark—"

He kissed her.

It wasn't a conscious act. Maybe it was just another delaying tactic, since everything she said was dead-center right. If he distracted her with a kiss, maybe she wouldn't realize what she'd figured out. Or maybe he just wanted to taste that too-smart mouth and get up close and personal with her ski slope of a nose. Maybe he just wanted to press her against the tree trunk and possess the woman who saw things too clearly.

She was startled. Of course she was. He'd moved with shifter speed because it had been the act of his grizzly. But she didn't fight him. After a split second of frozen surprise, she softened against him. Her gasp opened her mouth, and he wasted no time tasting her. And now was when he expected her to bite his tongue off or shove him away. Instead, she pushed at him with her tongue. Hot and fierce, they dueled while her hands gripped his upper arms, squeezing them enough to make him growl with hunger.

Then she did it. A little whimper of a sound that came from deep within her. He felt it pass through her lips and knew it for what it was: *yes*.

Lust roared through him, hard and hungry. His hands found her waist, tiny in his massive hands, and he spread his fingers as he pushed them upward. Her coat separated, the buttons popping free, and he felt the soft texture of her blouse. Tiny rib cage, full breasts held in an underwire bra. He hated the hard ridges that restricted the lush mounds. He squeezed her breasts, feeling the hard points of her nipples even through all the layers.

And all the while, he ravished her mouth. He used his height to dominate as he invaded between her teeth and explored every part. And then he began to thrust. Not just above but below, where his groin pressed thick against her soft belly.

She'd said yes, and he was going to take her right here in the middle of his homeland at the beginning of spring. His bear knew this to be right, and the man in him was powerless to stop the drive to pin her against the tree and take her every way his beast wanted.

Soft belly. Hot mouth. Hungry lust.

Especially when she moaned against his mouth.

It wasn't his rational mind that smelled the bear. He'd lost all thought the moment she'd opened to him. But something in him smelled *another*.

Male bear.

Coming near.

Young.

Easily conquered.

He spun around, using his body to keep her against the tree while he peered through the darkness.

There.

A dark silhouette of a bear beginning to shake. He recognized the signs of a shifter at the edge of his strength. And as he watched, the body started shrinking into itself, becoming an adolescent human. The grizzly hump slid down, the head grew more round, and the thick arms and legs became slender. A boy shifter exhausted as he headed toward home.

It was good that the child diminished himself. He would not tolerate another male bear near Becca. Not now. Not before he impregnated her. But this boy was no threat.

He turned back to his woman, using his hands to strip open her blouse. He would lick her breasts and belly. He would bury his tongue between her thighs. He would taste every part of her, letting her know that he was the only one to own her scent. And in so doing, he would mark her as his.

He smelled her arousal and knew she was fertile.

Now.

Boy.

Something about the boy niggled his brain, but he swatted the thought away. Becca was moving against him, her hips pulsing against his superior power, her breath coming in panting gasps as he tasted her neck.

But there was something else in the air. Something dark and rancid that was not Becca and not the boy. It was faint in the still air, but he knew it as *wrong* and that was enough to still his movements. He would not mate in a place that was unsafe.

He turned his head, sniffing the air. Becca stilled as well, and he pressed a finger to her lips. The night was quiet, the breeze negligible. Where was it?

A dark shadow moved in a distant tree. Was that it? He couldn't tell. It was too far away to scent or to see properly. Which is when he focused on the boy.

The boy who was down on the ground. Unmoving.

Alarm pierced through him. Procreating was a primal task for his bear, but so was protecting the young. The Wrong was out there. The young was vulnerable.

Therefore, he attacked.

CHAPTER 6

Becca blinked away the lust in time to see unbelievable things flash across her retinas. They were dark shadows, indistinct to her confused mind. So she did what she always did in a crisis. She made a list.

First was the sudden chill of being half dressed in Michigan at midnight. It didn't matter that it was spring. It was still damned cold on her bare belly and heavy breasts. Next was irritation that the man who'd been keeping her flushed and happy was suddenly gone. Her body was pulsing, her mind overridden by desire.

She was not a woman to be distracted by such things. Not usually. But occasionally a man pushed all her buttons and she lost sight of reason. And her clothes. She wasn't proud of the fact, but there it was. She kept herself so locked down that when a man breached her defenses, she went nuclear meltdown into passion. Clearly that's what had happened.

Which is when her vision finally cleared.

Holy shit, he was a bear.

Item number two. Carl was a freaking *huge* bear. Seeing Marty shift had been mind-blowing enough, but now, in the moonlight, she saw what had to be Carl running full-bear grizzly at something. She pulled her coat together, buttoning it quickly as she tried to make out form from shadow. Carl stopped at a dark lump on the ground, nosing it gently.

A boy!

"Theo!" she screamed and ran forward.

Carl was straddling the child, but at her cry, he turned toward her and roared. Not just a quiet grumble, but a full-out bellow that knocked her back on her heels.

Oh shitshitshitshitshit. He was going to eat Theo!

"Get away from him!" she screamed.

She had no illusions that she could frighten a five-hundred-pound grizzly, but maybe she could get through to the man inside the bear. She didn't think Carl would ever hurt a child, least of all Theo, but who knew what a bear would do?

"Get away!" she screamed again as she ran forward. Straight at a grizzly. What the hell was she doing? She didn't even have a weapon, and her damned coat had popped open again. But she couldn't stop. Theo needed her.

So she ran while Carl roared at her again.

"Get away!" Damn it, she needed a gun. Or a big rock. Something to…

She heard a pop. It was barely audible over the pounding in her ears, but something had happened. She saw Carl turn his head toward a tree far in the distance. *Good. Look somewhere else.* Maybe she could drag Theo to safety while Carl was distracted. It was a vain hope. No way would an animal let her drag away his dinner while he was looking at a tree, but it was all she had.

Her heels thudded on the cold ground as she just now realized how far it was. The whole clearing was probably the length of two football fields with Theo lying in the center. Carl had cleared the distance in twenty seconds, but she was huffing at only half-way there.

Then she heard Carl roar again, but this time it was at the tree. He leaped forward on all fours as he cleared half the distance to the tree.

Good! Go away!

Another breath and he reached the edge of the clearing. She heard another pop, this one distinctive because she'd been listening for it. A gun? No, she'd heard guns. That wasn't it. But it was something like that, which meant there was someone in the tree shooting at Carl.

"Don't shoot!" she screamed. "He's…" *What? A nice bear?*

But Carl reared up on his hind legs, roaring as he tore into the bare branches of the tree.

Shit, shit, shit!

There was nothing she could do for the stupid hunter. Thankfully, she'd reached Theo and skidded to his side on her knees. "Come on, honey. Get up. We got to move, honey."

She was babbling even as she saw that it wasn't her nephew. This was an older boy with a square jaw and freckles on his dirty face. Something about his nose reminded her of Marty, so she guessed she was looking at Justin. Didn't matter. Either way, she had to get the child to safety.

She leaned down and tried to pick up the boy. Adrenaline helped, but not enough. She managed to flop him around a bit before her arms gave out. Fine. She'd drag him.

"Come on, kiddo." She grabbed his wrists and started pulling. "We gotta go."

It was forever away to get back to the weeping willow. The tree line was closer. Getting under cover was the better choice, even if it wasn't nearly far enough away from Carl and the idiot with the gun.

She was just starting to get traction when she glanced down at the boy.

What the hell is that sticking out of his chest?

At first, she'd thought it was blood, but it was a different color of red and...

A dart? What the hell is a dart doing sticking out of him?

The answer hit her, and she started pulling for all she was worth. A tranquilizer dart. Someone had shot the boy...

Oh, shit. He was shooting Carl, too.

She looked back to the roaring grizzly shredding the tree. Her mind raced through all the horrible reports she'd heard about psycho militants holed up in compounds throughout Michigan. That's the only people she could think of who'd be shooting tranq darts in the middle of the night. Psychos with an ax to grind. Maybe against shifters.

Was Carl slowing down? How many times had he been shot? She hadn't heard any more pops, but that didn't mean anything. Given the noise Carl was making, she wouldn't have been able to hear a heavy metal rock band.

She needed help. She needed her damned cell phone.

Pocket. Coat.

Hell, she was an idiot. She had her cell on her. But she couldn't just stand there in the open. Not with someone shooting at them. But it was too far to the tree line. Which meant her best bet was to lay low while she called in reinforcements.

She dropped Justin's arms and flattened herself down between the boy and where Carl now stalked through the trees. She didn't think bears could stalk, but he seemed to be, and she could hear his low growl like the angry rumble of a pissed-off train.

At least he was conscious.

She dragged out her cell and dialed 911 with shaking fingers. Then she held it to her ear while she pulled the dart out of Justin's chest. The drug would already be in his system, but no sense leaving it sitting there in case it hadn't.

"911. How can I help?"

It was that same too-chipper voice that she'd heard earlier tonight. Before, she'd hated the woman for being in Carl's pocket, but now she was grateful. "Help," she rasped. "I'm at Carl's checkpoint. Justin's here. He's unconscious. Carl's gone bear at the trees and someone's shooting."

"Keep calm, Becca. Help is on its way." She heard clicking sounds of a keyboard in the background. "Now tell me exactly what you see."

Becca looked up, searching for Carl. She couldn't see him and had no idea what that meant. He could have been knocked unconscious by who knew how many shots. Or he could be happily feasting on dead hunter.

"I don't hear him," she said into the phone. Though there was a mechanical noise. "I can't see—"

Then she did see. Three guys with hoodies on motorcycles heading straight for her. Their headlights flashed across her vision, temporarily blinding her, but she'd seen enough. They came from different directions, though generally south of her position. And they'd seemed to boil out of the trees fast enough that she choked on her fear. They were a ways off, but at that speed, they'd be on her in under a minute.

"Becca!" the voice said. "What's happening?"

"Three motorcycles," she gasped as she leaped to her feet. She had to get Justin out of the way. If she dragged him far enough to the side, maybe the bastards would roar right past. She fumbled with the boy's arm, dropping the phone in the process, and heaved with all her might.

A foot's progress. Then another.

That was all she got when she saw one of the riders point at her. She had time to recognize moonlight on a gun and know that she was about to die. The very idea froze her up like a Popsicle, and she just stared. Nowhere to run with the bastards only a few dozen feet away from her and closing fast.

Then she heard that roar again. Carl in full grizzly tearing through the trees nearest her. Forty feet away at most, but the sound was loud enough that everyone flinched, including the guy with the gun.

Bang.

Not a tranquilizer this time. She prayed it missed. Couldn't be easy to aim from a motorcycle on rough terrain, right? Since she wasn't screaming in pain, she assumed she was okay. But now what? She couldn't abandon Justin, and she couldn't just stand here and die.

She crouched down, adrenaline pouring through her body. If she could get that bastard's gun, she could shoot at them. Ridiculous thought to jump at a guy on a motorcycle as he sped past, but what else could she do? Distantly, she heard the wail of sirens. Thank God. She'd just have to hold out for a minute or two.

Then there was Carl, all bear as he tore into the dirt right in front of her. The nearest motorcycle swerved when the bear swiped, skidding dirt as he flew past. She had a moment to register long, sharp claws, but then there was only grizzly as Carl backed up until he was practically on top of her and Justin. He was protecting her, she realized. And thank God, because now she saw the net.

It was a dark blob stretched between the two remaining motorcycles. Were they trying to catch Carl? They'd need a net the size of a Mack truck. Except Carl wasn't looking too steady. He tried to rear up onto his hind legs, only to flop forward again. Which is when she saw four little red blobs on his body. Tranquilizer darts. Shit.

Where the hell were the police?

The guys with the net swerved around, clearly regrouping. The third one was out there somewhere, too, and she spun around, looking for him.

There! With another gun, this one longer and

thinner. The tranquilizer gun, and it was aimed at Carl.

"Oh, no you don't!" she bellowed. Then she did the stupidest thing her terrified brain had ever imagined. She leaped up to protect a grizzly bear. After all, if they took down Carl, she was helpless. So she leaped. And by some miracle of luck and adrenaline, she'd guessed right. She felt the dart hit, the impact like a baseball against her ribs. Pain bit—sharp—and she fell backward from the power of it.

She hit Carl's butt, bouncing harmlessly off his fur. She felt him spin around, his claws flashing in the moonlight. Another roar and the sirens and the smear of starlight as her head bounced crazily on the ground.

And then...

Nothing.

CHAPTER 7

Becca woke to the sound of muted voices—one male and one female—arguing in heated whispers nearby. Her first thought was that neither one of them was Theo or Carl. The second was that they were arguing over her. Something about it not making sense.

Thank you, Ms. Obvious. Nothing about her last twenty-four hours made sense. As she scrolled through her memory, she ticked off all the ridiculously impossible things.

Theo disappearing—possible, but improbable. He was not a boy to run away, not when he knew how freaked she'd get.

Grizzly bear shifters—impossible. No explanation needed.

Theo returning to Gladwin State Park like a salmon swimming upstream—impossible. His home was in Kalamazoo and always had been.

Kissing Carl—completely and totally impossible, except that statistically speaking...nope. Still impossible. She did not fool around with people in Theo's life. It was just too awkward and Mr. Max was firmly in Theo's life. And yet of all the impossible things in her brain, that was the one that made her heart race and her stomach clench. Why did she pick now of all times to suddenly discover her hormones? Idiotic!

People on motorcycles shooting at her—impossible. She just wasn't a person people shot at. She made castle cakes for little girls' birthday parties. She lived in central Michigan, where nothing happened to anybody except maybe frostbite.

So there it was. Everything was impossible, and yet she remembered every gut-wrenching, heart-pounding, erotic moment. So either she was impossible or the rest of the world was. End of discussion.

She sat up, belatedly realizing that she should have opened her eyes and oriented herself a bit first. Especially since the world began to spin the moment she moved her head. She slammed her eyes shut. It was the only thing to do when Carl's man-cabin living room spun like a theme park ride. Fortunately, it was enough to tell her where she was, if not why.

"You're awake." Female voice. Tonya. The police officer she'd met before.

"Take it slow. You've had a rough go lately." Mr. Obvious, aka Carl's brother, Alan.

She swallowed and forced out the word. "Theo?"

"Still missing." Officer Tonya. "But we've got people looking for him everywhere."

"You had people looking before. What's different now?"

"We've got *more* people looking. And these people have guns."

Becca winced, not sure if that was a good thing or not. "I need to call home. Maybe he's gone back there."

"I just talked to Amy. He's not there, and none of his friends have seen him."

A warm mug was pressed into her hands. "It's ginger tea," said Alan gently. "It'll settle your stomach and then we can work up to broth."

"Thanks," she said as she finally opened her eyes. Alan looked like shit. His face was pale, which didn't do any favors to the lean cut of his jaw. He looked haggard, though his expression was kind.

Officer Gorgeous still looked gorgeous, even with her lips pressed tightly together. Becca looked away rather than feel unequal at a time when she needed all her resources. A glance outside showed early dawn and she frowned. "What time is it?"

"Almost five," Alan answered. "You got hit by a tranquilizer dart. The doctor's been here and will come back in an hour. But if you're having any pain or discomfort, I can call him now."

She processed that slowly as she sipped her ginger tea. Not bad. "Why aren't I in a hospital?" That would be the usual procedure, right?

"Because you're fine," Bitch Officer said. "And because the paperwork is…inconvenient."

"I don't give a rat's ass about your paperwork."

"Fine, then tell me why guys on motorcycles snuck up on Carl."

Becca frowned, then slowly turned her head to stare at the officer. Sure, the woman had looks, a badge, and attitude to spare, but that didn't mean

Becca had to take shit from her. "I don't know. Maybe you could ask them."

"I'm asking you."

"They're in the wind," Alan answered.

Of course they were. Too much to ask that they had caught one of them. "How is the boy?" Becca asked. "Was that Justin? Marty's son?"

"He's fine," said Alan as he brought over a box of Ritz crackers. "Just sleeping it off. That's normal after a First Change."

Becca nodded and ventured another sip of tea. "Where's my cell? I need to call Theo."

"Right here." Alan handed it to her, then everyone waited in taut silence while she dialed. Straight to voice mail. She sighed, then flipped through her email and texts, hoping for some news. Nothing.

She sighed, then turned to the officer, forcing herself to give the woman some respect, if only because she carried a badge and seemed to have been awake all night, presumably looking for Theo. "Tell me what to do to help."

The woman seemed to unbend a bit as she stepped forward. Then, as if consciously trying to force herself to be personable, she sat down on the coffee table so she could be more level with Becca. "Tell me what you remember, from the beginning."

Becca nodded, closing her eyes as she forced herself to remember. She relayed everything as methodically as possible, but damn it, guys with motorcycles and guns had been shooting at her. It was like a bad *Mad Max* movie in a park. And when she finished, she gulped down the last of her tea and tried her best not to freak out.

"You're doing fine," said Alan.

She nodded, but knew the real critic was Officer Tonya. The woman sat rigidly straight as she studied Becca's face. Then she slowly leaned forward.

"Let me explain some simple facts to you," she said, each word crisply distinct. "Carl is our alpha. As Maximus, he's our best warrior. He's big, he's smart, and he's careful. You're saying that the first you noticed Justin, he was lying on the ground. That's not possible. Carl would have seen him walking up, either in bear or human form. Plus, there's the sound of motorcycles. Any shifters can tell the sound, especially since there's no good reason for them to be in the park at that time of night. Carl would have heard it and called it in long before any attack."

Becca frowned, thinking back. Oh, she remembered why Carl hadn't seen Justin before or reacted to the motorcycles. She knew what they'd been doing, but she hadn't thought it important for Officer Bitch to know. What she was trying to think of was when the sounds had first come into her awareness. Had they been there long before Carl went grizzly? She couldn't remember. She'd been too absorbed in letting her hormones get their first fix in years.

"Miss Weitz, what really happened? And this time, try telling the truth."

"That is the truth!" she snapped, pissed that she would have to confess this private detail. It was bad enough that she'd been sucking face while Theo was missing, but to tell it to Tonya was beyond humiliating.

And then a voice came from the other room, the

rumble deep and gravelly, but Becca would know it anywhere. It was Carl, his voice rough in a totally sexy way.

"I was distracted." He sighed and rubbed a hand over his face. "I was...we..."

Stunned silence filled the room. And in that moment, Becca's gaze caught and held Carl's. In his eyes, she saw guilt and embarrassment. Probably an exact echo of her own. But more than that, she saw a quiet longing in the way his eyes never wavered from hers. His hands clutched the doorframe to his bedroom; he was clearly swaying on his feet, but his eyes—damn, his eyes—were locked on her.

"How are you?" he rasped.

"I'm fine. I didn't get a half dozen tranq darts in me." She scanned his body for wounds. He was in sweatpants and without his shirt. Except for the few bandages that dotted his torso, she could see every carved hill and valley of his chest and abdominals. Stunningly beautiful and covered in scars. A zillion of them, some very old. If anything told her exactly what kind of bizarro world she'd landed in, it was his body. Raw and powerful, but also carrying the memory of wounds she could barely comprehend. She wanted to shy away from it. All those scars were like a sign saying Danger! But she couldn't. He mesmerized her.

"I'm fine," he repeated when she finally looked back into his eyes. "Bears can take a lot."

Which is when the other two seemed to unfreeze. Alan was on his feet, crossing to where his brother sagged against the doorframe. "A tyrannosaurus rex can't take that much," he said as he wrapped an arm around Carl's bare trunk. "Let's get you back to bed."

"No. The couch. And I can walk."

"Sure you can. But humor me and let me help."

"I spend my life humoring you," Carl groused and his brother grinned in response.

"Because I'm the only one who tolerates your pissy moods."

The two bickered as only brothers can while Becca cleared a space on the couch. Tonya just watched everything with her coldly assessing gaze. She didn't comment or help while Alan asked his medical questions.

"Any pain?"

"Yes. You."

"What about headache, nausea?"

"I'm fine."

"What day is it?"

"The day you tell me what the fuck happened after I passed out."

"You're a pain in the ass, you know that?"

"Yes. Have we heard from Theo? Is Justin okay? What are we doing to find them?"

Which is when the officer took over, reporting as she might to a commanding officer. It was mostly names and locations rolled out with variations on the phrase "they haven't seen anything unusual." And while Carl got up to speed, Becca had a chance to look closer at his injuries. His torso was a mass of bruises and small cuts, but one bandage on the top of his arm stood out. It was small by comparison, but it had a dark red spot in the middle.

"What happened here?" she said as she touched the bandage.

She hadn't meant to interrupt. The question just slipped out. It was a measure of how much his mere presence took over her brain that she lost all awareness of everything but him. And while the room went silent, Carl set his hand over hers.

"I have no idea," he said.

Then Officer Bitch answered. "That's a bullet hole, Miss Weitz. By someone who doesn't understand how to shoot shifters."

A bullet. Right. The guy with the gun who had missed her when Carl roared.

She felt bile roll through her gut, thoughts mixing with memory, and all of them leading up to horror.

"Oh, shit," said Alan as he grabbed the wastepaper basket. He was just in time. She barely missed him as she emptied her stomach, ginger tea and crackers pouring out of her in choking gasps.

And while she was still retching, Tonya fired rapid questions at Carl. "Who shot you? What do you remember?"

"There was one guy in the tree. I took care of him. Then I heard the others but couldn't circle back in time. Too fucking slow."

"You were hit by eight tranquilizer darts," Alan said as he helped Becca stand and head for the bathroom.

"Then three guys on motorcycles. They were slowing down. Heading for Becca and Justin."

"Why?"

"What?"

Becca was in the bathroom then, listening through the open door.

"Why did they want Becca? Who shot you?"

"I don't know. And I don't remember. I was fighting. Did you get any of them?"

"Three escaped. The other is in pieces. We're working on an ID, but it'll take a while."

Silence.

Pieces? Oh. She meant torn apart by a bear. By Carl. Who was a bear. She was going to be sick again. Meanwhile, Officer Tonya wouldn't let it go.

"What was Miss Weitz doing when you were shot?"

"Tonya, she didn't shoot me. She was already down when I got this."

"You sure?"

"I...yes. I felt her go down."

Becca could tell by the silence that the woman didn't believe it. Meanwhile, she dried her hands before turning to where Alan waited by the door. He was taller than Carl and had golden brown eyes instead of green, but she could see the family resemblance in the square jut of his jaw and the odd perk to his ears. But most important to her was the way he seemed to understand all the nuances without judgment. Of everyone she'd met in Gladwin, he seemed the most approachable, simply because he listened. So she touched his arm and spoke in a soft undertone.

"What does she mean by someone who doesn't know how to shoot shifters?"

Alan's eyes were on the others, but at her question he turned to her. "Extremities shrink down when a bear shifts back to human. We don't know how it works, but only a shot to the torso will do permanent damage. The rest just seems to disappear."

She looked through the doorway at the stark white bandage on Carl's arm. "His didn't."

"It was a pretty big shot. Lethal on a human. And he took it in the meat of his upper arm. It'll be gone the next time he shifts."

What did she say to that? Lucky him? Except he didn't look so lucky. And she still felt sick at the idea. Meanwhile, Carl was arguing with Officer Bitch, who seemed to think the worst of Becca. And as soon as Becca could breathe without fearing she'd hurl, she was going to give the woman a piece of her mind.

"She didn't attack me, Tonya. I got distracted. It was stupid and irresponsible, but that's on me."

"Maybe you were drugged."

"With an aphrodisiac? Do you even hear yourself?"

"It makes no sense, Carl. Why the hell would guys on motorcycles attack you?"

"Not me," Carl said grimly. "Justin."

"What?"

Becca had come back into the room and Carl wasted no time in looking straight at her. His eyes were hooded, so she had no clue as to his emotions, but at his words, that didn't matter so much anymore.

"Someone's been taking shifter kids right around their First Change. That's why Bryn was in Kalamazoo. The wolves have lost two already."

Becca didn't react. She couldn't even process the

words. That didn't seem to be a problem for Officer Tonya, though.

"Abductions, Carl? And when in the hell were you going to tell me about it?"

"I just found out yesterday!" he snapped. Then he frowned. "Er, two days ago."

"You could have—"

"It was just the wolves east of here. Even Bryn thought it might be a coincidence. You know there are always a few who shift and never come back. I honestly thought the wolf was being paranoid. You know how he loves conspiracy theories."

Becca abruptly found her voice. "And what do you think now?"

Carl grimaced. "I think we need to find those other three bastards. They weren't some yahoos out on a drunken hunting party. They were coordinated and they had a net."

Alan's voice was low with horror. "They wanted to capture Justin. Why?"

"Bryn thinks they're being studied."

"Studied?" Becca gasped. "Like rats in a cage? Like why you can shift into a bear and we can't?"

"Yes."

"And you think they've taken Theo?"

He didn't answer, but when he met her gaze, fear was in his eyes.

Which is when Becca lost what little was left in her stomach.

CHAPTER 8

There wasn't anything he could do to help Becca. Carl sat in the living room listening to the woman losing not only her lunch, but her dignity, too. No one threw up with class. It was a violent physical reaction to the horror she'd been through in the last forty-eight hours. And there was nothing he could do to ease her pain.

So he sat there listening, his guts twisting as he scrambled for a way to make it better. There wasn't anything except all the things he'd already planned. Mobilize the clan, the police, and all his resources to find Theo. Contact the other alphas and find out if Bryn's pack was the only one noticing a problem or if there was more to the story. And do that all without unduly alarming his own people or accidentally revealing themselves to a dangerous someone who might just start the very thing he feared: scientific study by a militant faction of baddies.

In other words, it was his normal day as an alpha. The only difference here was that Becca was ten feet away being emotionally and physically torn apart by his world.

He looked at Tonya. Her gaze was on the bathroom, too, but her expression wasn't sympathetic. He could almost hear her brain shifting Becca from "Possible Threat" to "Too Weak to Survive." As a cop, Tonya couldn't afford to babysit the weak. She was too busy defending them from motorcycle psychos with nets. And true to form, she turned away from the bathroom and flicked on her smartphone. A moment later she was showing him a digital map of the area.

"Here's what I've got in place," she said as she rattled off people who were all part of the Gladwin clan safety net and their locations. "It's everyone and I can't think of anything more to do."

"I can," he said, as he grabbed his tablet. He stared at the electronic device, knowing just how to access the information he needed. But his heart and mind weren't there. He was in the bathroom wishing he had the right to comfort Becca. The need was a physical ache right behind his breastbone.

"Fuck the right," he grumbled to himself. He didn't need permission. He needed the tools to ease her pain, and in that, he was sorely lacking. He just didn't know what to say. So he left the nurturing to his fully human brother, Alan, and became the Maximus the clan needed.

"Here's who we need to contact and what we're going to get from them," he said as he pulled up a map of Michigan that marked all the shifter clans and their territories.

He started outlining his plan. It took ten minutes for Tonya to get the full scope and another two before she was out the door implementing his thoughts. Add in another twenty to get a snarling Mark on the phone and to set his nearly feral best friend on his job. Next came calling all the shifter alphas nearby and waking them at dawn to probe into sensitive areas about how they manage their young. And once that was done, he had to ask for their help. Not the easiest task, especially since diplomacy wasn't a typical grizzly strength.

And he did it all while keeping half an eye on Becca, constantly searching her for clues about her thoughts and feelings.

The hours ground away. Phone call after logistical meeting after Internet call. It was all needed and tedious in the extreme. Especially since every response was in the negative. No, they hadn't lost any young that they'd admit, though a few teens were not currently in sight. No, they hadn't seen Theo, but would do their best to contain the youth safely if they did. And no, they would not support any grizzly incursion on their territory without proper assurances, etc., etc.

It was the assurances that took the bulk of his time.

That and keeping himself aloof as Becca seemed to shrink into herself, growing more panicked with every passing moment. She was about to break, and everyone knew it. Alan had been alternately feeding her and encouraging her to rest. The doctor had visited and given her a sleeping aid, which she didn't take. Even Tonya had let her speak to the Kalamazoo police as they detailed what they were doing to locate Theo without anyone mentioning shape-shifting.

And now it was nearly three. His body was an allover ache from his injuries and his stomach alternated between ravenously hungry and queasy from the lingering sedatives of those damn darts. The last reports had come in negative for Theo and even Justin had woken with no news. All the kid remembered was walking home as a bear and then waking up in his bedroom as a man. Which left them doing nothing more than sitting around waiting for more reports and praying for good news.

Which is when Becca finally broke.

He'd just gotten off the phone with Bryn and was dreading having to report more non-news when he saw Becca drawing on her coat, her lips flattened into a hard line of determination. The man in him braced for an argument, while his contrary bear cheered her attitude. Bears generally didn't balance pros and cons in a logical fashion. Anything that smacked of action had them cheering. Usually as a bystander as someone else went impulsively into destruction, but no one ever accused a grizzly of being a deep thinker. It was his job as Maximus to manage the two halves. And at this moment, it meant keeping Becca calm.

Coward that he was, he looked around for Alan. Sadly, the man was out doing all the things that Carl was letting slip while coordinating the search for Theo. Which meant it was up to him to see that Becca didn't do something stupid.

"Going out for a walk?" he asked. "I could use a stretch, too. Let me grab my coat and I'll join you."

"What? Um, no." Her eyes skated away from his, and he realized she was standing next to the wall where all the keys hung. Sure enough, his truck keys were missing and he'd lay odds she had them tucked into her tiny hand.

He stood, making sure to go slowly, as if he were much more wounded than he actually was. No sense being injured and not playing the please-nurse-me card. Of course, since he actually was hurt, he didn't have to pretend the wince of pain as he straightened. "Tonya's going to check in soon." Not for a couple hours actually, but he was still in the business of delaying Becca until they knew more. "And Mark could show up any minute. He's sneaky in his own way. He may have news that no one else does."

She took a deep breath and met his gaze squarely. Uh-oh.

"Look," she said, her voice tight. "I know you think you're doing the right thing. No one could say you weren't pulling out all the stops."

"Theo is one of us. Of course I'd throw all my resources—"

"That's just it," she stressed. "There's no evidence that Theo is one of you. He's never…changed. Not like you guys. We're just normal people. We don't…*Mad Max* is just a movie, you know?"

He did know. He also knew that she had bravely faced down three guys with guns, which made her the rarest of rare: a normal person with *hero* inside. But even heroes had to get past a healthy, rational denial of magic.

"So what's the plan here, Becca? Where you going with my truck?"

"I'm going home, Carl. Back to Kalamazoo, where Theo is probably playing video games with some new friend and he's forgotten to call."

"Does that sound like Theo?"

She looked away. Of course it didn't. "This isn't my world," she said, the words choking out of her. "We're not part of it. So I'm going home, where he'll be at the bakery studying."

"Wouldn't Stacy have called if he was there?"

She turned toward the door, her shoulders rigid with stubbornness. "Maybe she's busy with customers."

Damn it, she was bolting for sure. "You don't believe that. You just don't want to believe this, either."

She froze, and he knew he'd hit on the truth. "I can't just sit here. I can't just do nothing."

"What would you do at home?"

She shrugged, the ghost of a smile curving her lips. "Bake. And worry."

"So bake here."

She shook her head. "There's no point. It's just what I do when I can't think of something more useful." Her gaze turned, tortured. "Do you really think Theo's been…taken by those…thugs?"

He wanted to lie to her, but he could already tell that she wouldn't accept a pat response. If she did, Alan would have calmed her down hours ago. So he crossed to her and stroked her arm.

"I think Theo takes after his aunt."

"What does that mean?"

"I think he's going to surprise us all. I'm going to find him, Becca, but I'll lay odds that when I do, he'll be a long way to rescuing himself."

"So you think he needs rescuing?"

"Don't we all? At one time or another?"

She slugged him weakly in the chest. "You're spouting greeting card philosophy and I'm barely holding it together here."

He grabbed her wrist and used it to reel her in. She came easily, needing the comfort as much as he needed to give it. She was such a tiny thing in his arms. Normal-sized for a woman, but he was on the huge side, even for grizzly shifters. And when she tucked her face against his chest, wetting his shirt with her tears, he marveled at how perfect this felt. Not the fear or the taut clench of her hands in his flannel shirt, but the inaudible click in his head as they synced together. Tiny as she was, she filled his arms. And together, they made a whole that he'd been aching for his entire life.

"Do you know what I remember of last night?" he said against her hair.

"Abject terror?" she asked. Then she moaned. "No, that was me."

He squeezed her. "It was me, too. The moment I saw you head out for Justin. I kept roaring for you to stay back."

She shifted in his arms. "Is that what you were doing? I thought—" She cut off her words, but he wouldn't let her get away with that.

"What? Believe me, I've heard it all."

She winced, and as close as they were, he felt the movement. "I thought you were going to eat him."

He sighed. Of course she'd think the absolute worst. "I was trying to protect him by standing over him. And you were safest hidden by the tree."

She shifted back and he reluctantly eased his hold. "So when you're a bear, you can think? Like a man?"

"I think like a bear with simple man words. Protect. Defend." *Destroy.*

"And you were protecting Justin?"

"I was protecting you both. I knew there was someone in the trees. So when you came out into the open, I had to become more aggressive. I had to take out the threat."

"Which is why you left us."

Again, she'd thought the worst. "I didn't know there were more hunters. I only sensed the one man."

She nodded and stepped farther back. "You thought you were doing the right thing."

"I *was* doing the right thing," he huffed. "That guy had a tranq gun. He could have picked us both off and then taken Justin and us without a fight."

She nodded, and he could see that her mind was telling her the same thing. But inside she was feeling something else entirely. It didn't take a genius to guess what.

"You thought I'd abandoned you."

She snorted. "I *wanted* you to abandon us. I thought you were trying to eat Justin."

Ridiculous to feel hurt. She knew nothing of their kind and so, of course, jumped to all the wrong conclusions. But did she really think he could do that? Even as a bear? "When did you realize the truth?"

She took too long to answer, which told him clear as day that she'd never understood. He'd never abandon her. Not while there was breath in his body.

"I should have called 911 sooner," she said. "I should have thought before I ran out into the open."

"You did the bravest thing I've ever seen, Becca. You had no defenses, but you ran out to protect Justin anyway."

She shook her head. "It was stupid."

"It was brave. And yeah, next time you're going to have a gun and a cell with 911 on speed dial." He touched her cheek. "I'll never forget the sight of you crouching down as they were heading toward you. You were going to fight." He pressed his forehead to hers. "That's when I felt complete terror. I knew I couldn't get to you in time to save you."

"But you did."

He nodded. He had. Adrenaline and all that. Plus shifter reflexes. "Don't run, Becca. Not where I can't protect you."

She jerked as he spoke, lifting her head back and away from him. "I don't need protection. None of this is my fight."

He could see she wanted to believe that. She needed to hold on to the thought that she could run back to Kalamazoo and none of what had happened in the last two and a half days would follow her. And maybe it was possible. Maybe Theo hadn't gone through his First Change and certainly hadn't been taken by whatever nut jobs were out there chasing down shifter kids. Maybe all of this was a big misunderstanding. But even if that were true, he'd already gone too far to let her go.

"There's something else I have to tell you," he said, hating that he was backed into another corner, but delaying this wasn't going to help. Which meant he needed to get it out there in the open.

She stiffened, bracing herself for more bad news. "What?"

"I've never gotten distracted like I did last night." She frowned at him, clearly not understanding. "Even as a teen, I never let a girl pull me away from my responsibilities. Not even once."

Her gaze canted away. And denied her eyes, he focused on her scent to give him clues as to her feelings. "You're talking about the kiss," she said, her voice low and her scent wary.

"I'm talking about ten or twenty minutes when I planned to take you in every way possible. I meant to mate with you right there against the tree and nothing—not even Justin—was going to stop me."

She frowned without looking up. "But you did stop."

"When there was danger."

"But—"

She wasn't getting it. "I'm the Maximus here. I've been bred and trained from the beginning to be responsible for my people."

"I know—"

"I don't get distracted. It's not who I am."

She was silent, and he could all but hear her thoughts churning. She was struggling to understand a world vastly different from her own, and he couldn't have been more pleased when her scent went from wary to aroused. From frightened to intrigued. Unable to stop himself, he touched her stubborn chin and steadily turned her until she was looking into his eyes. The man in him knew he needed to give her more time, but once her arousal colored the air, the grizzly demanded he possess her now that they were alone in a safe environment. It was an insanely aggressive physical push to own her as the war between grizzly and man ratcheted up exponentially.

So he chose to explain rather than to take. To tell her things he barely acknowledged to himself, much less to anyone else. But his grizzly gave him no choice. She had to know who she was to his bear.

"There's only one thing that can distract an alpha like me. Only one time when the primal drives override everything else."

Her eyes widened, but she didn't ask. He willed her to form the words, but she didn't. So he had to fill in the last piece for her.

"It's when his true mate appears. It doesn't happen often, but when it does, it's undeniable. It's some magical alchemy of animal and man and the special pressure of being clan leader. To be honest, I didn't think it more than a fairy tale."

She took a step back, the motion a sure stab into his heart. Her scent was muddled now, holding notes of confusion, fear, lust, and delight. "That's all this is. A fairy tale. A nightmare or a fever dream or... I don't know. None of this is real."

She needed to believe that because it was coming at her too fast. He sympathized but his bear would not let her run from this. "It's real, Becca." He snared her elbow and kept her close without dragging her back against her will. "You're my Maxima."

"I can't be. I'm not even... We don't even know that Theo—"

"Don't care," he said, his temper getting short. The more she fought him, the more his bear got pissed off. And right now, all it wanted to do was drag her back into his arms and stake his claim. But that was the bear in him. The man knew to insist she listen, but not force her to do more. "I know this is coming at you too fast."

"Ya think?"

"But I also know I can't let you leave. Not until we find Theo. Not until you give us a chance."

"A chance? To what? Mate like animals in the woods?"

"Yes! No!" He grabbed hold of his temper with an act of will. "I am not an animal, Becca, but I do have certain instincts."

"Instincts!" She threw the word at him like an insult.

"Yes." He drew her face up to his. "And they tell me that you're the one for me."

"Do you hear yourself? Do you hear how insane that is? There is no destined queen for you. There is no soul mate or fairy godmother or Beauty to tame your Beast. None of this is real!"

That was it. That was where his temper broke and he gave up trying to talk logically to her. This wasn't about rational thinking anyway. It was her denial, and he couldn't let her have it. There was too much at stake.

They were at stake.

So he kissed her. He hauled her into his arms and he slammed his mouth down on hers. It wasn't how a man kissed a woman. It wasn't even how an animal claimed its mate. It was some combination of that plus more. It was need. He needed her to acknowledge him. He needed her to accept that they were real. He needed her to want him as insanely desperately as he wanted her.

Which made no sense at all. They barely knew each other. And yet it was real.

She fought him, but only for a moment. She stiffened in his arms, she pushed at his chest, and she tightened her mouth against him. But somewhere between one heartbeat and the next, she surrendered. He'd barely touched her lips when she began to open to him. He hadn't even gotten his arms around her when her hands changed from pushing him away to clutching him closer. And then she whimpered, a sound that was both lust and surrender.

And now she understood. She hungered for him as fiercely as he lusted for her. She didn't want to. Neither did he. A human Maxima caused all sorts of problems. But this was undeniable. And so they kissed.

Hard. Hot.

He wrapped his arms around her waist and picked her up. The bear in him had taken over. She belonged in his bed. And he was going to claim her.

Now.

CHAPTER 9

I've lost my mind. That was all Becca could think as she felt Carl lift her up. Of all the insane things that had happened in the last few days, this had to rank as the most bizarre. She was kissing a man who turned into a bear. She was kissing a man who had dragged her unwillingly into his terrifying world of magic. And yet she couldn't stop.

He'd protected her when she'd thought he'd abandoned her.

He was marshaling people throughout the state to find Theo.

And he kissed her like she was his last breath.

Maybe it was the adrenaline. After all, she'd been keyed up all day, with no way to expend her energies.

Maybe it was because she hadn't been touched in a long time, and certainly not the way he was touching her. Even his gaze was like a physical caress, and she'd been feeling it on her since she'd woken up in his bedroom eons ago.

He set her on her feet beside his bed, simultaneously kicking the door shut. Then he unbuttoned her blouse while pressing tiny, licking kisses across her cheek and jaw.

"I can't stop," he murmured against her ear. "I can't. Tell me you want this, too."

Her fingers curled into the soft fleece of his red checked shirt. Then she began to pull apart his buttons. "Yes," she said. And when his hips jerked in response, pressing the hot ridge of his cock against her, she tilted her head up to look him in the eyes. "No diseases, right?" she asked, before she lost all reason. "No weird shifter thing I should know about beforehand?"

"All human normal," he said, his eyes dark and intense as he looked at her. Then he flashed a wicked smile. "Though my endurance might be legendary."

He tugged her blouse off her shoulders, and she hated that she had to let go of him to strip it away. Then he slid his palms around her rib cage to unhook her bra. He was so big, it felt like he could touch all of her.

"Legendary?" she said breathlessly. "That's quite a statement."

"I like filling a woman," he said. "The feel of her wet and hot around me." Her bra released and he tossed it aside. "I can stroke her all day until she can't stand it anymore."

The idea made her insides clench in hunger. The way he said it though—with a growl low in his throat—set everything in her to wild. She wanted to climb onto him, spreading her legs so he could take her standing.

Meanwhile, he moved to press tiny licks across the curve of her shoulder. "You taste amazing."

She had his shirt unbuttoned, but couldn't do more than press it off his shoulders. At least she could feel the muscled strength there, the broad expanse and—Ooh!

He abruptly cradled her head and shoulders while lifting her knees. She upended into his arms so he could lay her out on the bed. It added to her topsy-turvy feelings and she embraced them willingly, shedding the last of her inhibitions. Nothing was sane. Nothing was stable. She might as well hold on to what she could: him. And the exciting way he made her feel.

He settled her on the bed, her torso bared to his mouth as he began to lick her nipples one after the other. He didn't bite, but when he chose to suck, lightning seemed to arc straight to her womb.

"Not enough," he said against her breast, and she couldn't have agreed more.

She felt his hands fumbling with her jeans. She thought about helping him, but had more fun stroking her hands across his chest and using her thumbnails to scratch at his nipples. He growled the first time she did it—a low rumble that made her smile. Half purr, half hunger. She could listen to that forever.

Then suddenly his touch disappeared. Her breasts ached at the loss, suddenly cold and erotically tight. He loomed over her, his gaze roving over her body. Then he moved, putting his hands on her jeans and jerking them down with a single flick of his wrists. She'd been stripped naked in a split second. Perfect. Then she helped him by kicking the pants away when they caught on her heel.

"You glow, did you know that? What I see..." He

stroked a hand down her quivering belly. "Golden bright."

She didn't know what to say to that. She could only stare at the wonder in his face. The moment felt startlingly intense to be the subject of such amazement. As though he worshipped her even as he slowly—firmly—pulled his hands down her hips and thighs to spread her knees.

He took a deep breath, his eyes rolling back slightly.

"Ambrosia," he murmured.

Then he dove in.

She felt no subtlety in his movement, and given that he was such a large man, he moved surprisingly fast. One moment he stood poised above her, his mouth curved in appreciation. Then next, his tongue stroked her core, licking her in wide swaths that had her arching in shocked delight.

No one had ever done that to her. Not with such voracious appetite. No question that he loved tasting every inch of her, and she sped to her peak like a freight train. He took her there without compromise, without pause, and when she exploded, she screamed his name.

She'd never climaxed so fast or so hard, her hips bucking against his hands as he held her contained on the bed. But rather than stop, he softened his caress. His tongue slid around, everywhere but her peak. And when he pushed his fingers inside her, she continued to clutch at him, trying to draw in more. Deeper, harder.

He pressed his lips to her thigh, nuzzling her gently.

"Do that again for me," he said as she felt more fingers push inside.

She couldn't comprehend what he was asking. She was still floating, her belly constricting in slowly diminishing pulses.

"Again," he said.

Then she felt his thumb across her clit. First a roll, then a slow circular motion. Her body jolted in reaction and he softened his pressure. It was too much…for a moment. And then it was just right. And then…

"Oh God," she gasped. "You really mean it."

"All day, Becca. God, I never want to stop." The fingers deep inside her shifted and pulled.

G-spot!

She hadn't even thought it was real, but he stroked it perfectly.

"I can't!" she cried, though she already knew she could. And that he wouldn't stop.

She threw her head back, her body lifting up to his. She closed her eyes while he stroked every intimate place. Once. Twice.

Her breath caught. She was almost—

He stopped.

He slowed.

Soothing her with another slow kiss and a gentle bite on her thigh.

"Yes," he murmured.

Her pulse pounded in her ears, sounding like a never-ending echo of "yes, yes, yes, yes."

Then he built her again. Her legs were spread as wide as they would go. Everything in her was liquid pulse, beating to his stroke. Inside and out, he played her. Rubbing, pushing, spreading, and even thrusting with his hand.

Then she felt him lean in. His thumb moved away from her clit and was replaced by his tongue. Slow. Gentle. He dropped the tension back down again until she was mindless with need.

"Carl!" she gasped.

"Say yes for me," he said as he did a slow lick all around her clit.

"Yes."

He sucked. One strong pull right on her peak.

Detonation!

And it went on and on and on.

She was still riding those marvelous waves when she heard someone come into the house. The bedroom door was shut and her pulse was still loud in her ears, but some sounds were hard to ignore. Especially when she heard Alan call out, panic in his voice.

"Carl? Carl! Are you all right?"

"I'm fine!" Carl barked from between her legs. "Don't come in!"

If she weren't still high from the best orgasms of her life, she probably would have been embarrassed. As it was, she just started chuckling. Though she did manage to drop her arm across her face to muffle the sound.

"Where are you? Tonya's been calling."

Carl abruptly left his position to dive at the door, clicking the lock a second before Alan's footsteps sounded outside the room. "I told you," Carl said. "Don't come in."

"Tonya is on her way over. She got an ID. Where's Becca?"

Her giggling abruptly stopped the moment she heard the word "ID." But when she straightened up on her elbows to answer, Carl shot her a desperate look and shook his head. She immediately swallowed her words, but that didn't stop the slow sink in her gut. Was he ashamed? Embarrassed to be caught blowing off steam in the middle of a crisis?

Meanwhile, Carl gestured to the bathroom, by which she guessed that he wanted her to go in there. "She's taking a shower. I'll be out in a second. Who was the ID?"

"Don't know except that they're getting warrants and coordinating with ATF."

ATF? As in the scary governmental agency the Bureau of Alcohol, Tobacco, Firearms and Explosives? The one that took out the wackos in Waco?

"She'll be here in twenty." Alan tried the doorknob. "Damn it, Carl, are you hurt?"

"Not in the least," he said with a grin. But then he quickly sobered as he helped Becca sit up. He leaned in and whispered into her ear. "Can you shower fast? I'm going to have to step in behind you."

Her eyes widened but she nodded. Then he practically lifted her up to her feet—aka weak noodles—and carried her into the bathroom as if she were the queen of England with broken legs. Then he bent down to her ear again.

"I'll explain later," he whispered. Then he paused as if to linger. She would have leaned into him. She was still rosy with afterglow, but he abruptly stepped back. "Quickly," he said as he gestured to the shower.

Yeah, yeah. She got it. She looked like she'd just

been fucked to heaven and back. Which she had. But he didn't want others to know about it, and the more she thought about it, the more she agreed. She wasn't exactly sure what craziness had led her to dive into sexuality for the first time in years, but that was stress for you. At some point, it all had to blow somehow. Might as well be fun when it goes.

But there was no time to linger. She flipped on the shower and stepped in before it warmed. The shock of that was enough to chase away any remaining glow. Which meant that all too soon she was thinking about Theo and the ATF and all the horrible scenarios her imagination kept creating.

She showered in record time.

And when she stepped out, Carl was there handing her a towel. "There's fresh clothes for you on the bed," he said in a low tone. It was almost enough to distract her from the fact that he was fully naked and hugely erect.

"Uh—" was all she got out before he leaned in and turned the tap to cold. Then he pulled on the shower and stepped right into the icy spray.

Well, if he didn't shrink up from that, he was one virile man.

Part of her wanted to stay and watch to see how long it would take. It was one of her longtime fantasies to see a fine man lather up. But that was just an indication of how far away from center she was. How could she even imagine doing something like that when Theo might be caught in the middle of an ATF battle?

She hurried out of the bathroom and was dressed a few minutes later in borrowed leggings and an oversize sweatshirt. A single whiff told her it was Carl's, and she buried her nose in it while she listened to the steady pound of the shower. Tonya wasn't here yet, so she had a moment to linger in *wow!* What they'd done—wow. The way he'd done it—wow. The fact that even now, her skin was still tingling from it—double wow.

Then she pulled on her shoes and left the bedroom, her mind already shoving the experience into a tiny little box labeled "What Becca Did to Blow Off Anxiety." It had no other meaning, which is why she felt excruciatingly calm as she faced Alan, who was just coming out of the kitchen with a sandwich.

"When was the last time you slept?" she blurted. He looked awful, with sallow skin and baggy eyes. And for such a handsome man, that was saying something.

"About the last time you did," he said, though it was obviously not true. She'd spent hours knocked unconscious. "Did Carl tell you? They got an ID on the guy that Carl killed." The words rolled out of him, then he abruptly winced. "I mean the guy who attacked...er..."

"I get it. The bastard with the tranquilizer gun."

"And a sawed-off shotgun. They found his motor-cycle stashed in the trees. Matched the license with the dental records and voilà, ID."

She nodded. "Who was it?"

Alan shrugged as he stuffed a badly done chicken salad sandwich into his mouth. She could smell the cheap mustard from across the room. "Tonya will be here in ten. She has all the details."

Meanwhile Carl came out of his room, still towel-drying his hair. He had on jeans slung low on his hips and an unbuttoned flannel shirt, this one green. It set off his eyes, which distracted her from the kissable expanse of his muscled chest. "How's it going out there? What's the mood?" he asked his brother.

"Tense. Everyone knows about the attack. They're worried for Theo and anxious about..." He shrugged. "Everything."

Meanwhile, Alan's eyes darted back and forth between the two of them while Becca did her best to keep a neutral expression. Nope, she hadn't just had a couple screaming Os while he was outside holding things together.

Carl tossed the towel into a basket by the door to the basement. It was overflowing with laundry, and his toss toppled a pile of shirts and socks onto the floor. Wow, these men needed a housekeeper badly. She was wondering if she had time to throw in a load—it was the least she could do—when Carl picked his phone off the counter and let out a low whistle.

"Okay, so ten calls from Tonya might be overkill."

"We thought you'd had a seizure or something."

"I was resting." Wow, the way he said that made it sound possible...not. Even she knew Carl resisted anything related to rest.

Alan didn't look like he believed it either, but he decided not to comment. "Anything from the wolves?"

Carl shook his head. "Nothing. Though Tonya probably has kept Bryn up to date."

Then there was more conversation about people she didn't know and how they were reacting to the situation. Becca listened, trying to keep track of the names while she dialed Theo's number. She didn't know why she kept at it. If he had his phone, he would have responded by now. So she listened to the sound of his recorded message just to hear his happy voice telling her to leave a message.

Where was he?

Carl's arm landed heavy and brusque across her shoulders as he pulled her into a hug. It wasn't a gentle movement or remotely subtle. But the sudden weight of him felt solid, and she leaned into his embrace.

"We'll find him. He'll be fine and have a great story to tell his grandchildren."

She chuckled, the sound more choke than laughter. "He's not even dating yet. Let's not leap straight to grandchildren."

"They'll be here before you know it."

Maybe, she thought, the idea both reassuring and depressing. She'd thought about what would happen when Theo went off to college, met a girl, and settled down. The idea pleased her to no end, but part of her wondered exactly what she'd be doing while Theo was living his life. He was the only family she had. Everyone else was gone. She didn't want to be a hanger-on in his life, but what else did she have? A business and the ability to make castle cakes for other people's children.

Fortunately, Officer Tonya chose that moment to burst through the front door. She moved efficiently as she held up a hand for silence. She was on the phone, listening intently, so everyone waited in silence for her. Which was helpful for Becca, who was busy tucking away all thoughts of her empty future in favor of finding Theo in the here and now.

"Excellent," the woman said into the phone. "I'll meet you there."

She thumbed off her phone, then looked at the three of them. Her eyes narrowed at Carl, who still had his arm draped across Becca's shoulders, but at her look he dropped his arm, stepped around the coffee table, and confronted the officer.

"What's going on?" His tone was all alpha, demanding a report.

She took a deep breath and obeyed his command. "Got the warrant. So the kid you killed was from a militant compound about thirty miles northwest of here. Moss family."

Even from behind and only looking at Carl's back, Becca could see him flinch at Tonya's phrasing. But the officer kept talking, apparently oblivious to any reaction.

"ATF has been dying to get inside there, and now we've got the excuse."

Alan piped up from the other side of the couch. "He tried to kill Carl. That's not an excuse. That's a felony."

The officer nodded in an offhand way. "Whatever. We've got the warrant and are moving on the compound now."

Becca stepped around Carl. "What about Theo?"

The woman hesitated for only a moment, then shrugged. "Everyone's still watching."

"Those that aren't about to raid a militant compound," Becca countered.

"We've got a ton of civilian watchers." Then she

squared to pin Becca with a hard stare. "Isn't it better to know if he's there or not? If he's been captured by these wackos, then we'll get him out."

"Or get him killed!"

The woman shook her head. "Not going to happen."

"You don't know that." Becca didn't know why she was being so contrary. What better option did they have?

Officer Bitch pursed her lips. "There are no guarantees, Ms. Weitz. But I can tell you this: we're trained professionals and we're going to do everything we can to keep your nephew safe."

Becca wished she found that reassuring. She didn't. And from that well of unhappiness, her next words just formed: "I'm coming with you."

"No." Then the woman turned to the men. "None of you are. This is not a spectator sport." Tonya took a deep breath and looked hard at Carl. "I recognize your authority, Maximus, but the government does not. I can't—"

"I know," interrupted Carl, and Becca could tell by the tight set to his body that he chafed at being sidelined. "That's why we're going to sit well back from the police and wait close by for news."

Tonya's eyes narrowed. "ATF will never allow—"

Carl spoke right over her. "If Theo's there, he might need to see his aunt. And I'll be there in case you need an alpha shifter. Doesn't matter the species, everyone responds to an alpha."

They did? Apparently so, because Tonya's expression tightened until she looked like she was sucking on a lemon. But she still argued.

"You're injured. Doc said you needed to rest for a week."

That thought alarmed Becca, but there was nothing she could do about it. Even she could see Carl wasn't going to be denied as he folded his arms across his chest. "Doesn't matter. You know I have to be there."

Apparently she did, because she shot him an angry glare.

"Besides," he added, as he headed for his coat, "you already knew I was coming. That's why you stopped off here."

"It was a courtesy stop—"

"Whatever."

Becca scrambled, too, pulling on her shoes and coat. Meanwhile, Officer She-Bear turned to pin Alan with her disgruntled fury. "You're not coming."

He didn't say a word. He just stood there looking at her, his entire body tall and absolutely still.

"It's dangerous work," the woman continued, punctuating it with a glare.

Alan lifted his chin. "I'm not the one you're angry with, Tonya, so bitch at someone else. I'm not in the mood." And with that, he set down his plate, grabbed his coat and car keys, and was out the door before anyone else.

Which left Officer Tonya standing in the middle of the room fuming silently. Becca almost felt sorry for her, but a moment later the woman recovered and fast marched out the door. She would have slammed it in Becca's face if Carl hadn't rushed forward to catch it.

"Don't worry about her," he said softly as he

gestured to his truck. "Hope that in an hour, this will all be over and you and Theo will be joining me for a hearty dinner of steaks badly cooked by my own hand."

"You're a bad cook?"

Carl snorted. "It's hard to mess up a steak, but I've done it several times."

"Then I'll cook. You just see that Theo is there at the table."

"Deal."

Then they rolled out right behind Alan's car and Tonya's squad car, all three of them heading to the Moss family compound of militant crazies. If she weren't so frightened for Theo, she probably would have laughed at the absurdity of it all. She was a baker with no military skills whatsoever. And yet here she was, rolling out in a convoy like she was part of a band of badasses.

CHAPTER 10

Carl was out of control, and he hated it.

It was one thing to go all Destructo on Nick's field. The man deserved it and worse, so Carl had let his bear go wild. But that was nothing compared to what the bear wanted right now. Unfettered sexual thoughts coursed through his grizzly, and he had no idea how he was going to control it. He didn't just want to mate with Becca, he wanted her to orgasm around his dick for a decade. He wanted to lick every part of her while he planted his children in her. And he wanted it now and damn the rest of the community, his position as Max, and her wishes in the matter.

That wasn't logic. That wasn't the man in him thinking. No, this was pure animal without restraint. Which made life all the more difficult because she was sitting in his truck smelling like sex while on the way to a dangerous raid.

"Get it together," he muttered.

"What?"

"Nothing," he snapped.

She sighed. "It's not nothing. None of this is nothing." She dropped her head back against the seat. "I'm so turned around, I have no idea where's up."

He looked at her, seeing the soft curve of her cheek, the pert lift to her nose, and the circles under her eyes. It would be easy to blame her exhaustion on just the last two and a half days. Certainly that had taken its toll, but she'd been pushing hard for a long time now. He could see it in the way she closed her eyes for maybe ten seconds, then took a breath and refocused. She put away the panic and the fear, closing it down while she soldiered on. No one got so good at compartmentalizing without a lot of practice.

"You've been on crisis control for a while now, haven't you?"

"What?"

"It's not just the shifter stuff, it's everything. I know you took over custody of Theo four years ago, and that couldn't have been easy."

"God, no. He'd lost his mother, and soon after that, my mom died of lung cancer. He was one frightened preteen."

So she'd lost her sister and mother and suddenly had to care for a grieving boy. "What did your sister do for a living?"

"She…Um…She temped sometimes. Had a stint at McDonald's for a bit. But Theo took most of her time."

So no money there. And he knew that there was no cash from the father or the grandfather. Sure, Isaac had wanted to help out, but his sons had left so many bastards there wasn't any way to keep up.

"Who supported them while she was looking after Theo? Was it you?"

"I wish. I was busy getting my business degree plus shifts at the bakery. That's where most of our money came from—my aunt's bakery. And Mom was a nurse bringing in a good income. It wasn't until Mom got sick that things got really bad."

"And it was you, wasn't it? You held everything together."

She opened her mouth to deny it or at least dismiss her contribution. But in the end, she looked down at her hands. "I got the education. That meant I had to bring in the bucks."

"I don't just mean the money, though that probably was a strain all itself. Who held Theo's hand when he was scared? Who took your mother to chemo? Who saw that the electricity got paid and there was food in the refrigerator?"

She looked at him, her mouth soft even as she narrowed her eyes at him. "What are you trying to say?"

That she'd had it hard. For a really long time. He'd been cursing himself because he was horny, but if anyone had a reason to curse, it was her. And yet here she sat, pulling it together for one more moment. One more crisis. One more day.

"Have you ever been allowed to think long term?" he asked. "Have you ever considered your future and your wants? Or has it always been about making sure the family survived?"

"My wants are my family." She winced. "Theo."

Right. Because the rest were gone.

"He's going to be fine. I won't let anything

happen to him." It came out as a vow, and he damn well wasn't going to falter, no matter how distracted he got. Besides, even if she weren't as important to him as his next breath, she'd become part of his clan through Theo. That made her his top priority.

She nodded, apparently grabbing on to his promise and holding it tight. They stayed silent a moment, and he watched her hands grip together. She was thinking things, worrying, and he needed to distract her. Naturally, his bear had all sorts of ideas, but that wasn't going to happen. Then she spoke, creating her own distraction.

"So what's going on between Alan and Officer Stick-Up-Her-Ass?"

"Officer..." He laughed, a choked sound. "Tonya's good at her job. She's just buttoned down. Her bear is really strong, and it's the only way she can cope."

Becca's gaze shifted to the patrol car ahead, and he could tell she was chewing on that information. Which gave him time to sort through the rest of her question.

"And there's nothing between her and Alan. We've all known one another forever. We get to squabbling like siblings."

"Siblings?" she said, her tone almost mocking. "If you say so."

"Of course..." He frowned. Was it possible? Did his brother have a thing for Tonya? If so, he was one doomed camper. She was never going to go for a man who couldn't shift. She was all about the grizzly heritage and pack leadership. She was six when she'd decided to become Maxima. Alan was so human he wasn't even hairy. "I hope you're wrong," he muttered.

"Tonya doesn't like him?"

"Tonya has her sights somewhere else." Until he officially proclaimed her his beta at the next clan meeting, she would still think about being his Maxima. And even that promotion might not deter her. She was one determined woman. And, to his surprise, Becca picked up on the problem without him needing to explain it.

"Tonya wants you," she said. It wasn't a question. And then she figured out the rest. "That's why you wanted us to shower. So she wouldn't smell us on each other." Then she looked down at her clothes. His clothes. "And any lingering scent could be explained by my wearing your clothes."

He'd wanted her to wear his things, period. He wanted her to settle into his bed and never leave while he fed her with his own hand from game he had killed himself. Which wasn't so much bear as Neanderthal. Meanwhile, he had to explain himself to her. "I'm not ashamed of what we did."

She didn't react, obviously keeping her emotions locked down.

"This isn't the time to declare a relationship," he said carefully. "I want to, but…"

"It's not a relationship," she said softly, her gaze shifting back to the open road. "It was blowing off steam. Let's not make it into anything more than that, okay?"

His hands tightened on the wheel and it took all his willpower to suppress his bear's howl of rage.

Nothing more than blowing off steam? Did she understand nothing?

Except logic supported her statement. After all, she wasn't the only one strung tight. Even before Theo's disappearance, he'd been on edge. The clan dissent and pressure to marry Tonya were growing exponentially. Of course he'd turn to the first woman who was outside of all that idiocy. Especially one who was soft and nurturing. Maybe after Theo was found and Nick was sorted out, he'd discover that they had nothing in common. What did he know about baking or a mundane life in Kalamazoo?

Maybe.

Except it sure as hell didn't feel that way.

"That's why I thought we should shower," he said. "To avoid distractions. But I'm not ashamed."

"Neither am I."

That was something. Especially since her scent confirmed the statement. She was determined. No shame stink on her. "After this is all over, I thought we could go out to dinner."

She looked back at him, her lips curving into an incredulous smile. "The man who just gave me the best orgasms of my life is asking me out on a date?"

"Um...yeah?"

"Um...okay." Then her expression tightened. "But afterward."

"Definitely. Not until Theo is at home and grousing about his geometry homework."

Her expression softened. "I like that you know he's taking geometry. Even if it is kind of stalkery."

He shrugged. "I make a point of knowing all the pre-shift kids. As much as I can."

Which was pretty much the end of their conversation, as Tonya took a turn onto a back road that he knew would eventually lead to a fenced perimeter and the Moss family compound. Way up ahead he could see patrol cars and a couple ATF vans. Tonya stopped well before they got there, parking her car sideways across the road before she jumped out. Then she stood there with her arms on her hips to reveal her gun. She took enough time to point to the side of the road where, presumably, they were supposed to park.

He did, though he resented not getting closer to the action. And his bear was beyond pissed that his beta thought she could give him orders.

"Guess we're supposed to stay well back," Becca said.

"Guess so."

He and Alan parked their vehicles and stepped out. Tonya didn't even give them the chance to speak.

"You have to stay here or I'll have to put you in handcuffs."

Alan mirrored her pose, showing off his holstered Glock. "You say the sweetest things," he drawled.

"Don't antagonize her," Carl snapped as he pulled a couple shotguns out of his truck and tossed one to his brother.

"I'm not antagonizing," his brother countered. "I'm inviting."

It was Alan's typical banter, but for the first time Carl wondered if there could be more to it. He glanced at Becca, who was watching Tonya with a tight expression.

"Can you tell me what's going to happen?" she asked, her voice admirably strong.

Tonya gestured behind her. "Over there is the Moss family acreage complete with barbed wire and honest-to-God gun turrets. We're going to knock on the front door and show them the warrant. They're going to let us in nice and polite because they have no choice, and no one is going to shoot anything or anyone."

Becca sighed. "Why don't I believe it'll go that smoothly?"

"Because you don't know us," Tonya answered. Then her expression softened. "If Theo is in there, we'll find him."

"Okay," Becca said softly. "Thank you."

Carl squeezed her arm and gave her an encouraging smile. "It'll be just like she said."

Becca eyed the shotgun on his hip with a wry expression. He shrugged.

"It's just a precaution."

Alan chimed in from the other side of the truck. "Absolutely. Don't plan to fire a shot."

Which was the God's honest truth...in part. They were here just in case the Moss family was larger than expected. In case things got out of control. In case...any of a thousand possibilities occurred. Meanwhile, Tonya got back into her car. He thought she'd leave without another word, but she dropped her window long enough to shoot Alan a glare. "That Glock better be registered."

"You can come check my paperwork anytime."

She didn't respond except to roll her eyes and then she drove farther down the road. Meanwhile, Carl couldn't keep himself from touching Becca. "It'll be fine," he repeated. "You'll see."

She nodded, probably knowing he was reassuring himself as much as her. And then she looked at his gun. "Why do you need that? Can't you go…" She raised her hands like claws and mouthed, "Grrrr."

It was adorable and he wanted to kiss her right then and there, but he held himself back. "Can't until I get some rest. Only the wolves can change more than once a day, and that's only around the full moon. Most of us can't even do that. It takes a ton of energy to switch forms."

"So you're stuck as a man?"

Only someone who'd never been around shifters would call it "stuck" being human. They all thought it was cool to suddenly become an animal. No one ever thought about the cost. Or that between animal and man, nothing in his head was ever peaceful.

"Some of us like it as a man," he said gently.

"Only someone who can shift easily would ever say that," groused his brother in a weird reverse echo of his own thoughts.

Then another voice spoke, deeper than theirs and thick with disuse. "And both of you suck in either body."

Mark stepped out from the trees. His dark hair looked shaggy, his face haggard, but his eyes were bright and his mouth was curled in a smile. God, it'd been years since Carl had seen that smile, though what it meant was anybody's guess.

"At least we don't smell," countered Alan. "When was the last time you took a shower?"

"This here is one hundred percent natural musk," Mark said as he clasped Alan's hand and drew him into a bear hug, much to Alan's gagging discomfort. "Not that froufrou shit you use."

Carl almost smiled at the exchange. It seemed friendly and human. But Mark didn't touch people if he could help it, which made that bear hug suspect. And sure enough, while he watched, Mark dropped something into Alan's pocket.

"Okay, morons," Carl drawled, his gut knotting as he guessed what was going on. "Cut that shit out. Tell me what's happening. And while you're at it, Mark, tell me when was the last time you ate with utensils and slept in a bed."

Mark shoved Alan away and snorted. "Yes, sir, Mr. Max, sir." There was no respect in his tone, just a teasing camaraderie. He started to speak, then sniffed the air, his gaze going unerringly to Becca.

Great. Even in human form, the man's nose was better than a wolf's.

"Hello, ma'am," Mark said as he held out his hand. "I'm Mark Robertson, the only bear worth shit in the Gladwin clan. Your Theo is a good kid. I'll get him home safe."

"Thank you," she said as she shook his hand, her tiny fingers completely engulfed by Mark's massive paw. "And please call me Becca."

"Becca," he said with a low, throaty growl that immediately spiked Carl's irritation. Without willing it, his body started to bulk and if he hadn't been too exhausted to shift, he'd have sprouted fur.

Which was exactly the reaction Mark had been watching for. Damn it. The man's gaze shot to Carl and his expression turned from blatantly sexual to vaguely pitying.

"You're a fucking moron," Mark said under his breath, obviously talking about the relationship between him and Becca. It was stupid on all sorts of levels, but it hurt hearing that condemnation from his best friend. And then Mark softened. "But she smells good and hasn't freaked. Plus, she raised a good kid. I'd say you could do lots worse." Then he turned back to Becca. "You're too good for him. Let me know if you want to explore other options."

Becca turned an adorable shade of rosy pink. Meanwhile, Alan scanned the tree line with a worried expression. "Are we really just going to sit and wait?"

"No," Carl answered. "We can be effective without screwing up the cops." He just had to figure out exactly how to help without jeopardizing Becca's safety. So he turned to Mark. "Report," he snapped.

Mark ignored him long enough to give Becca a final low, sexual growl. It was all for show. Mark would never poach on Carl's territory—female or otherwise—but Carl had watched scores of women fall for that deep purr. He'd be damned if he let Becca fall prey to the lure that was his hypersexed best friend.

And then, just like that, Mark flipped to being all business, reporting in a flat tone. "I'm on perimeter search. Definitely something weird there."

"Weird how?"

"They're undermanned. I see a bunch of women and a few preteen boys dressed up to look big."

Carl frowned, pulling out his cell phone to access Google Earth. He wanted a satellite view of the area.

"I got it," said Alan, as he reached into his car and pulled out his tablet. A moment later, they were looking at a clear image of the local area, complete with three big buildings and a half dozen smaller ones, four of which had gun turrets.

Mark crowded in, pointing as he spoke. "They've got people here and here," he said. "Roof, too, and one in every turret." Then his finger circled a dirt track on the east side. "Smells hinky as shit here."

"A little more precise, please," Carl said.

"Medical smells. Anesthetic, blood, urine. But weird, too. Animals: dog, cat, monkey."

"Monkey?" Alan asked. "They have a monkey?"

"More than one."

Definitely hinky.

"I'm going to scout this last side. Try not to shoot each other."

"Mark, wait—"

Too late. The man had already headed off, moving quickly and silently through the trees. Carl wanted to grab him by the scruff of the neck and shake the man. The idiot was too close to the end, his bear dominating everything. It was in his scent, his quick movements, and his short, tight sentences. How much time did his best friend have before he became all bear? Until he went insane and Carl had to kill him? This was not the time for the idiot to rush into danger that might trigger that last change into animal. And even worse, what if his best friend was hoping to trigger the change so that ATF would put him down? It would spare Carl, but damn it, that was not what anyone wanted.

Meanwhile, Alan came to his side, speaking in a low undertone. "He ate at the cafeteria sometime around dawn. Told Marty the stew needed more beef."

"Probably said it was overcooked, too." Grizzlies like their meat raw.

Alan didn't answer, so Carl shifted to glare at his brother. He didn't like it when the two people closest to him kept secrets. "What did he give you?"

"Asphyxiation?" Alan quipped as he shoved his hands into his coat.

"Don't you fucking lie to me," Carl snapped. "And that's a goddamned order!"

His brother's expression shuttered down, his jaw tightening in fury. But it lasted only a second before he answered by pulling a set of keys from his pocket. Carl immediately started swearing vehemently enough that Becca jolted.

"What's wrong? What happened?"

"Nothing!" both men said together.

"Sorry," Carl said as he gestured for his brother to put away the keys.

Becca folded her arms and glared at them. "Do I look stupid to you?"

Alan raised his hands in surrender and backed away. "This is a job for Mr. Max."

God, it sucked being in charge.

"Those are keys to Mark's underground den."

Her brows arched. "He has a den? Like a bear—"

"Think of it as a big techno-marvel man cave. He's actually one of the most brilliant computer programmers in the world."

She blinked, understandably surprised. Mark came off as a huge bear of a guy, short-tempered with men and hypersexualized with women.

"He's brilliant," Carl stressed. "But he also has too much bear DNA in him. He's going feral and he knows it."

Her lips pursed in a silent *O* of understanding. "That's why you asked about eating and sleeping as a man. You want to know how close he is to turning completely animal."

He nodded, misery tying up his insides. "He gave over his keys because he knows he doesn't have long." He jerked his chin toward his brother. "Alan's the one with the law degree. He handles all the wills and stuff."

"Because he's going to die as an animal? Don't they just live…as bears?"

No point in sugarcoating it. "The human mind can't handle that much animal. Spend too much time as a bear and the mind goes insane. A crazy bear is a destructive killer and needs to be put down. There's no way around that."

"My God," she whispered. "And Alan will have to do that?"

"No," he said flatly. "Alan handles the legal stuff. As Max, the killing is my job."

She gasped as she turned to him, her eyes wide with horror. "Is there any way to stop it?"

He shook his head. He'd spent every spare moment of the last decade looking for a solution, but so far he'd come up with a big, fat nothing. He wasn't a scientist, though God knew he'd tried. He diverted as much money as he could to funding quiet research into the question, but it hadn't yielded anything useful. The most he'd come up with was an ancient spell book that talked about bonding magic to quiet the beast. It had been used to some effect in other clans, but as far as he could tell, it just shifted the crazy to someone who was easier to kill. Which left Mark handing the keys to his life to Alan, while Carl waited for the moment he'd have to do the unthinkable to his best friend.

Crazy-making all around.

Meanwhile, Becca stepped into the circle of his arm, setting her soft hand on his face. "I'm so sorry. Is there anything I can do to help?"

And just like that, his bear went from growling to purring. The heat from her palm eased the tension in his jaw. His gut loosened even as his dick thickened. And when he touched the back of her hand, pressing it closer to his mouth, everything in him settled into one thought: How can I make her mine?

"You're doing it," he rasped. "You understand."

He was looking at her mouth and thinking about kissing her when he heard the noise. Angry words, shouted voices—loud enough for him to hear but not clear enough to make out the words. Mark reappeared a moment later, prowling up behind them, unnaturally silent for a man his size. And when Carl turned, Mark's eyes had a subtle glow to the golden brown, saying to those in the know that the grizzly in him was coming out to play. Goddamn it. He had to do a dominance display, forcing Mark's grizzly to retreat. Problem was he'd shifted too recently, so he couldn't change. He'd have to do this as a human. So he thickened his shoulders and bared his teeth.

"When I tell you to stay, you stay," he growled. "Got it?" Then he clocked the man as hard as he could, right in his jaw. Mark's head snapped back and his eyes flared bright. Behind him, he heard Becca gasp and Alan step in to hold her back. Good. This was too dangerous for her. Hell, it was too dangerous for Alan.

He tensed, focusing everything he had on forcing Mark to submit. Which meant even before the man recovered from the first blow, Carl stepped in and grabbed his friend's short hair. He jerked Mark's head to the side to bare his neck. It was hard. Mark was shorter than Carl, but layered in muscle. And then he put his free hand straight on the bared flesh, digging his nails in like he was going to rip the man's neck apart with his bare fingers.

"Submit," he growled.

Carl didn't know if it was an order or a plea. Both because he sure as hell knew that one day soon, Mark wouldn't. And that would be the end.

Mark's neck bunched, as did his fists. His breath huffed out in two hot bursts of air. If he went grizzly, then Carl would lose. He couldn't shift, so human against grizzly this close would be the death of him. But he was counting on Mark's control. On Mark's ability to beat the grizzly back one more time.

"Submit, you fucker!" he barked as he dug his fingers in with all his strength.

And then it happened. Mark's eyes lost the hot

glow behind the golden brown. His muscles went lax, and his breath eased out on a slow, almost human exhale.

"I submit," he said in a thick, low growl.

Carl held the pose for a few beats longer. It never worked to give over quickly. But after a slow count to ten, he was able to ease off. And Mark, thank God, didn't fight him. But he couldn't completely relax, either. He had to follow this up with hard commands.

"Can you hear what they're saying?" He jerked his chin at the Moss compound.

Mark grunted and turned his head to listen more closely. "Moss rhetoric. Evil government. Over my dead body. Standoff."

So a piece of paper wasn't enough to open the Moss gate. No big surprise there. But there was more than one way to get through the doors. "You say they're shorthanded. Still seem true?"

"Yeah," Mark said. "I think the men are off somewhere else."

"Then we need a distraction. Make them even more shorthanded as they send people to check things out." He moved to the back of his truck. "I've got a couple grenades. Low grade. Just enough to make a few booms."

Alan shifted to peer into the trunk. "You carry grenades?"

Carl didn't answer. He wasn't in the habit of explaining how difficult and dangerous it was to take out a feral bear. Or to deal with Nick Merkel.

Meanwhile, Mark didn't even blink. "How long to get in position?"

Carl looked at the tablet, pointing out the best place for maximum distraction. "Ten minutes."

"Make it five. I'm breaching here and then heading here, where it smells weirdest." Mark stabbed at the tablet with one finger while shucking off his jacket and shirt with the other. Beneath his clothes, his cell in a neoprene pouch dangled from a large lanyard, so he wouldn't lose his phone while running around as a bear.

"It's too soon!" Alan said. "You went grizzly less than eighteen hours ago."

Mark grinned. "You keeping track?"

"Yes!" both Carl and Alan said together.

"How sweet," he returned. Then he looked hard at Carl. "I need the release, Max. I got it under control."

He was asking permission from his alpha. A good sign, but Carl still didn't like it. But a good leader knew when to trust his men, so he nodded. "Be careful."

"Don't have to be. I'm good." Then his grin abruptly widened into a muzzle.

Holy shit, Mark turned fast. He hadn't even fully pushed down his pants when a grizzly suddenly kicked the jeans away.

"Stay in control!" Carl growled, but he had no idea if his friend heard. The man was full grizzly and moving fast into position.

To one side, Becca breathed his biggest fear. "He has a death wish."

"No," Carl countered. "He has a death sentence. And he wants to go out doing some good along the way." Meanwhile, he pulled open the box of grenades, handing one to his brother, who was just putting away his phone.

"I texted Tonya what we're doing."

Smart man. Then, with a quick nod, Alan took off, heading through the tree line to the edge of the Moss compound. Which left him alone with Becca, trying to decide what was safest. Did she stay with him, close to danger? Or inside the truck down on the floorboards?

Becca decided for him. She set her chin and opened the truck door. "I'll only slow you down." Then she fixed him with a glare. "But first thing tomorrow morning, I'm heading for a shooting range."

What a woman! Logical and smart enough to look ahead. But damn, he didn't like leaving her alone. "Here," he said, handing her his keys. "Drive home. I'll call you as soon as I can."

She took the keys but didn't put them in the ignition. "Go! Save Theo and Mark."

Time was ticking away, but he couldn't leave yet. He leaned in and kissed her quick and hard. Then he took off, running as fast as he could through the trees to where Alan waited for him.

Two minutes later, he heard Mark crash through the barbed fence, roaring. He'd be sliced up, but it wouldn't be lethal. A split second later, he and Alan threw their grenades. The shooting started almost simultaneously, but the bullets went wide at seemingly random targets. He and Alan were safely hidden, but Mark was right there in the open, barging through like only a grizzly could. Fortunately, they'd guessed correctly that kids were manning the turrets. None of the shots landed where they were supposed to, and Mark made it inside the nearest building by ripping open a metal door with his claws.

From there, it was wait and pray while the rest played out. After long minutes, the shooting stopped, women peered out of windows to investigate, and then Carl's cell phone chimed. He thumbed it on, his grip so tight it was painful.

"Mark? Are you okay?"

"Yeah," his friend said, his voice thick and heavy. "Tell Tonya she's got probable cause."

Alan huffed from nearby. "She has a warrant. She doesn't need—"

"And whatever you do, don't let Becca down here."

CHAPTER 11

Becca heard the explosions, the sound jolting her enough that she squeaked in alarm. Then gunfire erupted, sounding a thousand times scarier than it did on TV. And then...nothing.

What the hell was going on?

She wanted to get out and see. She wanted to cower on the floor and hope that no one spotted her. She wanted to be in Australia looking at kangaroos with Theo at some nature park. Instead, she just stayed where she was and prayed.

Then her phone buzzed. She was so grateful she fumbled, flipping it around in her hand. But by the time she could see it, all she read was a short text from Carl:

The worst is over. Stay calm.

She read that a thousand times while her heart steadied to about twice its normal rate. And while she tried to control her breathing, she decided that "stay calm" were the most useless two words ever. If she was panicking, they wouldn't help. If she was calm, then they were completely unnecessary. And if she was vacillating back and forth between the two, then "stay calm" just pissed her off.

She wanted answers, damn it! Was everyone okay? Had they found Theo? Did they need help? Why hadn't she chosen to be a nurse or a cop? Some profession that was useful at a time like this? No, she'd gotten a business degree and baked castle cakes.

But rather than give in to her wildly shifting moods, she kept herself calm enough to respond. She didn't want to distract Carl with questions he couldn't answer, and she sure as hell didn't want him staring at his phone while bullets were flying. So she keyed in a simple response, though it took her shaking fingers three tries to get it right.

Okay. I'll wait for news.

And that's what she was going to do. She was going to sit there in the cab of Carl's truck. His calming scent surrounded her in the leather seat and the extra-soft sweatshirt he'd loaned her, and she was going to wait for him. And then later, when this was all over, she was going to learn first aid.

Hell, she should start right now. She could pull up any number of websites from which she could learn basic field medicine. So she did. Reception was weak, but thankfully not dead. And though the pictures were gory and nauseating, especially since she kept imagining Theo or Carl in them, she held it together long enough to read the same page seven times.

Retention was obviously not working well.

Then she saw Officer Tonya walking steadily to the truck, her expression grim. Though, to be fair, the woman's expression was usually grim.

Becca jumped out of the cab, rushing forward. "Did you find Theo? Is it over? Is everyone okay?"

The woman held up her hand, and Becca slammed her jaw shut. She needed answers and would not do anything to interfere with that. The woman nodded, a flash of gratitude on her face.

"First off, everyone's fine, as far as I'm aware. Though Carl and Alan are going to hear from me regarding that stunt. Not to mention Mark." The woman glared in the same direction the men had gone.

So that was good. No one shot. "But did you find Theo?"

The woman took a breath. "No. We don't think so."

"You don't think so? What does that mean? I'm going in there. I have to see—"

A male voice cut through her words. "Becca, wait!"

Carl.

She spun around to see him, her gaze checking everything she could think of for injuries. Face fine. No blood. Moving smoothly. Everything fine. Good. That meant she could stop worrying about him.

She tossed him his keys and turned to Officer Tonya. "Show me."

The damned woman didn't move. Instead, she waited while Carl made it to her side.

Becca glared at them both. "What aren't you telling me?"

"Tell me about the clothing Theo had on," Officer Tonya said in a crisp tone. "You said he was wearing a University of Michigan sweatshirt, is that right?"

"Yes." Oh God.

"Was there anything distinguishing about it? A rip or a stain? A lot of kids wear U of M stuff."

"No, no. It was just a sweatshirt."

"What about his jeans or shoes? Do you remember the brand?"

"No! I already told you—"

"But would you recognize them? If you saw them?"

Becca took a deep breath and leveled the woman with her steadiest expression. "You need to take me to those things right now."

Carl answered instead. "It's not a place you should see. It's not a nice basement."

She swallowed. "Was Theo in there?"

"We don't know," Carl answered.

"But you suspect."

Officer Tonya exhaled slowly. "It's an active crime scene. I can get pictures—"

"A picture isn't going to do it. And what you're doing right now? It's making me insane. Look, I may not look as strong as Officer Tough as Nails here, but Theo's my son. For his sake, I'd walk into hell itself." When that didn't seem to sway them, she tried a different tack. "Theo and I have a shorthand between us. Symbols and stuff that wouldn't mean anything to anyone else, but I'd recognize it if I saw it. If you think Theo might have been in there, you have to let me look."

Becca froze her body into the most coldly determined stance she could manage. Her chin was lifted, her brows lowered, and her hands were clenched at her sides. And while she kept her expression fierce, she looked at Carl. He was the Max, so he was the one she had to convince. "I've dragged my sister's drunken ass out of bars at two a.m. I took care of Theo every time he had the flu. And I've nursed my mother through lung cancer. I'm not going to freak at a scary basement."

Carl sighed. "It's not the same thing."

"I don't care. If Theo was there, I need to see it."

He had to agree. He just had to. And in the end, he huffed out a breath. "I'm going to be with you every step of the way."

"And you're both going to do exactly what I say," Tonya snapped. Then she touched Becca's hand. "And call me Tonya. This kind of thing is easier with a friend."

Becca nodded and tried to smile. No point in letting her nerves show as Carl helped her into the truck. They drove to the front gate of the Moss compound. It looked all rather normal to Becca for a large Michigan ranch. Except for the barbed-wire fencing. And the squad cars and ATF vehicles everywhere. It took forever to get past all the people checking IDs and the like. Tonya got them through while Becca gripped Carl's hand and tried not to panic. She didn't even know when she'd grabbed hold, but their fingers were intertwined, and she sure as hell wasn't going to let go until this was over. Plus, no matter how hard she squeezed, she was pretty sure his hand could take it. So she held on and kept moving steadily forward.

Until she came to the basement.

A set of stairs descended into a huge concrete

nightmare, complete with bloodstains on the floor and four large animal cages.

"Don't you dare puke on my crime scene," Tonya snapped.

"I won't," she said, willing it to be true.

"I was talking to Mr. Max."

It was a lie. That had definitely been directed at her, but she liked Tonya all the better for pretending otherwise. Meanwhile, Carl pulled her tighter against his side.

"If this gets too hard, you just say the word. I'll have you outside in a second, okay?"

"Okay."

She couldn't see much. Tonya was blocking her view, which was just as well. The glimpses she'd gotten were bad enough. And the smell was worse. A foul, nauseating scent of bodily fluids and antiseptic. She glanced at Carl's hard expression and wondered what his grizzly senses were telling him. Nothing good, by the look on his face.

Then Tonya moved, gesturing to a pile of clothing in the corner near the stairs. Not just a University of Michigan sweatshirt, but jeans and shoes. A bloody tee and...

A body. Not in the pile of clothes, but just to the side.

Oh God.

A boy misshapen beyond belief. His face was distorted into a kind of muzzle and there was fur on his arms. But the body was a boy's, and one leg was human, the other a distorted thing that was part animal. She choked back a cry as she slammed a hand on her mouth.

She would not be sick. She would not be sick.

It helped that she knew immediately that it wasn't Theo. Awful to be grateful when she was looking at some boy's death, but she was so relieved that somehow she was able to cope.

"That's not Theo," she managed.

"Good," Tonya said. "Now look at the clothes. What can you tell me about them?"

Becca leaned down, but Carl stopped her with a quick squeeze on her arm. "You can't touch them."

Right. Trace evidence. She straightened as she studied the pile. She didn't have to keep looking, but she wanted to be sure. She wanted to pretend for just a moment longer that what she was seeing couldn't possibly be true. But in the end, reality pressed hard against her mind and she needed a second breath before she could speak.

"The Nikes are Theo's. As is the U of M sweatshirt and those jeans."

"You're sure?"

Yes. "Not a hundred percent, but that stain on the sleeve there? That's ketchup. He did that…" She thought back. "Thursday. I didn't get a chance to wash it, and he didn't care."

Amazing that her voice didn't break on that. It wobbled a bit, but she squeezed Carl's hand and managed to steady herself.

"Okay, that's all we need," Tonya said, but Becca turned back.

"No. Not yet." It was time for her to see the entire basement. And that meant each cage. And anything else that was in this place of horrors.

"You sure?" Carl asked.

She didn't bother to answer, but clenched her jaw and stepped around Tonya. She looked at a row of smaller cages, recoiling when she saw a couple with dead monkeys in them. What the hell? She averted her gaze from them. She doubted Theo had anything to do with that. She had to look at the larger—

"There," she said, and this time her voice did choke. There in the dirt by one of the cages was a dark, circular smudge. She went closer, her eyes tearing up as she recognized a lovingly drawn sunflower with a smiley face in the middle of it.

"What is it?" Tonya asked.

"It's the sunflower from Plants vs. Zombies," she said as she turned into Carl's arms. She couldn't look anymore. She'd seen too much already. "We used to joke that everything would be better as soon as there was more sun," she said, her voice strong as long as she kept her eyes closed and only breathed Carl. "He gave me the mug for Christmas."

That last bit took away her control. Her voice broke, and she shuddered. Carl held her tight, cocooning her in his arms. "That's good news, Becca. I know it doesn't feel like it, but it shows he's alive."

He was right. Theo was alive. She had to hold on to that. So she took a moment to gather her strength. To wipe away her tears and breathe the power that was all Carl. And from that place, she forced herself to turn around. She would see, damn it. And she would help them figure out what had happened to Theo.

Except she wasn't more help. No matter how much she looked, no matter what horrible thing she imagined, there wasn't more information she could reveal. Tonya insisted that she'd already given them a lot. They now knew that Theo had been here and that the bad guys were invested in keeping him alive. That last part was a guess, but Becca held on to it. It was all she had.

CHAPTER 12

Carl couldn't stop touching her. She'd cried for hours, curled quietly against his chest. He'd tucked her close and let his shirt sop up her tears. There weren't any words he could say to her. The whole situation haunted them both. Any boy trapped like that was bad enough, but holding a new shifter in a cage was beyond horrifying. The animal was strongest during the First Shift. To lock it in three square feet of space would make it choke on its own claustrophobia.

So they'd held each other while they waited for news. Eventually exhaustion claimed her, and her body fell lax against him in sleep. He could have left her then, but he had no desire to. She fit right where she was. And in time, his own eyes drifted shut until dawn, when she stirred against his side.

He woke immediately, delighting to see her eyes flutter open, the sunlight warming them to a brilliant blue. He watched awareness enter, then embarrassment. "I'm sorry," she said as she pushed up onto an elbow. "Your arm must feel awful."

"You don't weigh hardly anything," he said, his voice thick with lust. Thankfully he was on his side, otherwise his morning wood would be tenting the sheets. "And I slept deeper than I have in years."

"You must have been really tired," she said.

He stroked the curve of her cheek, watching the skin turn rosy under his caress. "I'm with you. It makes things...settle." He said the words because it was true, but the meaning reverberated in his mind. Man and bear were quieter around her. The war in his head went still for long moments. She had no idea what a miracle it was. In truth, he was only now beginning to understand the scope of it.

She didn't answer, just held his gaze. Then, because he was sure she was thinking, he gave her a quick update.

"The police didn't finish processing the crime scene until late last night. Tonya will call as soon as there's news, but the earliest we can expect anything is noon tomorrow. They've got their hands full getting all of Bryn's information. That other boy was his nephew."

She winced. "How awful."

"Yeah." There was nothing more he could say to that, so he didn't. He just held her gaze and lost himself in the way her hair fell across her cheek and the soft curve of her breast in his borrowed shirt.

Then she moved, rolling out of his arms and his bed. "I'm just going to use the bathroom."

"Use whatever you like."

She went in, shutting the door quietly behind her while he lay in bed and listened. The sounds were normal domestic noises. Running water, the sound of brushing teeth, even the flush of the toilet had him smiling with a soft yearning. How strange to want those noises in his life. How bizarre to want them with someone who—up until a few days ago—hadn't even known shifters existed, much less understood the burden of being an alpha.

He'd always assumed that when he mated, it would be with a woman who comprehended the nuances of being a shifter. Who knew the complicated dance of being his Maxima. He'd assumed that she'd be a fierce grizzly fighter who could go toe-to-toe with any bear in his clan. In truth, he'd thought often of Tonya, but the only thing he liked about her was her grizzly. The woman left him cold. Becca, on the other hand, was all woman, and that seemed to suit his man and his bear just fine.

Go figure.

He was still mulling over the strange twists of fate when she returned and looked at the bed. Thankfully, he'd already rearranged the blankets to hide his erection. He turned to her as casually as possible, making sure his eyes were half lidded, as if he weren't painfully awake.

"You should try to get more rest," he said.

"Don't you want your bed to yourself?" She glanced at the door. "I could take the couch."

"You'll sleep here," he said firmly. Then he started to sit up. "I'll go."

"No! No, I won't throw you out of your own bed."

He flashed her a slow smile. "Guess we'll just have to share."

She looked at him a long moment, her thoughts unreadable. "Is that what you want?"

"More than you can possibly imagine." Well, that was a bit more honest than he'd intended, but it worked. Her lips curved into a beautiful smile and she climbed back in the bed.

He held out his arm to her, and she set her hand on his chest. Tiny palm, slender fingers. It burned straight through his shirt like a brand.

"You sure I'm not too heavy?"

"You do know I'm a grizzly bear, right? Three of you wouldn't be too heavy."

She chuckled, a low sound that had his dick leaping toward her. "Good to know."

He wanted to offer her food. He wanted to provide for her in the most basic way, but he didn't want to disrupt the way she settled back into bed. She crawled up into the open space between his chest and his arm. She sank slowly into the mattress, tucking her hand beneath his chin as she snuggled her hips against his. She accidentally bumped his dick, and his breath caught on a gasp. He held himself still by an act of will, but, damn, his lust ratcheted up another hundred percent.

Her scent perfumed the air. It saturated his clothing and made his head dizzy with want. But he kept himself frozen. He didn't want to frighten her.

Meanwhile, her hand stretched open, flattening against his chest. God, could she hear how his heart thundered for her? Did she know how much he wanted to—

"Carl?"

"Umm?"

"It's a weird situation, isn't it? Between us, I mean."

Understatement, much? "It's only weird if you want it to be. I just want to be here with you. No strings attached."

She nodded, a shift of her face against his ribs. Her hand drifted over his left nipple, and one of her fingers moved, sending lightning straight down to his groin. She was killing him, but he'd be damned if he moved one tiny inch. And if he was really, really lucky, she'd do it again.

"So do bears have strong sexual needs? Or are you the buttoned-down type?"

If he'd been drinking, he would have choked. As it was, his breath caught and his head nearly exploded from the sudden triple beat of his heart. "Um, it depends on the bear, I suppose. But usually the drive is pretty strong. Especially in spring."

She was silent a moment, and—praise God— she moved her fingers again. Twice more across his nipple, and his hips jerked involuntarily. It was a tiny movement, but undeniable.

"It's spring now," she said softly, and he scented arousal. But was it his or hers? Then she pushed up from the bed, her hand exerting a soft pressure as she levered up to look at him. "So do you think you could have sex with me?"

Yes! Yes! *Yesyesyesyesyesyes!*

"Um, I think you can already tell that answer," he said. He'd thought the way she'd curled against his groin had been accidental. Apparently not, and the joy of that blew his mind. But he didn't move yet. He couldn't. He would leap on her like an animal.

Meanwhile, she smiled, the expression both shy and filled with mischief. "It's no strings, I promise. I just…" Her expression faltered. "I want to be touched." She reached up to stroke his jaw, brushing fire across his beard-roughened skin. "I want you to touch me."

He lost his control then. It snapped like a rubber band pulled too tight. His arm tightened where it was wrapped around her, hauling her up and over until she lay across his torso. Her mouth opened on a gasp of surprise, but he caught it with his own. Then he invaded the dark, wet recess with his tongue, and he plundered her like the animal he was.

She murmured a sound of appreciation, deep in her chest. She began dueling with him, tongue to tongue. And she wiggled against him, making his cock buck for attention.

He wanted to ask her if she was sure. He wanted to be gentlemanly and hold back. This was a stressful situation. She wasn't thinking straight. But he couldn't make himself stop.

So he grabbed her hips, stilling her as he rocked his dick against her core. Even through his jeans, it felt heavenly. And her eyes widened as she took in the size and girth of him.

"Be sure," he rasped, praying that he could stop if she asked it of him.

She smiled and ground her pelvis down on him. His eyes rolled back in pleasure. "I am sure," she said. Then she supported herself on one hand as she pulled something out of the front pocket of her shirt. A roll of five condoms unfurled from her hand. "I found these in your bathroom."

"Did you check the expiration date?" God knew it had been a while since he'd needed one of those.

She nodded. "We're okay, if you're okay."

"Baby," he growled. "We're headed for something exponentially better than just okay."

* * *

Becca felt laughter bubble out of her as the world suddenly flipped upside down. He'd done nothing more than roll them over, dropping her on her back in the middle of the bed with him on top. His groin settled perfectly between her thighs and she had a sense of forces working beyond her control. Ever since he'd walked into her bakery, she'd been riding a roller coaster of worry, joy, terror, and peace. But the moments with Carl had been beacons of sanity even when she felt upside down and inside out.

She'd tried to hold herself together, but as of last night, she'd given up. The most she could do was ride the experience, and if that meant grabbing onto the distraction that was Carl, then who was going to judge her? Not him, certainly. And not herself. Nobody else mattered.

So she kissed him. She let him unbutton her shirt. And she reveled in the glorious magic that was his tongue on her breasts. His hand shaping her and twisting the nipple. The suction and nip of his teeth on the other side. And the keening hunger he built inside her.

Tension coiled toward release. He built it inside her. He took all the emotions that were tearing her apart and shaped them into sensuous overload. Hands and teeth on her breasts. Glorious pressure at her groin. He thrust at her and she ground back at him. They both had on jeans, but that just added to the experience, especially as he circled his hips, driving the thick seams of her clothes into areas that made her gasp.

He lowered himself onto her body, his mouth leaving her breast to press kisses into her belly. She burrowed her fingers in his lush hair while her eyes shut to better experience every touch of his massive body. And when his hands framed her hips, slowly stroking across the top ridge of her jeans, she tugged his face up.

"Carl?"

He lifted up enough to look at her, his green eyes dark and gloriously intense. "Yes?"

"Can we go fast the first time?"

His nostrils flared and his hands tightened on her hips. "Baby, we can do it any way you want."

She reached down and unfastened her jeans. There wasn't a lot of room until he lifted off her, shedding his clothing in record time. Then he stood there in the dawn's light, large and golden, his penis thick and dark red as it jutted between his thighs. She'd thought he'd be grizzly furry, but he was no more so than a normal man. Enough for her to trace the inverted triangle on his chest, flowing down to the steady point of his erection. And that aimed straight at her.

He held still, watching her as she looked at him. Uncertainty flashed in his eyes, and she gave him a slow smile. "I haven't changed my mind."

He released a breath and grinned as he moved forward.

"You're just...um...largely proportioned."

He paused with one knee on the bed. "Is that a problem?"

"It's a compliment."

"Good. Because I know we'll fit."

"Pretty sure of that, are you?" She liked that he was so confident. And to be fair, so far he'd been an exceptional lover.

He leaned over her, caging her with both arms and legs. She'd kicked off the last of her clothes, and lay back on her elbows, fully exposed to him. But she wasn't self-conscious about her nudity. The way he looked at her banished any doubts. Instead, she let her head drop back as he gazed down at her.

"You're beautiful," he said.

She flashed him a grin as she drew a hand up his flank. "You're very virile."

His brows arched at that and she chuckled.

"I didn't think you'd like me calling you beautiful. Besides, you're too manly to be called handsome."

He nodded. "I'll take that." Then he leaned forward and pressed a kiss to her lips. He went slow at first, which was frustrating. He teased the edges of her lips, he nipped at her mouth, and when she opened completely to him, he barely pushed his tongue forward at all. This wasn't fast. And worse, just when she was about to grab him and force him to go harder with her, he abruptly straightened away.

"What— Oh."

He grabbed a condom off the bed, ripping it open with quick movements.

"Do you need help?" she asked.

"Not this time, baby." He flashed her a grin. "Let's save that for round three."

Goodness, that was ambitious. But she simply tossed her hair back and gave him a wicked grin. "If you want to wait that long. I decorate cakes, you know. I excel at all sorts of hand techniques."

He growled in hunger and she laughed. The moment his penis was covered, he stepped between her knees. Then he leaned forward, both his hands stroking quickly up the inside of her thighs, separating her legs even as he began to finger her.

Oh! Oh yes!

His fingers were thick and nimble. He pushed into her wet opening, spreading the moisture everywhere, and he did it with hard, circular strokes that had her arching into his pressure. Her arms gave out and she dropped back onto the bed.

"Now. Oh God, now," she pleaded.

He leaned forward. There was a moment's delay while she stretched for him, lifting her knees and arms as she tried to grab hold of whatever part of him was nearest. It was all within reach. Every glorious muscle, every hard bone, and most certainly his jutting organ.

And then he thrust home.

Her breath caught on a delicious cry. He filled her to perfection. There was enough stretch to make her feel his every glorious inch, to make her clutch him as he pulled back. And to make her arch almost off the bed as he slammed into her again.

And then he stopped. He held himself still as he leaned down to kiss her. He pressed her mouth hard, his movements unsteady, his breath short and hot against her lips.

He wanted something from her, but she didn't know what. She opened her eyes and looked into his dark ones. Which is when she realized he was holding back. Even though she'd asked him—begged him—to take her hard, he was still keeping himself from losing control.

"How can you be so calm?" she asked. She was insane with want.

He leaned down and scraped his teeth lightly across her jaw. Tiny bites that made her clutch him above and below.

"So sweet," he rasped. "I could devour you."

She wrapped her arms around him as far as they would go. "So do it," she said. "Please."

"You don't understand," he said against her ear. "I don't want to hurt you."

She pushed him back far enough that she could look him in the eye. "Why do you think I'll break?"

His eyes darkened and his hands clutched her waist. "I'm a grizzly, Becca."

That made her pause, but geez Louise, he was already inside her. What more could happen? "Do you get bigger?" That kind of boggled her mind.

"What? No! At least I don't think so."

"What are we talking here? Claws? Fur? Humpback or something?"

He snorted. "No, no, and absolutely not!"

"Then I think we're okay." She stroked his face. "Isn't it usually the girl who makes it complicated?"

He shook his head. "It's not complicated. I don't want to frighten you."

"I'm not frightened," she retorted. "I'm bored." That wasn't remotely true, but he seemed to need her to demand more. To give him permission to let his animal out. "Bring it, grizzly. Show me what you've got."

It wasn't enough. He still stared at her, fully embedded and yet completely still. Which pissed her off. She was not some fragile little bird. So she did something new. Something she'd never done before, but which he seemed to need. She grabbed his right nipple between two fingers and twisted.

"Ow!" He reared back with a jerk, but below she felt him grind against her.

Oh yes!

But then—damn it—he stopped again. She saw his nostrils flare, she felt the tension in his body, but he was still holding on too tight.

So she did it again. This time harder.

That did it.

Some restraint broke inside him. He released a roar of fury, and then he bore down on her. Not up top, though his eyes darkened and his face dropped to within inches of her. It was below that he thrust hard enough to raise her off the bed. Then he grabbed hold of her hips and held her right where he wanted her before pulling back and ramming her harder.

Oh yes!

He slammed into her again and again, his breath coming out in harsh growls each time. It took three slams for her to climax. The waves crashed through her while he kept going.

Sometime in there he must have released. While

she was bucking in his arms, he roared again, but if there was a pause, she barely noticed. Her whole body was riding waves of ecstasy.

But then she felt him lean over and unceremoniously flip her over. She was completely boneless and her face planted with an oomph in the pillow. She heard another foil packet rip. She was just wondering why he needed another condom when he grabbed her hips and raised her up.

Bam! He slammed into her. And this time he leaned over her, caging her as he took her from behind. Everything was wet and slick, but he ground a thick finger against her clit and set off more sparks. More waves when the first had barely slowed.

Over and over he pumped into her, making guttural sounds that thrilled her. He wanted her. He was consumed by her. And she in turn felt as if her every cell was marked, owned, and wrung to its fullest.

It was animal possession at its most base level, and she reveled in it. There was no room for doubt or fear. There was only wave after wave of pleasure.

She lost count of her orgasms. It could have been a dozen. It could have been one long one that he perpetuated forever. After he'd taken her from behind, he rolled her over again and began feasting on her. He licked every inch, keeping her body pulsing. She never managed the dexterity to help him with another condom. He took care of that, too. And when he pushed into her again, it was like she'd been made for this and for him.

It made no sense. She was a strong, independent woman who would never dream of giving everything over to a man. And yet he made her want to. He made it so she loved to.

And when he was finally finished with her, he settled beside her, tugging her into his arms until she was cradled against his chest. It was so perfect, she never wanted to leave.

Crazy.

Bliss.

CHAPTER 13

Carl woke on alert, leaping out of bed before he even realized why. He was naked, but not for long. He'd either be covered in fur soon or...

"You mother-fucking-whoreson!" It was Nick Merkel bellowing outside, fury and profanity in every breath. Guess his wife had given him the bad news. But just in case, Carl called through the door to his brother.

"Alan! Is everything locked down, legally speaking?"

His brother threw open the door while pulling on his shirt. "Yes. Ruling came down yester..." His voice trailed off as he took in Becca naked in the bed.

Carl whirled on his brother, his mouth lengthening into a snarling growl. His brother's eyes widened as he hastily backed out. "Sorry. I wasn't thinking. I—"

Carl kicked the door shut in his brother's face. Then he reined in his temper as he turned to Becca. "I should have locked the door. I'm so—"

She held up her hand. Thankfully, she was covered by the blankets so only her head and one beautiful shoulder had been exposed to his brother's stare. "It's fine. I'm not ashamed."

Right. He was the one who'd tried to hide their relationship.

Nick continued to rant, his bellows coming closer as he left the circular street and moved up the walkway to the house. "I'm going to carve out your fucking heart and…" blah blah blah.

Becca's gaze turned to the window. "He sounds really pissed."

"Yeah. I've been expecting this." He needed to get out there, but he didn't want to leave her yet. "Don't be afraid. You're not in any danger."

She pushed back the covers. "Don't worry about me." Then she winced as Nick launched into another streak of profanity. "Go take care of…um…is that clan business?"

"Yeah." God she was beautiful in the morning, with her skin flushed and hair mussed. "I know we need to talk, but—"

She stretched up on her toes, kissed him hard and fast, and then pushed him away when he would have pulled her deeper into his arms. "Go!"

He wanted to argue with her, but she was right. He had to deal with—

Alan's voice cut through the tirade, along with the sound of a shotgun loading. "That's far enough, Nick. This is private property."

"You tell that mother-fucker—"

"You know you're in a kids' camp, right? Calm down. Mr. Max will be with you in a moment."

Carl grabbed a pair of his tearaway pants and yanked them on. He didn't like having to wear stripper pants, but he wanted to be prepared to go grizzly. Shifting while still wearing jeans was a mistake bears made only once.

Beside him, Becca was drawing on her clothes with swift motions. He didn't want her clothed at all, but didn't have time to indulge that particular fantasy. So, with a quick apologetic glance, he quit the bedroom, shutting the door quietly behind him.

A half dozen steps later, he was outside, barefoot, bare chested, and wearing only his stripper pants. He always felt stupid doing this. Like the sight of his manly chest would mean anything to Nick. But it was how most Gladwin Maxes appeared when addressing the clan, though his uncle had skipped the pants altogether.

"Good morning, Nick." He looked at the sky. Almost noon. Damn, he'd slept like a baby.

"You mother-fucking…"

He rolled his eyes, not even bothering to stop the tirade. Nobody won in a shouting match. Besides, the best thing to do was to appear bored. A true leader appeared calm, almost casual, against a threat so that when he struck, it was fast and decisive.

Great strategic thinking, except his grizzly thirsted for blood. Nick was defying his alpha, disturbing Becca where she rested, and being a goddamned pain in the ass. For that, Carl was a half breath away from tearing out the bastard's throat. At least there weren't any kids watching. They were all in school. A half dozen onlookers had gathered, keeping well back on the circular road, but they were all Gladwin family. Which meant he could go all Max without fear of outsiders misunderstanding. Unfortunately, Nick didn't seem to be losing any steam. Well, not until Becca came out with an extra mug of coffee in her hand. She passed it to Carl with a smile.

Jesus, that was perfect. Nothing cut off a temper tantrum like the sight of people not giving a shit. He leaned against the porch railing as he let his gaze linger on her. He knew his expression was warm and intimate. And it shut Nick up mid-profanity.

"Jesus fucking Christ, you're screwing a human?"

Carl didn't bother to answer that except to let his expression shift into an extra-wide grin. Then he pushed himself off the porch, setting his coffee mug down as he went.

"Now that you've finished whining, let me make this official." He raised his voice, pitching it so all could hear. He knew that Alan would be recording this for an email sent to the whole clan, so he made himself as pompous as he ever got. "Nick Merkel, you have disobeyed a direct order to clean up your toxic waste dump. Therefore, you are now expelled from the Gladwin Bear Clan."

"The fuck you—"

"Your property has been given to your wife, Pam, to manage as she pleases. If she chooses to harbor you, then that is her choice. If she wishes you tossed out on your mangy ear, then I will assist her because she remains one of us and I have sworn to protect her from harm. As for this location..." He gestured to the main campground. "You are no longer permitted here."

Then he turned as if his business was done. His

bear rebelled in every single cell of his body, but in this, his mind ruled. It had to look as if he'd ended the confrontation—at least for the camera—even though they'd just begun this particular dance. Carl knew that no way, no how, was Nick smart enough to accept banishment. A shifter without a clan wasn't necessarily going to die, but he was a target for every magical weirdo with a grudge. And Nick's pride would see it as going from big bear in the clan to crazy loner in the woods.

Carl's back prickled with awareness, knowing exactly what was about to happen. But he had to allow Nick to swing first, especially since it was all being caught on camera.

He heard Becca squeak in alarm, and that was enough to spur him into action. Nobody scared her. And certainly not an uneducated redneck of an asshole like Nick.

Carl spun around, easily sidestepping Nick's swing. Somehow the man had hidden a huge wrench in his dungarees and had just tried to bash in his alpha's skull. Well, that established the legalities. Whatever happened next was self-defense. Meanwhile, all he had to do was taunt the idiot a little more.

"A wrench? Seriously, Nick? You think you can take me man to man?"

Nick straightened, a wild grin on his face. "I just needed you closer." Then, faster than Carl thought possible, the man started to shift. He must have been practicing, because it took serious focus to morph that quickly. But it didn't matter. Carl had him by the throat and shoved up against the nearest tree trunk before he got more than a snout going. And then he banged the bastard's head backward a few more times just for good measure and to stop the guy from shifting fully to bear. Right now he was just a hairy man with a long nose.

"You're a sorry excuse for a man," he growled. "But I'm going to let it go because of how you're mentally incompetent. That's why everything's in your wife's name now."

Then he stepped back, showing the camera that he was stepping away while Nick was still standing and plenty healthy enough to start spewing filth.

"You fucking..." Blah blah blah. It went on for a while with the man swinging wildly and Carl easily sidestepping everything. Everything in Carl wanted to end this now, but he couldn't do it yet. One more piece had to fall into place. Alan had won in court, declaring Nick legally incompetent. Pam must have given the bastard the news, which is what triggered the tirade today. But Nick's kids had to...

There.

Mark pulled up in his truck. A second later, Pam and her two sons got out of the cab, looking wide-eyed and terrified.

Finally, Carl could end this. He'd needed to have the boys here to show them that a man stood up for what was right. And that their father wasn't an all-powerful monster. So he focused back on Nick and dodged one last wild swing.

"We can do this all day, Nick," Carl taunted. "Or you can calm down and walk away."

"Fucking whoreson!" Suddenly, Nick swung paws the size of hams, complete with claws a foot long. Nick was shifting, and his dungarees were large enough to accommodate him in his grizzly form. Carl had two seconds to act before he lost his opportunity.

So he swung twice. One blow straight to the diaphragm to stop Nick's breath, and the other under the jaw to snap his head back. It worked. Even as a grizzly and twice Carl's weight, Nick's head whipped back and he staggered. Three more blows and the bear lost his footing and went down. Carl slammed his bare foot down on the furry neck, angling as best he could to choke off the guy's breath without exposing his own body to a swipe from those massive claws.

"You're an idiot, you know that?" he growled. "You think you can disobey me and I'm going to just ignore it? Jesus, power isn't about the size of your claws. Just because you can intimidate a woman and two boys means jack shit. I've beaten you as a *man*, you moron. Do you seriously want to take me on as a *bear*?"

Nick started to growl, but Carl shoved his heel harder against Nick's windpipe.

"I could snap that now, but I was trying to be kind to your family. I don't like killing someone for being stupid."

Nick stilled, but he wasn't cowed by any means. Now was the time to get the last of it out. For the video. For the clan. But most of all, for the boys and Pam. They needed to hear just what was going to happen.

"You've been declared legally incompetent. Pam has control of everything." He looked up at her. "What do you want, Pam? You want him with you or gone?"

It took her two tries before she found her breath, but she got the word out clear enough. "Gone."

Finally. He'd tried to get Pam to defy Nick for years, but she and her boys had steadfastly stood by the bastard's side. It was the only thing that kept Carl from interfering before. But once Nick started poisoning the land, he'd finally had a reason to end it.

"So be it." He leaned down and spoke low and quietly. "Leave now or die." Nick reacted the only way a man like him does: with violence. He swiped with snout and claws, but Carl jumped back and away. Then Nick was up on his feet, rearing to his full grizzly height. He roared loud enough to be heard a county over. A call to his side. The challenge of an alpha to another. Except that no one, not even his boys, who'd both had their first shifts years ago, came to his side.

That left Carl standing alone in his stripper pants against a bear nearly twice his size. There was a moment when Nick seemed to realize he was standing alone. A moment when he seemed to think about the stupidity of his actions. But then it was gone. Whatever ability he'd had to reason things out failed him. So he attacked. And Carl finally got to let his grizzly free. Nick was all in—to the death.

CHAPTER 14

Becca had never enjoyed violence. She didn't like *The Fast and the Furious* movies, only watched cute puppy videos on YouTube, and if there was blood on the TV screen, then she took those moments to check her email. Yet here she stood, rooted to her spot on the porch as two grizzly bears tried to kill each other in front of her.

When Nick had first lunged at Carl, she'd taken a step forward to help, but got no farther. Alan had gripped her arm to hold her back. And then she'd watched Carl's amazing display as he held himself in human form while the grizzly Nick attacked. It was beyond impressive. It was a demonstration of control and calm like she'd never imagined.

But then it had changed. Nick went from angry to all-out war. She couldn't have stated what the difference was. It was all fur and teeth with Nick, not to mention roaring. But, suddenly, the atmosphere seemed to thicken and the seven-foot-tall beast became deadlier. Beside her, Alan cursed under his breath and, worst of all, a look of resignation settled on Carl's face. And then he, too, became a bear.

She'd seen him in bear form before, she told herself. No need to be so shocked now. But back then she'd been in the midst of a bizarre attack in the woods at night. This was in the broad light of day out on the front porch. Carl was standing there all golden skin on a muscled torso, and then she saw his head shift. His nose elongated, his shoulders thickened. And while she watched his whole body grow, he pulled off his pants, abruptly standing as tall as a full bear.

Mahogany brown with a distinctive streak of silver gray on his back, right between his shoulder blades. He was slightly taller than Nick, who was a darker color and had thicker arms and uglier-looking claws. That's all she saw before Nick lunged and suddenly the two bears were grappling.

She felt Alan's hand tighten on her arm, holding her back. Had she seriously been trying to move forward to intervene? No one was getting between those bears.

The air filled with grunts of exertion. She saw blood fly but couldn't tell whose it was. Her brain couldn't make sense of the mass of claws and teeth, not to mention fur and limbs. The two rolled in dirt, and the onlookers backed up to give them more room. God, there were boys watching. Nick's adolescent sons, if she had to guess. And how awful would that be to stand there and watch your father fighting for his life.

Then Nick gained the upper hand, pinning Carl

with his body as he hauled back an arm—claws flashing evilly in the light—to eviscerate Carl. Becca would have screamed, but she hadn't the breath. She ought to do something. Throw a chair, maybe, but Alan's grip was like iron.

And just when Nick was most extended, his arm raised like a spiked mace, Carl moved. He must have gotten his feet under Nick, because in the next second, he threw the bastard five feet away to slam into an oak.

Then Carl rolled to his feet and stood there, watching as the older grizzly shook his head as if stunned.

"Stop," Alan rasped under his breath. "Stop it now."

Becca looked at Carl. He wasn't moving. "He's not doing anything."

"Not Carl," Alan said, his voice tight with worry. "Nick. Nick has to stop and accept his banishment. He has to."

There was something in Alan's voice that made her turn slightly. Just enough to see the man's face. "And if he doesn't?"

"Carl will have to kill him."

Oh, shit. But Alan wasn't done.

"The last thing Carl needs is another soul on his conscience. He's already killed three ferals. This won't help him sleep at night."

Oh, hell. That suggested all sorts of things, none of which were good. She looked to the combatants. Nick had regained his senses and looked around, his gaze landing unerringly on his children. Both boys shrank away from him until they stood protectively in front of their mother. Pam set an arm on each child.

"You shoulda fixed the platform, Nick. You were poisoning the land." She wiped the tears from her cheeks. "You shoulda done what you were told." Her voice quavered as she spoke, but there was a firm set to her jaw that Becca respected.

That was it for Nick. Instead of slinking away like he should, he lunged forward on a roar. But he didn't go at Carl. Instead, he went for Pam and his two sons. Becca didn't even see the move coming. One second he was leaning against the oak as he steadied himself, the next he was mid-leap right at his own family. Pam's face registered shock—eyes wide, mouth open—but there was no time for more.

And then Carl landed on Nick from the side, rolling the two of them away until they flattened into the hedge. And this time, the change was in Carl. Before he'd been grappling with Nick, defending himself but keeping the fight contained in the yard—away from the onlookers. Now he was all fight and blood.

No restraint as he clawed at Nick. The first swipe took out a huge swatch of Nick's thigh. Blood spurted over everything, but the older grizzly didn't stop. He rounded on Carl, snapping his jaws, barely missing Carl's neck.

So Carl clawed across Nick's chest, making deep furrows that welled bright red.

"Run," growled Alan. And the one word was echoed all around.

Nick didn't listen. He kept fighting, coming at Carl again and again. But it was a hopeless battle. His leg was hobbled, and he was losing blood.

So Carl didn't waste any time.

Two more blows ended it. One thunked against Nick's head. The other sliced straight across the grizzly's throat.

Nick fell, crumpling in agonizingly slow moments. He twitched on the ground, blood pouring like a thick, dark river.

Becca stared, waiting for the moment that he reverted to human form. That's what happened in the movies, right? Werewolf turns back into a naked dead man while the credits roll? But this wasn't a movie and Nick didn't shift back. He remained a bear, lying dead at Carl's feet.

Carl was the one who shifted, shrinking back into himself until he was a man covered in blood who turned to the boys now clutched in their mother's arms.

"I'm sorry," Carl said, his voice sounding gravelly. "I tried to find a different answer. I didn't want to kill him."

Pam clutched her children tight, and this time her voice rang clear and strong. "And that's why you're a terrible alpha," she said. "You shoulda killed him months ago and saved us all this trouble."

Carl flinched as if struck, then stomped forward, his eyes blazing and his hands poised to become claws. He didn't shift, but if ever a man could look like a bear, Carl did.

"I would have done this years ago, but you begged me on your knees not to." Then he looked around at everyone, pinning every onlooker. "Is that what you want? A bloody, violent tyrant in charge? Yes, my uncle would have killed him months ago, but he wouldn't have stopped there. He would have snapped your boys' necks, too, raped you until he tired of it, and then taken your property as his own." He loomed over Pam. "Is that what you want?"

"N-no, Mr. Max," she stammered. The boys just flinched and kept their eyes down in submission. Carl rolled back slightly on his heels, but he kept up the glare until Pam spoke again. "Th-thank you for your help, Mr. Max. I'm sorry if we caused you any trouble."

Carl took a deep breath, and as he exhaled, he seemed to settle further back into himself, though Becca could see the struggle in him. She saw his muscles ripple, the hump between his shoulder blades thickening and retreating, then thickening again. He was fighting to keep himself under control, and she held her breath, waiting to see if he would manage it. Eventually, he blew out a hard breath. "You have until Friday to get that platform fixed."

"Yes, Mr. Max."

"And you'll pay Alan for all the legal work he did on your behalf. Every single dime, if it takes you ten years."

Pam was bobbing her head like a puppet. "Yes, Mr. Max."

Then Carl looked down at the terrified boys. "And you two will come to camp after school every day. Every single day I want you doing your homework right there." He pointed across the circle to the cafeteria. "You're going to get the grades I expect out of every Gladwin member. If you want, we'll help you with college, but you have to prove to me that you're smarter than your father. Is that clear?"

Both boys scrambled to answer. "Yes, Mr. Max."

Carl looked at Mark, who had been watching with almost casual disinterest from the side of his truck. "Can you see that they get home?"

Mark didn't even speak. He just pulled open the door of his truck and waited while Pam and her sons climbed inside. Meanwhile, Tonya stepped up beside Carl, her expression flat.

Becca did a double take. When the hell had she gotten here?

"Alan got it on video," Tonya said. "And I was here for the last of it. There won't be any problem from the police. It'll be reported as a bear attack. I'll get animal control to deal with the body."

Carl nodded. "Thanks."

Tonya kept talking, her voice all business. "Let me handle this and then we've got to talk. We've gotten some of the forensics back from yesterday."

Becca saw Carl's shoulders tighten, then slowly ease back down. "Good. That's good."

"So why don't you go clean up? Maybe put some pants on, and I'll be inside in a minute."

There was a moment's silence, and then Carl answered in an almost humorous tone. "Well, it is getting a bit chilly."

Tonya smirked as she glanced significantly at his crotch. "Couldn't tell by me."

It was that smirk that woke Becca up out of her trance. How dare the bitch make comments like that now? Becca might be new to this shifter clan stuff, but she knew hierarchy. Comments like that were inappropriate from a woman to her boss. It had to be ten times worse in a pack structure, no matter how complimentary the comment.

So Becca stomped forward, holding Carl's coffee in one hand and picking up the discarded stripper pants with the other. "I'm sure he finds your tits appealing, too, Officer, but let's try to keep things professional, shall we?" Then she offered Carl both items and waited while he decided what he wanted to do.

Well, that's what she intended to do. She held to the plan long enough to see Tonya's dark flush of embarrassment, but then she turned to face Carl and that's when things went all to hell.

She got an up-close-and-personal look at his face.

His mouth and jaw were dark with drying blood. Plus, the coppery scent was thicker here right over the body. And now that she saw the front of Carl's torso, she got too close to all that gore.

Holy shit.

She was going to be sick.

CHAPTER 15

Disgust. Horror. Nausea.

Carl saw all that and more fight for dominance on Becca's face. Her eyes widened, her mouth grew slack, and he knew the moment she fought the urge to vomit.

He hadn't been self-conscious about his physical state until that moment. Bear shifters were fairly casual about nudity, but Becca's reaction filled him with shame. All of the judgmental thoughts he kept locked down rushed forward, swamping his consciousness. He was a violent predator, unfit for civilization. He disgusted normal people, and they were right to shun him. He'd lost control again, and now he was exposed as a monster.

His jaw grew tight and his grizzly growled. He hadn't intended to make a sound. Hell, he'd thought he'd completely locked himself down. But apparently he'd made a noise. It must have been bestial because Becca's eyes shot back up to his. She was pale, and he saw her swallow convulsively.

On instinct, he reached out to steady her, but she flinched back.

Well, that answered that. Up until that moment, he hadn't realized how deeply she was embedded in his life. He hadn't consciously decided to propose to her. He hadn't faced the Gladwin shifters and declared her his mate. But he'd been thinking about it.

She'd flinched back from him. Which meant that she'd seen him for who he really was and was revolted.

He struggled for something to say, anything that would ease the moment or reassure Becca that he wasn't a monster. But he *was* a monster and his grizzly wasn't going to let him apologize for it. Neither was the alpha in him. Which left the man standing there, mute and embarrassed.

He let his hand drop away from her elbow, then awkwardly reached for his pants. But he couldn't put the damned things on over all the blood. And he sure as hell wasn't going to strut his bloodied self inside. So he turned to Tonya, who was watching the entire byplay with banked intensity. At least she understood the monster inside him.

"Mind holding the hose?" he asked as casually as he could.

Her brows arched in surprise. "It'll be cold."

"Whatever," he answered. He wondered if he'd even feel it. He felt totally numb inside.

"Sure," she said as her phone buzzed and she quickly answered it.

It took him a moment to grab the hose from the garage and hook it up to a spigot beside the driveway. He was excruciatingly aware of Becca watching from just off the porch, her eyes still huge and her mouth pressed tightly closed. He wondered what she was thinking. Was it like staring at a train wreck? She just couldn't look away? Or was there something more to the way her gaze followed him whatever he did? She didn't say a word and he couldn't guess.

Meanwhile, Tonya put away her cell and grabbed the spray gun part of the hose. "So how'd you do it?" she asked.

"What?"

"Declare him legally incompetent. You did it so Pam could have everything, right? Otherwise she and the kids would be out and penniless."

He nodded as he positioned himself at the top of the driveway. "He thought he was a bear."

Tonya frowned. "But he is a bear. Or was."

"The judge didn't know that. And neither did the therapist who evaluated him. And if he hadn't been such a blowhard, he would have known to shut his mouth when being videotaped."

Tonya's laugh was the last thing he heard before icy water hit him full force. It should have cut off his breath. It should have had him cringing against the frigid cold. Instead, his gaze ended up on Becca, still standing by the porch with his coffee mug in her hand. She watched him steadily, her eyes slowly softening as her mouth lost its tight cast.

What was she thinking? What did she want?

He almost went to her. Fuck the wet and the blood, he needed to touch her right then. But he didn't get far. The very moment he took a step toward her, she flushed and turned away. He wanted to call her back, but she didn't give him a chance.

Long before he figured out what to say, she disappeared back inside the house.

* * *

Becca didn't know what to think. Worse, she didn't know what to feel. The sight of Carl covered in blood had made her physically ill. She held herself together by willpower alone, but by the time she'd been able to function, Carl's eyes had gone flat.

She knew that look. She was raising a boy, after all. It was that moment when they just turn off and you know nothing you do or say will get through. So she stood there waiting, racking her brains for something that would make it better. But before she'd found it, he'd stepped under the spray of water. It was spring in Michigan, which put the temperature at a few notches above freezing. He hadn't even flinched when the stream caught him. He'd just stood there taking the punishment while all that blood washed away.

Never before had she seen anything more beautiful. A man covered in gore, slowly cleansed in the sunshine. Inch by glorious inch, his body had emerged, flexing golden in the light, his muscles rippling with power. She knew every curve and hollow of that body, had kissed every part of him last night. She had lain underneath, felt him strain above her, and had climaxed around him. This beautiful man had worshipped her last night, and she had reveled in it. In him.

That was the man who was revealed to her beneath the spray. That was the man who looked at her with such yearning that she had felt herself go wet and achy. Her nipples had tightened and her belly had contracted just from the way he looked at her.

But they were in public and he'd just killed a man in front of her. Hell, the grizzly body lay just a few feet away. And yet she'd wanted to strip naked and step under the water with him. She'd wanted to feel the cold sluice down her while his body warmed her. And if he had bent her over and taken her right there on the front lawn, she would have loved it.

She was that aroused.

Which was insane.

So she'd run inside rather than give in to such an immodest display. She rushed inside and headed for the kitchen without any thought of what she was going to do or say. She couldn't even figure out what she was feeling. Lust? Certainly. Disgust? Maybe. But not at him. She was appalled by herself for wanting someone who was so violent it terrified her. She was a civilized woman, and now she saw him as a primal man in all his brutal glory. She wanted him even as she was repulsed by the violence of him.

She could have reconciled the two if this were a simple attraction. Who didn't love a hot, dangerous man? But the real problem was the power of her desire. This wasn't a lukewarm interest. Or even a fascinating diversion. No, this was hunger—deep and raw. This was desire without inhibition. This was a need that went beyond anything she'd ever felt before and it terrified her.

She'd never be able to control a passion like this. She couldn't imagine fitting it into her regular life. This was something that would consume everything around it. Her life, her nephew, herself. She could lose herself in a man like Carl. And as a single parent, she had no business losing herself in anything except Theo.

"Are you okay?"

She looked up from the kitchen sink to see Alan standing in the door, his expression wary.

She swallowed and cleared her throat. "Um, yeah. I'm fine."

He took a step into the room. "Forgive me, but you don't look fine. You look scared."

"Do I?" *Get it together!*

Alan was quiet as he poured himself another mug of coffee, but then he leaned against the counter to study her with a quiet intensity.

"He'd never hurt you."

That was something she felt to her bones. "I know."

"It's natural to be freaked out. I grew up here, and challenges like that still bother me."

"The violence?"

He nodded. "It's pretty raw."

He understood. She flashed him a weak smile. "It's primal, and I'm not used to that."

"No one is. Not even them."

That was reassuring in a twisted kind of way. So she took a breath and reached for the coffeepot to refill her own mug. Except the carafe was almost empty.

"I'll make some more," Alan offered, but she stopped him.

"Please, let me get it. I think I need to be useful."

He started to argue with her, but something in her

face must have changed his mind, because he backed off. He pointed to the cabinet right above her head. "Everything you need is in there."

"Thanks," she said. And then she went about the business of making coffee. It was a simple task that gave her hands something to do. Which allowed her fears to ease their grip enough for her to talk a little more rationally. "So when you shift, how exactly does that feel? Do you think? Can you control yourself? I mean, could you be a bear and drive a car?"

He snorted at that image, and she flashed him an awkward smile. "I'm sorry to be so ignorant."

"It's not ignorance. They're reasonable questions, but you're asking the wrong person."

She finished pouring the water into the coffeemaker and switched it on. "What do you mean?"

"I don't shift."

She looked up, startled. "What?"

"It's a genetic lottery. Shifters have human and animal DNA. Too much animal, and they shift young and often go full beast by adolescence. It's the hormones. When they kick in, the beast can be too much to control. Or in my case, I seem to have only the human side. I've never shifted." He shrugged. "I'm not even all that hairy."

"Oh." *Jeez, what a stupid response.* But she didn't know what to say. Congratulations, you're not half beast? I'm so sorry you can't kill people with your claws? Did shifters like running wild in the woods and digging honey out of beehives? Or did they want to hang out with a girl at prom and not worry that they'd start sprouting fur if things got too intense?

"You should ask Carl."

She nodded. She should, but her emotions were too close to the surface to even consider that yet. She felt too exposed and too wild around him to broach the topic. Then, as if the thought summoned the man, the front door opened and Carl came in.

He was wearing the tearaway pants and nothing else. His hair was dripping wet and slicked down against his body. She looked up at him as he entered, and the lust slammed against her hot and hard. She drank in every sculpted muscle, every lithe movement of his body, but she didn't leave the kitchen. If she did, nothing would stop her from jumping him in the bedroom. And from there, it was the tiniest step to giving him everything.

Carl didn't stop as he came into the room. He saw her, of course. And there might have been a slight hitch in his stride but no more as he headed straight for the bedroom.

Ouch. Even though she knew she was the cause, the awkwardness between them hurt. But she couldn't think of a way through it. Not until she felt more settled. And more capable of controlling herself when she was around him.

Meanwhile, Alan spoke, his voice low. "You need to talk to him, Becca. If you two are going to make a go of this, you have to love the bear as much as the man."

She jolted at the word "love." It wasn't that she hadn't flirted with the idea. Hell, she'd been fighting tooth and nail to *not* think the word. "We just met," she said. "We…He and I…" Hell, she couldn't get the words out. "It's a no-strings-attached kind of thing."

"Is that what he told you?"

She jerked her gaze back to Alan. She'd been staring at the closed bedroom door, but suddenly she was staring at Alan with her chest so tight she could barely breathe. "What do you mean?"

For the first time this morning, Alan looked chagrined and he rapidly started backing out of both the conversation and the room. But she couldn't let him go. She grabbed his arm and held firm. He could have escaped, of course. She wasn't that strong. But he didn't push the point as she held tight.

"Talk to me, Alan. I need to understand."

He huffed out a breath. "The very first night, he put you in his bedroom, Becca. His *den*. He hasn't done that with anyone before."

She shook her head. The last thing she needed was to realize that Carl was feeling as intensely about her as she was about him. That made it a scorched earth kind of relationship: wild, passionate, and completely destructive of the world around them. She knew. She'd seen her sister go through them often enough. By all accounts that's how Theo had been conceived. Maybe that's how all shifter relationships went.

"We just met," she said, denying everything he'd said in three words.

"Maybe you feel like you just met. He's been watching Theo from the very beginning. That's his job as Max—to keep an eye on potential new shifters."

"But that's Theo, not me."

Alan held up his hand, freeing his arm and silencing her in one motion. "He's been aware of you, Becca. And if what I saw this morning means anything, he's fully invested in you. Carl doesn't do things halfway."

No, no, no! It was too fast! But Alan didn't stop.

"You have complete control here. You can say yes or no. He won't force you in any way. But don't imagine for a second that he's just being casual with you."

She leaned against the counter and closed her eyes. Her hands were wrapped around her empty coffee mug as if it were a grounding wire to reality. It wasn't. Which left her reeling from too much too fast. Hell, Theo was missing. Shouldn't she put all her attention on finding him? On getting him home safely?

But what more could she do there except wait? And while waiting, all these other things had happened with Carl. She didn't know how to cope. And then she felt a hand, large and gentle, on her arm. Her eyes shot open to see Alan looking at her with sympathy. His expression was kind, but his words were anything but.

"I know this is a lot, Becca. And I don't want to pile more on, but you have to make a decision. Because I'll be damned if I let you hurt my brother."

"What?"

He took a breath. "You can't use my brother to distract yourself from what's going on with Theo. It's cruel enough to play with someone's emotions like that, but it's deadly if you do that with an alpha. Don't fuck with his head. Certainly not when he's doing everything he can to find Theo for you."

Was that what she was doing? Was she just

screwing Carl as a way to pass the time? Everything in her rebelled at the thought, and yet in a situation like this, who knew what tricks the mind played? "I'm not doing that on purpose," she said, knowing it for a weak excuse.

"Don't do it at all. For any reason." Then he straightened and stepped away, his gaze cutting to the right.

She followed his look and saw Carl standing awkwardly in the middle of the living room, his gaze heavy on her and Alan. His hair was towel-dried now, curling every which way. He had on jeans and a flannel shirt and there were socks in his hands. She met his gaze, flinching slightly at the raw emotion that swirled there. She couldn't read it, had no idea what he was thinking. But whatever it was, it was wild and powerful. And it was only in his eyes as the rest of him stood statue still.

She swallowed, wanting to go to him, but holding herself back. Alan's warning rang loud in her head. She didn't want to use him for her own selfish needs. And until she got some clarity about herself and him, she didn't want to lead him on. So she held herself back and wished with all her might that she had time to take a breath.

And then, like magic, he gave it to her.

"Tonya's got some leads. She and Bryn have figured out some locations where they might be holding Theo."

Her heart jolted inside her chest. "Where?"

"There are a dozen different places. They're checking as many as they can, but need help. So she and I are going to the ones around Gladwin."

That made sense. Tonya would have authority as a police officer and Carl would be there as Max.

"What can I do?" she asked.

"Just wait here. I'll call if there's any news."

"But I want to—"

"Just wait here, Becca." It was half order, half plea.

"Sure," she said. What else could she do? Maybe he needed some time to sort things out, too. So this was the perfect solution for them both. Except it didn't feel like it. In fact, it felt awful as she stood there watching him pull on his socks and boots. Worse, he then crossed to a locked cabinet and pulled out a handgun. She wondered at first why he needed it when he was Max Grizzly Bear, but then she remembered that he'd already shifted today. He wouldn't be able to go back into that kind of fighting mode again until after he'd rested.

Damn it, that made him extra vulnerable, and that scared the hell out of her.

"Wait!" she called as she headed for the door.

He froze mid step.

"You've got fifteen minutes, right? I mean you don't have to leave this second, right?"

He frowned. "Tonya's still coordinating with her team. I have maybe ten minutes. What did you have in mind?"

A million things flooded her brain, half of them pornographic, but out of all of them the need to make him as strong as possible was the loudest. "You haven't eaten and you shifted this morning. You must be starving."

"We'll grab a doughnut—"

"Don't be ridiculous. Or cliché." She opened a

bottom cabinet and found a skillet shoved in the back. God, it had dust on it. "I'm making you breakfast."

"You don't have to do that…" His voice trailed away at her glare.

"Sit," she ordered. Then she went into short-order cook mode, pulling together a breakfast fit for a starving lumberjack. All the protein and tasty carbs she could shove in his body in ten minutes.

He ate every bite, murmuring appreciative grunts throughout. There wasn't time for them to talk, which was just as well. She had no idea what she wanted to say. It took twelve minutes in total, and he left with a full thermos of coffee and three slices of buttered toast to eat on the road.

And then he was gone. She heard him and Tonya talk as they climbed into the squad car. Then she stood at the window and watched them drive away, feeling irrationally jealous that Tonya got to sit with him and not her. Five minutes later, Alan left as well. There were legal things to handle after this morning's fight.

Which left her alone with her thoughts.

Which—she now realized—really sucked.

CHAPTER 16

Carl ached. There was no other word for the exhaustion that pulled at his heart and mind. It began with a physical burn from the fight earlier today. Plus, shifting left a residue in a body. A kind of toxin that had to be worked out either in bear or human form. It was normal, but it often required ibuprofen or a hot tub to soak the misery away. Carl had neither.

Next came his frustration at their lack of progress. He and Tonya had visited every possible site in the county for another secret lab to no avail. With modern satellite imagery and their combined knowledge of the area, they'd been able to investigate a dozen possibilities but had found nothing. Well, not quite nothing. They'd stumbled over three small pot fields, but Carl hadn't cared enough to deal with that. Even Tonya had just texted the info to her boss and moved on.

But now it was after dark. Tonya had moved past cranky hours ago and was now into grunt-and-point mode as she dropped him off at his home. Which left

Carl heading up the walkway to face Becca and the ache that had filled his heart for most of the day.

She was repulsed by him. He didn't blame her. After all, it had taken him years to come to an armed truce with the animal inside him. The thing was brutal and violent. All it knew how to do was destroy. That was useful, so long as his intelligence kept it under control. He'd learned in his first years as Max to open the cage and aim the creature at whatever nasty had to be taken out. Then the moment the danger was past, the grizzly went back into lockdown.

But this morning had required him in full grizzly. Which meant she'd seen him at his most brutal. He'd felt her revulsion like a physical blow. And when she'd turned from him? It was like being kicked to the curb by civilization. She was a soft kind of girl, raised in the city, educated well, and living in an area that didn't even have crime. Of course the sight of him covered in gore would make her ill.

So he'd stayed away, searching for her adopted son as the only way he could help her. But he'd stewed about what had happened, worrying it like a diseased tooth until he was as surly as Tonya. And now he was home, his body tired, his mind still churning, and his heart aching because the woman he wanted had rejected him.

What a pathetic sack of shit he was.

He pushed open the front door, expecting the place to be deserted. Alan liked to work in his room, and Becca was probably hiding from him. Except instead of the typical dark, the living room was bright with light. Alan was sitting on the couch watching TV and Becca was at the dining room table working on a laptop. They both looked up when he entered, but if they said something, he lost it amid the smell.

Garlic bread and lasagna. He'd know that scent anywhere, and it drew him inside like nothing else. It was his favorite meal, and he hadn't had it home-made since his mother died when he was sixteen. His stomach growled, loud enough to be heard over the TV. Becca smiled and gestured, but she needn't have bothered. He went straight to the kitchen cabinets for a plate and silverware. It was a triumph of civilization that he didn't just pick up the pan and gobble it whole.

Becca joined him in the kitchen, her scent an odd combination of his soap, tomato sauce, and gun-powder. He wrinkled his nose, trying to understand if he had that right, but then lost the thought as she scooped up a huge serving onto his plate. And when he started to dig a fork in, she pulled it out of his hand.

"It's cold. You need to microwave it for a minute." She fitted the action to her words and he almost howled at the loss. Then he stood there like a child counting down the seconds on the machine while he waited. His stomach growled three more times, though she poured him a glass of something and he drank that just as a way to wait.

Raspberry iced tea? From a jug?

He frowned at the container on the counter, and Becca answered before he could ask it out loud. "I made some sun tea this afternoon. Is it cold enough?"

He didn't even know what sun tea was, but he nodded as held out his empty glass. Twenty-three more seconds until lasagna. Twenty-two. Twenty-one.

While Becca poured him more tea, Alan turned off the TV and leaned against the kitchen door. "I take it you didn't have any luck."

Carl shook his head, his gaze not on his brother but on Becca's face. She kept it neutral, but he saw her disappointment. Her lips tightened and she even swallowed as she put away the tea. Meanwhile, heaven came at the sound of the microwave finishing. *Lasagna!*

He took it out and shoveled in his first bite while it was still too hot. Didn't matter. Heaven in a single bite.

"This is good," he managed.

"I can't believe you didn't just burn your tongue."

He shrugged. "Hungry." And wasn't he doing a great job of acting like a mature man? A caveman spoke better than he had. So he forced himself to swallow and hold off shoveling in a new bite. "Thank you for the dinner. You can't know how much I appreciate it."

She smiled, her cheeks warming to a rosy pink. "I had to do something. Alan said your mother used to make lasagna. I found her recipe. I hope you don't mind."

Mind? He was ready to worship at her feet for this. But he didn't say that. It was too brutally honest. Instead, he looked around the counter. "Recipe? Where—"

"The box was in the cabinet up there." She pointed to the corner cabinet, which was filled with stuff they hadn't used in years: a food processor, a couple casserole dishes, and he didn't know what. And—obviously—his mother's recipe box.

"Make anything you want, anytime you want. I'll pay for the food. Whatever you need. Please." *Was that too much like begging?*

"How long has it been since anyone's cooked for you?" She looked at both men.

Alan shrugged. "We usually eat whatever the kids are being served." The after-school program had snacks every afternoon. And since shifters tended to eat a lot, even before their First Change, the meals were heartier than the usual crackers and a slice of cheese. They got burgers, hot dogs, and pizza on a regular basis. For Carl and Alan, that meant that weekends were filled with leftover burgers, hot dogs, and pizza. All of which added up to homemade lasagna as the nearest thing to heaven in a very long time.

"I made salad, too," she said, then chuckled. "But I can see that you'd rather eat the pasta."

He was already serving himself more. At least this time he managed to wait somewhat patiently as the microwave worked. Meanwhile, Becca leaned against the refrigerator, obviously working hard to appear casual. "Did you learn anything at all?"

He could see the worry in her eyes and hated making it worse, so he tried to put a positive spin on the situation. "We've eliminated a lot of possibilities. That's good progress. The entire police force is working on this. They'll figure out the next step."

She nodded, her gaze canting away. "Nothing new, then."

No way to answer that directly without confirming her worst fears. So he touched her chin, pulling her gaze up to his. "We'll find him. I swear it."

She searched his face and he kept it as open as he knew how. Let her see his absolute determination to find Theo and punish the bastard who created the situation in the first place. Whatever he showed her must have been convincing because eventually she nodded.

"Thanks."

Jesus. "Don't thank me, Becca. This is what I do. It's the Max's job to protect everyone here, especially the young." And it killed him that he'd failed in that. "Thank you for the food." Now that there were calories in his stomach, he noticed that the pile of laundry was gone and that someone had tidied up their home. That sure as hell hadn't been Alan. "Thanks for everything," he said, gesturing at the clean home.

"I have to do something or I'll go insane."

"She also went to the gun range today," Alan said, his voice excruciatingly dry. It was his lawyer way of criticizing. "I told her we'd keep her safe, but she insisted."

That explained the scent of gunpowder. "You don't have to be afraid here," Carl said. Though he could hardly blame her for being worried, what with grizzly wars taking place on the front lawn.

She sighed. "Turns out a gun didn't make me feel safer," she said as she handed him a slice of garlic bread. "I'm a sucky shot."

"You're a great cook," Carl said, and she couldn't

know how much he needed that. How he wanted a woman who wasn't about destroying. Whose focus was on building and nurturing.

Meanwhile, Alan continued to poke. "Did you run into any trouble today?"

Carl glanced at his brother, hearing the underlying question there: Is Tonya okay? "Nothing we couldn't handle. We're going to start at dawn tomorrow. Start searching farther afield."

"Everyone wants to help. Marty's coordinating food baskets for the people at the watch points, but beyond that I don't know what else we can do."

Carl couldn't think of anything either. "No more teens in their First Change?"

"No one's old enough. It's just Theo now."

Right. His gaze went back to Becca's pale skin. She was holding it together better than many mothers would, but the strain was showing. "You should get some rest," he said to her softly.

"I…" She shrugged. "I can't sleep." Then she gave an awkward shrug. "I made pie. It's not fancy, but—"

"Pie?" he interrupted. He shoveled in the last bites of his lasagna. "Where?"

"Blueberry." She opened the refrigerator. "I can heat it—"

"Nope." He took it from her hand. "I love it cold. I used to sneak it late at night after everyone had gone to bed. Always ate it cold then."

"Told ya," Alan quipped to Becca as he straightened off the wall. "I don't know about you two, but I'm beat. Dawn comes early for lawyers, too."

Carl frowned. "Anything I need to know about?"

Alan waved absently behind his back. "Not unless you enjoy the finer details of estate taxes."

"Kill me now."

"Exactly how I felt this afternoon when I started with it." And with that, Alan climbed the stairs to his bedroom, leaving Carl and Becca alone with blueberry pie.

A third of the pie was gone—probably what Alan had eaten—and Carl could easily finish the rest. But he figured it would be crass to eat the thing straight out of the pie tin. So he once again pretended to be civilized and got himself a plate. "Want any?"

"I had some earlier," she said.

He paused, frowning down at the plate. He knew his brother. Alan took the missing chunk. "Did you make two?"

She shook her head. "Just the one."

He set down the pie long enough to look at her hard. "Don't lie to me, Becca. It makes me nuts."

She opened her mouth on a gasp, then slowly closed it. "Sorry. I don't know why I said that."

He did. "Because Alan probably pushed you to eat when you didn't want it. So it's easier to lie to me than go through that again." He leaned forward, needing to press his point. "Except it isn't easier because I can tell. Just say you don't want it. I won't force you."

She nodded. "Is that a bear thing? Does my scent change or something?"

Yes. No. Her scent was a constant bouquet of temptation for him. It probably did change when she lied, but if he started focusing on her scent, he'd be hard and horny by the next breath. "Not this time," he said. "But I can still tell."

"I won't do it again." Then she gestured to the pie. "Want any ice cream with that?"

He didn't care about the ice cream, but he didn't want her leaving his side. Not yet. So he used the excuse to keep her near. And while she scooped, he looked at the laptop open on the dining room table. "Is that yours?"

"It's Alan's old one. He set it up for me. I've been catching up on emails and..." She shrugged. "Killing time, mostly."

As hard as today had been for him, how much harder had it been for her just sitting around waiting for news? He'd texted when he could, but there were only so many variations on "Nothing yet. Hope for a lead soon."

Still, he had to care for her somehow, so he pulled out an extra spoon and bowl for her. "Why not scoop a little for yourself?"

She shot him a glance. "You said you wouldn't push."

Oh, right. "It was just a suggestion."

Her expression turned wry, but then she pleased him by taking the bowl from his hand. "Maybe a little."

A few moments later, they settled down at the table, each enjoying the dessert. It was ridiculous how happy the domestic scene made him. He couldn't remember the last time he felt so content at the end of the day. Certainly never after a day as bad as today. But then Becca started to shift uncomfortably in her chair. She opened her mouth twice as if to say something, but then abruptly shoved a spoonful of ice cream in instead. Clearly she wanted to talk to him, but wasn't sure how to broach the topic. And given how happy he'd been a second ago, he wasn't sure he wanted her to break the peace. But in the end, he had to know. So in the split second between one bite and the next, he gave her an opening in the most offhand way he could think of.

"You can tell me anything." He smiled at her and wished for the thousandth time today that their morning after had gone differently. That he'd had time to hold her in his arms and wake her slowly in the way of a skilled lover.

She flushed and looked away. "It's more of a question."

He nodded. "So ask."

"It's personal."

He huffed out a breath. Didn't she get it? He'd give her anything she wanted and that included all the intimate secrets of his life. "Ask."

"What's it like to shift? Is it just you with a different body? Like putting on a different coat? Or are there other changes? Do you think like a man? Or…"

"Like an animal?"

She nodded. "I don't mean to be offensive."

He snorted. If she thought this was offensive, she hadn't met any of the crass members of the community. "These are normal questions. The kids ask all the time. I just…" He shrugged. "It's hard to explain."

She looked down and fiddled with her empty ice cream bowl. "Oh. Okay. Forget I—"

He touched her hand. "No, I'll explain. It just may not make any sense."

"You transform into a bear more than double your weight. I think we left rational behind a while ago."

He nodded. "It's like opening a cage door inside and just letting it have free range. The bear takes over, and I sit in the back and kind of watch. The body change is secondary. Suddenly, everything's instinct and action. What words I have are simple. Want. Need." *Kill. Destroy.*

She tilted her head as she looked at him. "You sound as if you're two different people."

"That's how it feels. There's me, the one sitting here talking to you. I'm the one who plans and strategizes. Who acts as Max and watches over the kids." He leaned back in his chair. "And then there's him."

"The grizzly part of you?"

"Sometimes he's so close to the surface, I worry he's going to explode out of me. It used to happen all the time as a kid. Now it's just…" *A constant war.* "A balancing act."

"It doesn't sound like balance," she said. "Actually, it sounds like what Theo was talking about with his friends."

"A bear under his skin?"

"Not the words he used. His football coach told him it was hormones. All that aggression and lust."

"I can relate."

"So it's like adolescence, only forever? Like your hormones take physical shape?"

He'd never thought about it like that. "I don't

know," he said honestly. "I've always been a shifter." But he spent a great deal of his time with kids, especially boys. They all had the wild inside them. Shifters just had to be extra careful when and how the wild got loose. "But I don't want you to think I can't control the bear. You're safe here."

Becca released a huff. "Why does everyone keep reassuring me that I'm safe? I never thought I wasn't. Well, except for when you kidnapped me, but that was just at the beginning."

He looked at her, his heart filling with emotions he couldn't control. "But what about this morning? What about…" He gestured vaguely to the front yard. He vividly recalled the way she'd turned from him.

"You protected me this morning. Me and the rest of the Gladwins. From what Alan said, Nick has been a problem for years."

"But weren't you afraid?"

"Not for me." She stroked her thumb across the back of his hand. "Were there others who haven't felt safe around you? Did someone get hurt?"

How to answer that without spilling his entire heart and soul? "We're all raised from birth to keep this quiet. Sure, we have normal friends, but we don't talk about shifting. And once we start dating…"

"It's a closed community," she finished for him. "Only look at girls who can shift."

"Or grew up around shifters. It's dangerous to share this stuff. Normal people tend to freak out."

She nodded her understanding. "Paranoia probably gets ingrained early."

She didn't know the half of it. "Our kind have been hunted since the beginning of time. But it goes the other way, too." He sighed. "People have a reason to fear. When shifters go feral, they destroy everything in their path. It's insanity at its most brutal and violent."

"You're talking about Mark."

He shook his head, his tone firming. "He's not there. Not yet." But he might be any minute now.

She flipped his hand over so that they could touch palm to palm, and that gesture pulled him out of his dark thoughts. "He seemed in complete control to me."

He flashed her a grateful smile. "He's strong." Then he forced himself to return to the main topic. She needed to understand the reason for all that paranoia. "We've all broken the rules at least once. We've told an outsider and had them lose it."

"Told them you can shift into a bear? Like you told me."

"Yes. You don't know how rare it is for someone to take it as well as you did."

She stood up, picking up their dirty dishes and carrying them to the sink. Her mouth was pursed as she moved, her expression drawn into one of concentration. "I did freak," she said, quietly enough he had to strain to hear. Then she returned to the doorway. "But you're not violent or insane. You're just people."

"I'm 'people.' My grizzly is a bear."

"Don't be ridiculous. You two are one and the same."

And here was the crux of her confusion. "No,

we're not. Not really. Because if the bear slips its leash, it's my job to kill it." His gaze shifted to the window. Miles away his best friend lived with that certainty. One day he would turn too much a bear and would go insane. And it would be Carl's job to put him down.

Then he felt her hand on his cheek, gently but firmly guiding his gaze back to her. She was standing above him as he sat in his chair, and she used the superior position to emphasize her words. "You are the same person," she repeated. "Bear or human, you are one person."

"You don't understand."

She sighed. "So explain."

"The grizzly is a wild creature. The man keeps him under control."

"Two entities in one body?" she asked.

He nodded.

"I don't believe it."

He stared at her. He couldn't fathom the audacity of her—a completely mundane human—telling him the details of who he was or how he functioned. It robbed him of words. And in the silence, she issued him a challenge.

"Can you let him out?" she asked. "Without shifting, I mean. Just let me talk to him if he's someone different."

He stared at her. Did she know what she was asking? "He's dangerous."

"You think he'd hurt me?"

"Absolutely not." The words were out immediately and emphatically. "He worships you."

Her brows arched, and her lips curved into a

smile. "Wow. I don't think I've ever been worshipped before."

"You were last night," he said.

"Oh, yes." Her cheeks pinked. "Well, that was fun." She frowned. "That was the bear?"

"No, that was me. And him. Together." That made it clear as mud.

"See," she said, touching his face. "You're the same person."

"We're different," he repeated.

Her expression shifted as she bit her lower lip. "Please?" she asked anxiously. "Is it possible? I'd really like to talk to him."

"He doesn't talk." He pulled her closer to him, thrilled that she let him wrap an arm around her hips. "He's instinct and action." And when she still didn't understand, he squeezed her bottom. "He wants you, Becca. And he won't be subtle."

He could see her process his meaning, but she was undaunted. "You want me to understand this shifting thing. You want me to feel safe with you."

He nodded.

"So show me. Let him out of the cage, Carl. I trust you to take control again if things get out of hand."

She trusted, but he didn't. Good lord, did she know what she was asking? "Last time I tried this, I lost control. Became a grizzly and tore apart my girlfriend's bedroom."

"How old were you?"

"Sixteen."

"And how did she react?"

He snorted. "Tonya shifted, too, and we..." He

cleared his throat. "Well, she didn't get pregnant, so we were lucky about that. But there wasn't much left of her furniture when we were done."

"Hot and hormonal. But you already shifted today. So that won't be a problem, right?"

He nodded. That at least was true. "This still isn't a good idea."

She leaned over him, stroking across his cheeks with a feathery touch. "I need to meet him, Carl. If you're two people, then I need to meet the other half."

"He doesn't talk," he repeated.

"Then it'll be a short conversation."

He could see that she was determined. And to be honest, he wondered if he could manage it. He hadn't tried to do this since that disastrous time with Tonya over a decade ago. But inside, he couldn't stop the dread that filled him. What would happen when she saw he was just a grunting, horny bear? Would he lose what little chance he had with her?

"It's not me who feels unsafe," she said softly. "It's you. You don't trust yourself."

"Because it's playing with fire." He looked into her eyes. "People have been burned. Badly."

"What people?"

"My mother." The word was out before he could stop it. Damn it, this is what Becca did to him. She made him lose control and words—secrets—came tumbling out.

"What happened?" she asked, her entire body stilled.

"My uncle was Maximus then. He was brutal,

like most Maxes of the time. But he seemed to enjoy it."

She waited, her body stilled as it pressed against him, but not in fear. She was simply listening and he found he wanted to explain.

"He was being cruel. He liked baiting children, torturing them until they got angry enough to shift."

"Does that work?"

"Only if the kid is ready to shift anyway. For anyone under the age of fifteen, it's just sadistic."

She pressed a kiss to his forehead. "Was it you? Was he torturing you?"

He shook his head. "Alan." The boy who was so human they knew it even when he was a toddler. But that hadn't stopped his uncle.

"How awful."

"She went Mama bear on him. She was a shifter, but not a strong one. She changed only three times in her life. That was her third."

"And he killed her for it?"

Carl nodded, feeling the burn of tears in his eyes. He still remembered the sound of them fighting. His mother's roar of fury. His uncle's lower, angrier growl. And then blood. Oceans of blood. And he'd been powerless to stop it.

"My uncle was mean, but even he had limits. He didn't plan on killing his brother's wife, but she attacked him." The words clogged his throat, and he pressed his face against Becca's breasts. They were full and soft, and smelled of the food she'd cooked. Lost in her softness, he was able to say the rest. "My father heard the noise and came running, but was too late to save her."

"What about you?" she whispered. "Where were you?"

"With Alan." He'd shoved his younger brother into a kitchen cabinet, then cowered nearby, planning to distract his uncle when the creature turned on them. "My uncle's bear was a monster," Carl said.

"Sounds like he was the monster—human and bear."

Maybe. Certainly. But in his mind, Carl had always associated the bloody death of his mother with the grizzly bear, not the man. "My father challenged him that day, but he was smart, too. He knew he couldn't beat my uncle bear to bear, so he called in the police to help. It was a human cop who shot the 'rabid' bear attacking my father. By evening, my uncle was dead and my father became Max."

He felt her hands on his face, stroking his cheeks as she pressed kisses to his forehead. "I'm so sorry."

So was he. And how awful to relive it even in memory. Except that it hadn't been so bad. Not with her holding him. Not with her hands on his body and her warmth cradling him. He ought to feel ashamed for burrowing into her embrace like a child needing a blanket. But he wasn't ashamed. And he needed her solid strength right then. Not for him, but for the child he'd been who had watched it all and had been powerless to stop it.

"That's why," he finally choked out. "That's why I don't trust the bear."

"But that wasn't you."

He shook his head. "Doesn't matter."

"It does matter." Then she stepped back far enough for her to angle his face up toward hers. "It matters," she repeated. "You aren't bad. Your grizzly isn't vicious."

"You were here this morning, right? You saw—"

"I saw you protecting your family. Yeah, all that blood freaked me out, but that wasn't you." Then she leaned down and pressed a soft kiss to his lips. He would have deepened it. He pulled her tight again to try to take her in the most human way possible, but she refused him. She held herself apart after one single kiss and she stared him in the eye.

"Enough," she said in the firmest voice he'd ever heard from her. "Let me talk to your bear. Now."

How could he say no? He would give her everything. So with a swift, silent prayer that he could keep things under control, he stepped back from his brain. He pulled away from the rational, human side, and opened the door to his grizzly.

It was there, ready and waiting to be freed. He was too tired to shift bodies, but mentally, the switch was a simple choice. Carl stepped back. The grizzly pushed forward. And in a split second of mutual accord, they both swore that Becca would remain safe no matter what.

But the grizzly made no promise to stay civilized.

CHAPTER 17

Becca watched closely, so she saw the change, though physically it was subtle. The clearest shift came in his eyes, which went from green to a dark brown. Then his nose seemed to stretch a bit, his neck and shoulders might have thickened, and nothing at all changed with his mouth. At least not until she caressed his lips.

He licked her. A long twist of his tongue around her first two fingers, and her nipples tightened in reaction.

Okay, so his bear was lust-inducing. That wasn't new. But the way he was looking at her was. Carl was right when he said the bear worshipped her. His eyes were fixed on her, steady in their absolute attention. There was no demand in his gaze, not that she could see. No thoughts either. Just pure…emotion?

She touched his face, stroking gently across his cheekbone. He turned into her caress, closing his eyes in appreciation but doing no more.

Carl had said that his bear was all action. He'd suggested that the creature might just take her to bed without thought or gentleness. But there was no forceful seduction here. Nothing beyond a quiet appreciation. And in that realization, all her fears faded away. Truthfully, she hadn't even known she was afraid, but now the release of tension was like dropping a heavy blanket from her shoulders. She took a deep breath for the first time since he'd come home.

"I told you I was safe with you," she said.

She'd barely gotten the words out when he changed. His eyes flickered and where before there was an unnamed focus of emotion, now she read yearning. He released a low moan of pain. The sound was heartbreaking and she immediately searched him for an injury.

"Is something wrong?"

She'd stepped closer to him and his arms wrapped tightly around her hips. He was still sitting, she standing, and he dropped his head against her chest, his breath shuddering in and out. She touched his hair, feeling coarse strands where before there had been only silky softness. Another manifestation of the bear, she supposed. But mostly what she felt was the way he held her, rumbling low and deep inside.

Carl had said the bear couldn't communicate, but he was wrong. There was language here, just not the human kind. She made it her mission to understand. She had a guess, but she had to see if she was right. So she pulled back from him. It was hard, because he wasn't going to let her go. But she insisted and eventually his arms eased. That gave her enough room to kneel down in front of him. And when their eyes were on a more even level, she touched his mouth. He licked her fingers again, but lightly. More of a hello than anything more.

"You have a mouth. You can talk. Tell me what you want."

"Becca," he said.

She smiled. "There you go. That's a start. Now tell me why you're so sad."

He clutched at her again, but she didn't let him reel her in. He was strong enough to override her wishes, but he didn't. He just ducked his head, another low moan pouring out of him. And when she pulled his face back up to hers, there were tears in his eyes.

It slayed her to see him like this. Carl was the definition of large and powerful. To see his eyes wet with pain made her chest tighten unbearably. But she didn't give in to the need to hold him. Not yet. He had to explain and eventually he pushed a word out.

"Alone."

She frowned. Did he want her to leave? Of course not. Which meant…"You feel lonely, don't you? Carl locks you tight inside, only letting you out to beat up on things." Okay, so she might be feeding into this idea that he was two separate people, but identities got sectioned off all the time. Sometimes she thought of herself as a mother and nothing else. Other times, she was a baker and a small-business owner. Different parts of herself functioning separately, but she still knew herself as one person. Carl, on the other hand, was taking this to an extreme. "But you're part of him, aren't you? And you need to be more than just a brute."

"Need you." He caressed her arm, squeezing it as if for emphasis.

"Why?" She had to know if this was just a mating drive or something more. But that was asking for complicated expression out of a bear. It just wasn't happening.

His hand trailed up to her mouth. "Becca."

So it was up to her to figure this out. No problem. She'd been dealing with a monosyllabic teen boy for a while now. She touched Carl's chest, flattening her palm there as she spread her fingers. She felt the ripple of his muscles beneath her hand and she imagined she felt his heartbeat. It was probably more her own, but she didn't care. Especially when he managed two more words.

"Love me."

Well, that was clear enough. And the startling truth was that she did. She loved the aching loneliness in the man before her. She adored the power that he contained and the gentleness with which he wielded it. But most of all, she loved the man who split himself in two so that he could manage the demands of his mind and the needs of his heart. And the bear, she now saw, was his heart.

"Becca?"

"Yes," she said. Then she kissed him. She pressed her mouth against his and teased his lips with her tongue. He waited just a moment—frozen as if in shock—and then he changed again. His mouth opened and he devoured her. Hot and hungry, his tongue invaded her, branding her lips, her teeth, even the roof of her mouth, with his need.

She purred against him, already arching into his

embrace. That seemed to be all the encouragement he needed because he scooped her up in his arms. Still with their mouths fused, he carried her to his room. Once there, he set her down on the bed, and when they separated enough to breathe, he began to pet her everywhere. Large strokes, whole hand, absolutely everywhere. There seemed to be no preference for any part of her body. Her hair, her shoulders, her belly, her breasts. He even palmed her ankles while she stripped out of her clothes. And once she was naked, she rushed to help him.

He was impatient with his clothes and the business of taking them off. His attention was on her, and when she forced him to move his hands away from her while she pulled off his shirt, he leaned forward to put his mouth on her. And when that was impossible, he rubbed his legs against hers. He wanted to touch her everywhere and with every part of his body. And once all the clothing was dispensed with, she happily succumbed to his needs.

He stroked her everywhere and with every part of him. It was a rollicking tumble all over his bed, and she began to giggle with delight. He liked their legs entwined every which way. He liked her torso in his hands. Not just her breasts, but spanning her rib cage and tracing her spine. He wanted to lick every inch, but inevitably found his way between her thighs. She'd thought he'd been thorough before, but he seemed to revel in it now. There was no skill in the steady build to orgasm, just sheer delight as he tasted her every which way.

Her orgasm—when it happened—was almost an afterthought to the way he was owning her. And though she came with a cry, gripping his shoulders with her thighs as she bucked beneath him, he just kept licking, his large palms squeezing her bottom as he feasted.

On and on it went until she lost track of individual sensations. Her entire body was pleasure, almost without form. Just touching and throbbing. Pulsing and laughing. And it was all joy.

Pleasure as his penis thrust inside her.

Happiness as she gripped him, her orgasm pulsing around them both.

Joy when he exploded inside her.

And ecstasy when he did it again and again.

* * *

Becca woke slowly, her body settled deep in Carl's arms and his heartbeat steady against her ear. She was resting on his chest and he held her half on top of him, half wrapped around his hip and thigh. Even their feet were touching.

She felt him press a kiss to her forehead and she released a low purr of delight. Then she murmured, "Good morning."

"Sorry to wake you."

She smiled. Of all the ways to wake up, this was now her all-time favorite. His hands were brushing across her shoulder and back. Long strokes that were less soothing petting and more a "wake up and love me." She was okay with that, and so stretched against him, lifting her mouth to press a kiss against his contoured chest.

A low rumble rolled through his body into hers

and she smiled. But then he tightened his hold and gently pushed her back a half inch. "I'm sorry. I have to get up."

He was already up. She felt his penis thick and heavy against her hip. But she knew what he meant, so she reluctantly slid off. He rolled the other way and sat up, rubbing his face as he went.

She blinked the sleep out of her eyes and studied his profile. All human, complete with a Roman nose and shoulders that were broad without being thick. Also, the way he moved was more efficient, less fluid. As if everything in him were locked down again.

"You need to be the bear more often," she said, startled by her own words. It wasn't like her to boldly tell someone what he should and shouldn't do with his life. But once started, she couldn't back away from the message. It was too important. "You've locked all your emotions away with him, and that's not healthy."

He turned to look at her, his eyes fully green in the muted dawn light. "He's gentle only with you."

"Bullshit. He's you, Carl. Your emotions and your instinct caged in a little box labeled Bear. They're part of you. You pull them out when you think you need them, but they're all you. And they need to be expressed."

"He doesn't talk."

"He talked plenty last night." And she'd heard him when he'd expressed loneliness and need. And he taught her about the joy of reveling in each other's physical bodies for the simple pleasure of being with each other.

Carl dropped his hand into his lap. "Even you talk about him as a separate person."

"Only because you do. Because you've locked that part of you away." She pushed up to a seated position. "Your bear is wonderful, Carl."

His expression lightened and he touched her arm. A single stroke that was both longing and connection. And then he spoke, his words shocking her into reality.

"He also didn't use a condom."

Becca froze, the words echoing in her brain. Mentally, she pulled up her calendar, trying to remember when she'd last had a period, but she didn't know. There'd been no need to keep track. Meanwhile, Carl squeezed her arm.

"Don't panic. Whatever happens, we'll deal with it. Whatever you want, I won't abandon you."

She looked into his eyes. Abandonment wasn't her fear. It was everything else. The choices, the possibilities, and the moral weight of it all. Could she fit a baby into her life? Did she dare consider giving it up for adoption or something worse? What would Theo think? And how the hell had she let this happen?

And yet, even as those thoughts scrambled for purchase, another wholly instinctive part of her settled into a purring contentment. Was this the animal part of her? If so, it was happily knitting booties and settling into Carl's bedroom as if it were a den made just for her and their child.

"Becca, really. There's no need to panic. Odds are nothing happened."

"That's what my sister said, and nine months later, Theo was born."

He touched her chin, drawing her gaze up to his. "We both have plenty on our plates right now. Don't add more before you have to."

"Good advice, except that life still keeps happening." She closed her eyes and dropped back against the headboard. "Jesus, I'm supposed to be the responsible one. I didn't even think. Last night, I just felt."

His voice was quiet, but she heard him clearly. "And how did it feel, Becca?"

She opened her eyes. "You know it was wonderful, Carl. But..." She swallowed. His question had been about more than just the night. It was about who they were together. "This whole situation is out of control. I have a normal life back in Kalamazoo. I have a business and a son." And what was she doing creating babies when Theo was missing?

He turned away, his expression carefully blanked. The bear in him was completely absent, which meant his emotions were locked down. "I need to shower before Tonya gets here. Then I'm going to find Theo and everything will be fine."

Was that even possible anymore? She didn't think so. So much had happened since Theo's disappearance that she wasn't sure she could find normal again. Not in a world where her adopted son was a bear shifter. And she was potentially pregnant with another.

She bit her lip, fighting the frustration. Every time she thought she had her life under control, something happened to destroy her peace. First it had been her father's abandonment, then her sister's pregnancy. Next came the deaths, Nancy's and her mother's, leaving her and Theo to find a new balance together. And now? Now everything was off-kilter again.

She couldn't take it. It was too much.

"Becca…"

She held up her hand, stopping him from talking. "First things first," she said. "Find Theo. I can't deal with anything more."

She didn't even look at him, but kept her eyes closed and her head down. She wouldn't look up until he was gone.

Twenty minutes later, she got her wish. He showered and left without another word. But once the door thudded shut behind him, she finally took stock. What was on today's plate? She would deal with that. Sadly, the only thing she had to occupy her time was meaningless chores and endless worry.

CHAPTER 18

Okay, you are officially a pain in my ass."
Carl jolted as he looked at Tonya. She was driving the squad car as they went to the next house on their list. "What?"

"You've been a shit all morning and that last conversation with Mr. Edelstein? Not necessary to put him against the wall."

"You?" he stressed, layering sarcasm in every word. "You're chewing me out for too much force?"

"Yes. Because that's my beat. You're the thinking one. Except today you're Mr. Get Outta My Face."

"Yeah, I am. So get out."

She snorted. "You'll have to get a lot more violent for that to work on me."

"Don't push me, Tonya. I mean it."

She huffed out a breath. "You playing the alpha card? Was that an order?"

He considered it. He was in that foul a mood. But Tonya had only so much obedience in her, even when given direct orders. A good leader knew when to call in his markers and this wasn't one of those times. So instead of answering, he looked out the window at the rapidly warming landscape. Michigan was hitting one of those hopeful spring moments. The smart ones knew it could change in five minutes, so they took the time to appreciate the weather now. He chose to stare at the landscape and pray that Theo wasn't out in it somewhere.

"That's not going to work either," Tonya said with a huff.

He turned and hit her with a hard glare. She stared at him for a moment, and then turned back to the road.

"Okay. So I guess that will work. So I'm going to do something radical here. I'm going to offer something I never do. Are you ready?"

He snorted rather than answer.

"I'm going to listen without judgment. Whether you realize it or not, you need to talk to someone. So talk. I'll listen. And I won't tell either, but you know that already."

Yes, that part was true. She was as close a confidante as he'd ever had. Except for his brother, she was the one person he trusted with his secrets. Which meant, after a time, he finally started speaking.

"Becca wanted to meet my bear last night."

Tonya frowned. "She already met your bear. When you tore apart Nick."

He winced at the memory. "Not like that. Unshifted. Just...you know, the bear."

"Jesus, you are the bear. Unless we're talking fur and claws, you were being you."

He snorted. "That's what she said."

"So she's smarter than she looks."

"Stop that!" he snapped. "She's brilliant. She understands a lot more than you do, that's for damn sure. She's gentle and kind. She's been raising a kid by herself, running a business, and you should see her cakes. They're works of art. She's amazing, and you show yourself as an idiot when you trash-talk her."

If his earlier silence had her staring, this little explosion had her gaping in shock. Bad news when they were speeding down a country road at seventy miles per hour.

"Pay attention to the road!" he snapped.

She did. Her gaze ripped back to the road and her mouth clenched in a tight line. But she didn't speak. Instead, she slowly blew out a breath. And then after he'd turned back to glare out the window, she finally ventured a couple sentences, albeit in a small, quiet voice that she never, ever used.

"So she met your bear last night and told you that you and the bear are the same people. What happened next?"

He sighed. "She may be pregnant."

She snorted. "Been there, done that." He glared at her again, but she held up a hand. "Not judging. Just saying."

He didn't respond. Nothing to say. Except apparently, Tonya had plenty on her mind.

"Okay, since you're not talking, let me be the one to say the things you're brooding about. We'll just get them out in the open and you can tell me to go shove it or not." He opened his mouth to tell her to shove it, but she rushed her words. "You've fallen for Becca. That much is clear from your tirade a moment ago."

He didn't argue. That much he'd already figured out.

"Maybe you even think you love her."

He hadn't gone to that word yet. Worship. Adore. Thank God for her every moment of the day. Those words he'd used, at least in his own head. Love? His bear certainly loved her. Maybe he could admit that the human Carl loved her, too. But crap, that was a problem. The woman hadn't even been able to look at him this morning.

"So you're moody," Tonya continued, "because you know it's a doomed relationship."

"What?" The word came out with a sharp bite.

"Don't snap at me for saying what you're already thinking. Look, she's fully human. She may be the adopted mother of a shifter boy, but she's not one of us and she never will be. Anyone else in the community, that's not a problem. But you're the Max. And worse than that, you like being the Max and you're pretty good at it."

"So maybe you should let me pick the woman I want and leave it alone."

"I will, but that doesn't help Becca. She's the one who'll suffer, not you."

"Don't be ridiculous. She'll be my Maxima. That's a position of status." He ignored the fact that she was a long way from becoming his wife. Hell, as of this morning, he wondered if she'd still be there tonight when he came home. He gave even odds that she'd have already bolted back to Kalamazoo.

"Now who's being ridiculous? She's an outsider

and that will never change. She'll be given lip service as your Maxima, but attacked in other ways. People won't talk to her, won't accept her help, and will criticize her every chance they get. She won't be able to function as a Maxima would because no one will let her. That will end up hurting both of you."

That was a bleak picture. Worse, he knew it was possible. Being alpha was akin to being mayor of a small, insular town. Everyone seemed friendly on the outside, but once you got to the inner workings of the clan? Well, that was a dicey political position indeed. He survived because he kept the various factions in balance. Marrying a fully human woman would hurt that standing. But then, maybe that wouldn't be so bad. Maybe he should give up being Max. It was never something he sought out specifically. He just hadn't wanted psycho people like Nick to take control.

"So be it," he said. "I don't need to stay Max."

"Bullshit. You love being Max. Sure, you complain, but you're the only reason the Gladwins have held together since your father killed your uncle."

He winced. That had been a devastating time for everyone. It started out just rocky. No one grieved his uncle's passing and they were relieved at the sudden release from the violent control that had been the man's MO. Everyone cheered his father's kinder, more gentle approach. But within a year, it became clear that his father just didn't have the organizational skills to keep matters running smoothly. He screwed up key negotiations with neighboring shifters—which planted the seeds of

Nick's discontent—and worse, he had no ability to manage finances. Even at eleven, Carl had understood the disaster in the making. He was the one who convinced his father to hire an accountant and a manager to oversee the daily affairs of the kids camp that had always been the heart of the Gladwin clan. Shortly after his twelfth birthday, Carl started listening in to important meetings.

It wasn't always smooth, but with his help, his father had managed to keep the Gladwins from disintegrating long enough for Carl to come back from college. The day after he graduated, his father handed him the title and four months later died from a heart attack. There'd been a challenge two days later, but Carl's bear was in its prime. The fight had been long and bloody, but he'd ended up victorious. He'd become Max in the most animal way. But the widow had been angry and started whispers. Sure, he retained the title, but the discontent had been a constant nagging problem that had eaten at his peace of mind.

But that was the job of the Max. To keep things running smoothly for the good of everyone. And Tonya was right. He was good at it. But that didn't mean he couldn't do something else.

"If I give up being Max, I could put more time into finding a solution to the feral problem. I could spend more time with the kids."

"You're not a scientist, and you spend time with the kids as Mr. Max. It doesn't work if you're not the alpha. It'll be the other Max's job. And speaking of which, just who do you think will replace you? Nick was the least nutty of the viable candidates."

"Why not you? The alpha doesn't have to be a guy."

She shot him a look. "Like I want to manage money or listen to an old lady's complaints about her neighbor's dog. I'm the least diplomatic person alive and you know it. One bad look from the wolves in Detroit, and we'd be at war with them. No thank you. I prefer to leave that kind of crap to the guy who kept us neutral three years ago when the cats and dogs started killing each other."

He'd done some fancy dancing then, when the werewolves and the were-cougars had gone at it. It was a short war—only about a year—but it had been bloody on both sides. The populations were still recovering and it had taken all of his human diplomatic skills to keep the Gladwins out of it. Especially since one of the most logical battlegrounds was Gladwin State Park. And what even Tonya didn't know was that he was the one who brokered the peace.

"I could be your diplomatic liaison," he suggested.

"Or you could keep doing what you're doing and not screw with success." She blew out a breath. "Look, I know you're feeling all these great things for Becca. She's everything warm and fuzzy that you adore. She's also sexy in that hot mama kind of way. But come summer, it'll change. Don't destroy both your lives for spring fever."

Was that what he was feeling? Spring hormones? It didn't feel like that, but hell, it'd been so long since he'd felt the hots for anyone, how would he know?

Tonya shot him a long look, trying to gauge his reaction to her words. He didn't give her any. There was too much to consider. Just because every part of his body and soul wanted Becca in his life didn't mean he was thinking clearly. Or that it was the best choice for everyone. After all, he could give up being Max. He could if it was for her. Plus, it would give him more time to do the things he cared about, like finding a solution for the ferals. But what if she would be miserable here? Tonya was right. As a full human, Becca would never completely fit in. He had only to look at his brother, Alan, to know that. The man did more for the community as a lawyer than any of them could possibly imagine, but he was still considered inferior because he couldn't shift. How much worse would it be for Becca, without any shifter blood in her at all?

He couldn't do that to her. She had a life and a business in Kalamazoo. Why would she give that up just to be shunned here? It didn't make sense, and he'd cut off his right arm before he made her miserable. Which meant the answer was clear.

He couldn't have her. He'd go back to what he had been doing, which was watching her from afar. Wanting her but knowing it was best for her sake to leave her be even as he taught her adopted son how to be a shifter.

If he'd cut off his right arm to make her happy, then how much harder could it be to cut out his heart?

CHAPTER 19

Becca had never enjoyed housekeeping. It's not like anyone truly wanted to spend their day vacuuming or throwing out cans of food that had expired ten years ago. But she found a kind of peace in setting Carl's home in order. And if nothing else, she knew Alan appreciated her efforts. He said so when he came home for lunch. But he was running late, so there wasn't much time for anything but the usual "Is there any news?" and "Oh my God, this tastes great!" Neither of them had more information and Carl texted a big "nothing yet" every hour, which was enough to make her seriously crazy.

By midafternoon, the walls started closing in on her. She had to get out of the house or commit hara-kiri. So, taking Carl's truck, she headed out to the supermarket. Forcing the men to eat some fresh vegetables would be a good way for her to burn off excess energy. And she could pretend she was cooking for Theo, too. For when Carl brought him home safe and sound this evening.

She pulled into the Walmart parking lot and

picked a spot well clear of other cars. She wasn't used to handling a truck and didn't want to damage it or another vehicle as she maneuvered the huge thing into a slot. An hour later, she was cursing the distance as she pushed her cart down the long row. The wind had picked up and her face burned from the cold. Odd that there were two more vehicles parked on either side of her, a truck and a van. There were lots of other spaces closer up and now she'd have to be extra careful not to sideswipe them as she backed out.

She was just running through her meatloaf recipe, trying to remember if there was any ketchup left back at the house, when the door to the truck on her right opened. A thick-jawed guy who seriously needed a haircut stepped out and nodded to her. She smiled vaguely back at him as she pressed the key fob to unlock the truck. And then she heard the door on the van and had her first stirring of alarm.

She turned to look, but it was already too late. Thick-jaw guy moved fast, slapping a foul-smelling cloth over her face. She tried to scream, but barely got out a squeak. Her heartbeat slammed against her throat and her vision started fuzzing out. She managed a kick, feeling gratified when she heard an annoyed grunt, but that was all she got. She couldn't claw his arm away from her face and she couldn't stop breathing, whatever it was that fogged her mind.

Seconds later, the world went black.

CHAPTER 20

Aunt Becca! Wake up!"
Becca groaned and pressed a hand to her forehead. What the hell had she been doing? She hadn't had a migraine this bad since she was fifteen.

"Shh! Don't talk yet. Just nod if you're okay."

No, she wasn't okay. She felt like crap and Theo… *Theo!*

Her eyes shot open, which apparently was a bad idea. Light stabbed through her eyeballs to attack her brain, and she slammed them shut again. Holy hell, she felt awful. But at least her brain was working.

"Theo?" she whispered, hoping like hell she hadn't imagined it.

"It's me."

ThankGodThankGodThankGod! He was alive. "Where are we?" All she'd gotten in her short blink was a flash of white on white and metal bars. It was that last part that bothered her. But Theo was alive and the relief of that had her lightheaded from joy. Or whatever shit it was they'd made her breathe.

"An abandoned salt mine. That's all I know. They're not real big on talking with the lab rats."

She nodded slowly, then decided to risk another peek. Shielding her eyes with a hand, she slowly cracked them open. Every once in a while her migraines were so bad they made her retch. She didn't think that would be a good idea right now. She was probably going to need all her wits pretty soon, and that meant slowly taking stock of her surroundings without putting her on her knees over a bucket. If there even was a bucket.

She squinted and peered around.

There was a bucket about two feet away from her. And that was about it for her in this metal cage on a gray-white floor. Abandoned salt mine, huh? Well, she supposed there were worse places to be, though at the moment she couldn't think of any.

Meanwhile, her eyes adjusted enough that she could look farther away. There was another cage beside her and in it, a young man was flopped on his back, his hair matted with blood. Somehow it would have been better if he'd been curled in on himself, but he lay as if dropped and unable to move.

She choked back a sob at the sight. It wasn't Theo, that much she'd seen instantly, but the boy looked near death and she wanted to go help him.

"That's Caleb," Theo said in a low voice. "He's not dead, so it's best if you just let him rest."

"Where are you?" she asked, slowly moving her throbbing head. But as she did, a sharp pain from the crook of her arm cut through her consciousness. She looked and saw a telltale bandage there and she cursed under her breath.

"I don't think they gave you anything. Just took a ton of blood to test," Theo said.

She was finally able to locate her nephew by the sound of his voice. Tilting her head up, she saw another cage, only this one was a great deal larger. Not big enough for a person to stand, but at least Theo had plenty of room to crouch forward against the bars.

"Theo," she whispered, scanning him from head to toe. He looked pale and bruised, plus his hands were raw. Even crouched as he was, she could see that he'd lost weight. No baby fat left on her boy anywhere. He had bandages at the crooks of both elbows and, now that she looked closely, she realized that he was naked and covered in raw welts. It took her a moment to place what might have caused them, and when she did, the fury was nearly blinding. "Did they…Was that…a cattle prod?"

He flushed and tried to cover his wounds, but there were simply too many. And that made her all the more livid. To think that he'd be ashamed of what they'd done to him. My God, she was going to kill them!

"It looks worse than it is," he said.

"Is there anything else? Are you hurt? Did they beat you?" She searched her memory for every scrap of medical information she had. There wasn't much. All she knew about emergency medicine she'd gotten from TV.

"I'm okay," he said, his words low and urgent. "Keep your voice down. You want them to think you're still asleep."

She nodded and pressed her lips together. But

the sight of his battered body made her want to wail. And find a gun. She did neither. Instead, she tried to focus more on their surroundings. There wasn't much to see. Just long rows of cages, all of them empty except for her, Theo, and Caleb. Then, twisting as much as she could, she picked out what she guessed were two doors, one on either end of the large room. That was the extent of her reconnaissance.

"There was another boy. Caleb's brother." Theo's voice choked up as he spoke.

"I know," she said. That must be the boy who'd died at the farm. "We found him, but were too late to…" Her voice trailed away. Too late to save the child. Too late to find Theo. And now she was trapped here, too. "They're looking for you—Carl, the police, everyone. We almost found you before. They'll find you now. We just have to hold on a bit longer."

Theo's eyes went wide with hope, and for a moment, he looked like that little boy who'd just lost his mother years ago. The one who had put all his faith and trust in her, even though everything had just been shattered.

"We'll be fine," she repeated as much to herself as him. "Carl will find us."

"Who's Carl?" he asked. Trust the boy to hit on the one awkward part of the whole conversation.

"He's Mr. Max. He's been part of the search from the very beginning." She stretched out her legs as much as she could in this narrow space. If she stayed on her side, bent at the waist, she could just do it. She was pleasantly surprised to see that she wasn't bruised or hurt in any way except at the elbow. That was something. Though God knew how long that would last. "What do they want with us?"

"I, um... We're being studied. Caleb and me." He took a shuddering breath. "I think they did something to me, Aunt Becca. I think they made me into something... awful."

She looked over at him. He was trying to be brave. She could see it so clearly on his face, even though he was terrified. But in this one respect, she had to tell him the truth. She couldn't let him look at himself like some kind of monster. "You mean because you can shift into a grizzly bear? Is that it? Because if it is, that's not something terrible. It's wonderful." She looked over at Caleb. "And he's a werewolf, right?"

Theo's eyes were wide and he could barely get the words out. "You knew?"

She shook her head. "Not until a few days ago. Right after you went missing, Mr. Max came and explained things. He said..." She smiled at Theo, trying to show him with just her eyes and her words that she would love him no matter what kind of biology he had. Human, bear, wolf, or anything else. "He said you were on the verge of your First Change."

"Into a bear? It's not... you know... lycanthropy or something?"

"No, sweetie. I don't think so. But when Carl gets us out, he'll explain it to you. He's a bear, too. As are a lot of people. He says your father was one of them, and they've been watching over you since you were first born."

Theo's eyes narrowed and his hands gripped the bars, twisting as if he could work them free. They didn't budge, and she could see his brows lower in fury. "My father did this to me?" he asked, his voice low and rough. "And Mr. Max?"

"No, no. They'd didn't *do* it to you. It's something you *are*. It's something they are."

"A freak?"

"Never! Theo, you have to calm down." But it was too late. She could see his emotions getting away from him. His hands were thick where they gripped the bars, and as she watched, they got larger and darker. She looked to his eyes and saw them turn golden brown. His nose lengthened and dark fur sprouted everywhere.

He was shifting and in that confined space, he wasn't going to fit. Plus, she knew if she and Theo were going to have a chance to escape, it wouldn't be with him unconscious after the bastards used their cattle prod on him. Carl had said that shifters could change only once a day at best. That the change took too much out of them. And it was clear that Theo needed to conserve his energy. He was thinner than she'd ever seen him and this wasn't going to help. So it was time for her to go into Mommy mode.

"Theodore Samuel Weitz, you will settle down this instant!" Her voice was sharp and cold. Theo's head snapped up immediately, his eyes pinned on her, but he didn't stop growling deep in his throat. "Don't you dare take that tone with me, young man. You will sit down on your bottom and think, do you hear me? You will use your brain, or so help me, I will climb out of this cage and flick you hard right on your nose."

The absurdity of that threat wasn't lost on her.

She couldn't get out of her cage and no way was a finger snap on his nose going to do anything. But it was the only physical punishment she'd ever used. It was the shame of it that settled Theo down when he was ten. And it was the tone—she hoped—that made it through to the bear.

It worked.

He dropped down onto his butt and stared at her. A moment later, his nose seemed to recede and his ears returned to full human. Odd how she was starting to pick up on the little changes more than the big ones. But she'd been studying Theo's face since he was a baby. Of course she'd notice every little thing. She didn't speak again until he was fully human.

"I know you're angry," she said softly. "I am, too. But you need to conserve your strength. We'll get our chance soon. I promise."

Theo swallowed and turned his face away. Then a moment later, he looked back at her, hope once again burning hot and wild in his hazel eyes. "Promise?" he whispered.

"I promise. Mr. Max won't let us down."

"But what if—"

"Hssst," she said. "Stop questioning that. You can ask about anything else, Theo, but don't doubt for a second that we're getting out of here. Do you understand?"

He nodded twice, just like he had when he was ten and she'd told him he was going to live with her and they were going to be so happy together. "I understand."

"Good," she said, her voice dropping to a quieter tone. "Now tell me everything that's happened to you so far. Everything. Starting from how they found you."

His story turned out to be remarkably like hers. He'd been walking to practice and then there'd been four guys on him and a cloth over his face. He'd woken up sometime later in the Moss compound basement with the two wolf boys. There was a mad scientist—his words—and lots of bastards with cattle prods. He'd shifted only once and that had freaked him out so much that he'd slept on and off for the next two days. He'd even slept for most of the move from the farmhouse to here, though he suspected that was because they'd drugged his food.

He'd woken a few hours ago when they brought her in. He'd watched when they drew blood from her arm, and then he'd waited until they'd left to try to wake her. Which brought them up to now.

She suspected that he left a lot of the details out. She didn't know whether to be thankful or to push him for every last detail so she could figure things out. But that was silly. She wasn't James Bond or even Tonya the pissy cop. She was a human baker who wasn't going to martial arts her way out of this mess. She didn't have the skills.

All she could do was keep Theo calm and wait for their opportunity. Because one would come. It had to.

Hurry up, Carl. Find us!

CHAPTER 21

"Head to Walmart." Carl's voice was clipped as he thumbed in Alan's phone number.

Tonya shot him a baffled look. "You have a sudden need for Cheetos?"

He shook his head. "Becca's not answering her phone."

"Maybe she doesn't want to talk to you."

"The phone is *off*. And the last I knew, she was at Walmart."

"Maybe she turned off her...Right." Obviously Tonya had realized that the last thing Becca would do is turn off her phone. "So how do you know she's at Walmart?"

He shrugged, and she rolled her eyes.

"Creepy stalker app, right? And it showed her last location."

"I asked her permission before I installed it on her phone." He didn't bother watching for Tonya's reaction. Also, Alan came on the line.

Their conversation went fast. The man had no

idea where Becca was, but he'd head home right away just in case. Then Carl answered the unspoken question.

"We've got nothing new on Theo." Nothing but a whole lot of frustration and fury.

They made it to the mega store in twenty minutes. Another five to scan the area to look for his truck. And then a stop at the security office. Tonya didn't even have to show her badge, because everyone in the area knew who she was. Then it was a long, slow process watching the parking lot video, but eventually it paid off.

They saw her.

And they saw her abduction.

Carl went white hot with fury. Hell, he was a half breath away from going grizzly and smashing up the place, but Tonya kept him calm. She was staring at her phone and using the security office landline to dial, but she paused long enough to shoot him an almost gleeful look.

"We got 'em."

"What?"

She jerked her chin at the monitor. "They took your truck."

Yeah, he'd noticed. "I disabled the GPS tracker months ago."

She shot him a grin. "I know. That's when I put a real tracker on it."

"What?" He didn't know whether to be furious or gleeful.

"I'm the highest-ranking shifter cop in the area. You're my alpha. Of course I'm going to put a tracker on your truck."

He stared at her. "And you called an app creepy and stalkerlike."

She grinned. "Doesn't mean I think it's a bad idea." Then she tilted her phone toward him. "That's where your truck is."

His expression flattened and his nails lengthened into claws. "I'm going, too."

She knew better than to argue.

* * *

It turned out that being held prisoner was boring. Though Becca was relieved not to be threatened by armed guys with big guns, she discovered that hours of absolutely nothing happening was incredibly tedious. Especially since she couldn't stand up straight in her little cage. She hadn't realized until now just how much she moved in an average day.

Fortunately, the break gave her time to talk to Theo the way they never did at home. Call it making lemonade out of lemons, but part of her appreciated the time to really converse with her adopted son.

He finally opened up about feeling the bear underneath his skin. At first he called it a monster, but by hour three, he sounded like he might like being a grizzly. He asked a ton of questions about the Gladwins and Mr. Max. She answered as honestly as she could, even hinted at the growing fondness she had for the alpha, but didn't go into more detail. The last thing she wanted was to upset Theo, and who knew how he'd react to a new man in her life. Hell, she didn't even know how she felt about the man bear except to spend every other thought on a prayer that he found them soon.

So time passed. If they hadn't been locked in cages and afraid they were about to die, it might even have been pleasant.

Becca was just getting Theo to open up about a girl he liked. She'd suspected as much way back in September, when he couldn't mention his lab partner without blushing fiery red, but he'd said nothing about her since then. Finally, the kid was hinting at the edges of his interest. He wondered how much of his feelings—like for a girl, maybe—were the bear and how much just normal human stuff. Honestly, Becca had no clue, but she certainly wanted to know exactly what he was feeling and what he thought about it and all that stuff boys never ever articulated.

Which made her doubly pissed when the door suddenly burst open and in walked a gangly guy with Einstein hair. Theo's mad scientist, she presumed. His eyes were definitely a little wild as he glared at all three of his captives and started issuing orders. She wasn't sure at first who he was talking to until a middle-aged woman sauntered into the room. Her steps were gracefully fluid and she seemed to move with absolute precision. But it wasn't until Becca saw her catlike, slitted eyes that she gasped.

"They're awake. Tie them up or knock them out. I don't care, but we need them both," Crazy Einstein ordered.

So much for pretending to be asleep. She'd been so involved in listening to Theo that she forgot she was supposed to be playing possum.

"What about the dog?" asked the weird cat woman. Her voice even had a low kind of purr that was seriously freaky.

"He's nearly gone anyway. Leave him."

"No," cat woman said. "Kill him. The less anyone knows—"

"Whatever." Crazy Einstein plopped down a computer case he'd slung over his shoulder, then scared the hell out of Becca by bringing out a smaller case of syringes and vials. "How much can you carry? Do we knock them out?"

Becca's mind whirled, making deductions as fast as she was able to, given the clutching panic that was churning in her gut. All she could tell was that they were leaving and that these two were trying to figure out the best way to transport them. Which meant two things. First, Carl had found them. Second, her best hope was a delaying action, and for that, she had to stay conscious.

"We won't fight," she said in her most cowed-woman voice. "Please don't hurt us."

Cat woman's gaze cut to hers, the look hard and cold. "Unconscious."

So much for pretending to be docile. "Where are you taking us? What's going on?" She didn't expect any answers, but rolling off questions kept their attention on her rather than Theo, who was gripping the bars and looking like he was about to tear them both apart limb from limb. She wanted to tell him to cool it, but frankly, what other options did they have? It's not like she could fight worth a damn. The best she could do was distract them to give Theo time to do something.

Sadly, cat woman wasn't that stupid. She completely ignored Becca and glared at Theo. "Settle down or I'll put you down," she practically hissed.

"No, no," said Crazy Einstein as he looked between Theo and Becca. "This is most interesting. He's trying to shift to protect her. Most interesting, indeed."

That a boy would try to protect his mother? Any other deductions, Dr. Obvious? "Leave him alone!" she cried. "Look, you don't have to cage us. We want to understand this stuff as much as you do." It was a guess, but it made sense that Psychos 1 and 2 here were trying to figure out the science of shifting. "We'll cooperate. I promise." Where the hell was Carl?

Meanwhile, Crazy Einstein pulled out a hypodermic and filled it with something that was probably knockout juice. "Grab her arm," he said.

"No," cat woman growled. "The boy first."

Einstein snorted, his gaze cutting to the door, where two wide-eyed adolescents walked in, both carrying guns. One was a handgun, the other a dart gun. "That's for the boy."

Great. She'd seen the effect of those darts. Theo was about to be down for the count unless they did something now. And since Carl had been able to take a half dozen of those darts while in bear form, their only answer was to give Theo more mass.

"Shift now, Theo! Go nuts!"

She saw her son's beautiful hazel eyes connect with hers, and then she watched them turn a burnished gold. He let out a roar that started human but grew deeper and angrier with every second. She wanted to watch the transformation. That kind of thing never got old, and she especially wanted to see what kind of bear Theo would become, but she didn't have the luxury of time. She needed to know what else was going on.

Cat woman was baring her pointed teeth and letting out a hiss. Totally creepy. She seemed to be part animal all the time. The thugs were back on their heels, holding up their guns with shaking hands. Both of them started firing wildly, which was good for Theo specifically, but bad for everyone in the room. Bullets and darts started pinging about the small space and Crazy Einstein started screaming.

"Don't shoot! Don't shoot! We need him alive!"

Cat woman didn't bother with words. She simply sliced the handgun out of the thug's hand. At first Becca didn't understand what she'd seen. It was all blood and screaming. But then she saw cat woman's hand was really a paw with razor-sharp claws. She'd sliced right through the guy's wrist while grabbing hold of the gun with the other hand-paw when it dropped. Obviously she didn't care much for her henchmen's health.

Fortunately, Becca didn't have time to process it. Her opportunity had just presented itself. In his screaming, Crazy Einstein had backed up against her cage. He was ducking from the gunshots, the hypodermic still clutched in his hand. And he was not paying any attention to her.

She surged forward, reaching through the cage to grab the needle. Adrenaline made her fast. Mother protectiveness made sure she didn't hesitate. She flipped the syringe around and slammed it as hard as she could into his thigh. He screamed and jerked away, but not before she'd pushed the plunger down. Hopefully it was enough.

Crazy Einstein stumbled away from her, and then in a bizarre twist of fate, he suddenly got a dart in his shoulder. Becca spun to see the thug, doing her best to process the tableau. Best she could guess, dart gun guy had seen his comrade drop and was trying to aim at the cat woman who was really, really pissed off.

And then the pièce de résistance. From somewhere down the hall, there came a roar. A full-bellied grizzly battle cry that had Becca grinning from ear to ear. Finally, Carl had arrived! But her joy was short lived as gunfire erupted as well. Apparently, crazy doctor had more men defending him. But then there was a second roar, which was higher in pitch than the first and equally pissed. Tonya? She could only hope.

Those roars were the final straws for Thug 2. He threw the dart gun at cat woman and took off out the door. The bitch caught the gun easily and spun around to glare at her.

"I am not going easily," Becca said. Neither was Theo, who was a cramped, pissed-off bear in his cage, tearing at the bars. One glance told her it wouldn't take him long to break free. Especially since none of the tranquilizer darts had ended up in him.

Cat woman didn't answer in words, but if looks could kill, Becca would be dead on the spot. Instead, she squatted down and grabbed drooling Crazy Einstein. It was impressive how easily she slung the man over her shoulder and still had the dexterity to grab the computer bag. Damn it, they were getting away. Becca had to try to delay them.

"You won't get away with this. We'll find you. What the hell are you anyway?"

On a TV show, she'd say something vital. She might even pause long enough for Carl to get here. But this woman was smarter than that. Beyond that first angry glare, she didn't give Becca a second glance. She was off and sprinting in the opposite direction and out the far door. Smart bitch, because at that moment, Theo finally broke through his cage. He burst out with a kind of gleeful rumble that turned into a yip as one of the bars tore through his shoulder.

"Slow down, Theo," she said. "They're gone."

Theo wasn't listening. His head had swung toward cat woman and his nose twitched. She could tell he wanted to chase the villains, but it was too dangerous. Cat woman had both guns, and who knew how many other men were waiting to shoot?

"You're fine. Stay here. I need you here."

Theo paused, his nose drawing him one way, his mind pulling him the other. She wasn't sure what he was going to do, but then the noise from the other direction grew exponentially louder. Suddenly more guys with guns burst in from the near door, and these guys looked coordinated. They had a leader barking orders and three others following in a clear retreat. Which would have been fine except Theo was standing there in full grizzly form.

The first guy pulled up with a gasp. The others flanked out and two of them aimed their weapons.

There was no time to react. Theo didn't have more than a split second to rear up. And in that frozen moment, she realized he was about to die. These guys were going to shoot.

She screamed. It was all she could do.

CHAPTER 22

Usually the waiting is the worst part. Carl had had to wait during the drive to an abandoned salt mine near Saginaw. That had been hard enough, but once they'd seen his truck parked near the opening, Tonya had tried to make him wait while local law enforcement mobilized. This was out of her jurisdiction and she—appropriately—didn't want to rush blindly into an underground facility. He'd nodded and told her she had ten minutes to cover the legalities and whatnot. Then while she was on the phone, he'd started "reconnaissance," checking things out as stealthily as he could.

He hadn't been stealthy enough. In his defense, there weren't a lot of places to hide in a salt mine. Plus the place was supposed to be abandoned. Twenty yards inside the opening, he was confronted by a paramilitary guy with an automatic weapon. Questions were asked. Vague answers given. And then a gun was raised.

Oops. But at least it had given him the excuse to proceed more boldly.

He'd knocked the man unconscious and rushed farther down the huge space. Five minutes later he'd smelled her. Becca. He knew her scent and the spike of her fear. Which is when he'd started running. She was here and he would find her. *Now.*

He didn't remember shifting to his grizzly form. For the first time ever, he and his bear were completely unified. The grizzly form was faster and could cover more ground in this massive place, not to mention it had the better nose. All he had to do was follow Becca's scent as it grew stronger and louder in his mind.

And then he'd heard her cry out, the words indistinct.

He'd roared in response and tore faster through the shaft, only to be met by more guys with guns. He was lucky. They were shit shots. Or they just hadn't expected a furious grizzly to tear through their ranks. Either way, he'd made mincemeat out of them. It helped that Tonya had joined him a few breaths later, adding confusion and more noise to the mix.

But it had cost him time. And a few bullet hits to his arms.

That's when he learned the worst part of a battle wasn't the waiting. It was the certain knowledge that he was too slow, too far, and too late to stop whatever was happening to Becca.

He knew she was close, but there were all these bastards in between him and her. He could hear her yelling and there might have been gunshots. He redoubled his fury until there were just four guys left. Then they did an organized retreat toward a door. A second later, he heard her scream, this time in terror, while he was still yards away.

He took off. She was there. She was in danger. And when he rounded the corner, he saw the worst sight of his life.

Becca in a cage, screaming for her life.

A young grizzly standing tall before her, his battle cry aimed at the guys with guns. Big target there. No way the bastards would miss. Carl did the only thing he could. He roared his own challenge, trying to startle the shooters, but they were too well trained.

Two spun to face him. Two fired at the kid.

And all the while, Becca was screaming.

Carl charged, knocking the two nearest him aside like they were bowling pins. The other two had taken down the young bear and were now scrambling over the body, where it had crashed against a cage with an unconscious werewolf in it. He smelled the acrid scent of blood and wondered how much of it was his own, how much the youth's.

Then he made it to Becca's cage and ripped at it with all the strength in his claws. She was screaming something, but it was hard to understand the words. He had to get to her. He had to make her safe.

Fortunately, the two shooters had made it over the young and out a far door. They'd run like rabbits and were no longer a threat. The bowling pins were still unconscious. That left this cage his only obstacle. Just the bars that separated her from him.

He decimated them.

She scrambled out as soon as he'd cleared the room. Her words were making sense now. She was repeating the youth's name over and over.

"Theo. Theo."

She touched Carl as she moved past, using him to scramble out. And as she went, he made sure she was whole. No blood. No pain scent. Just the fear for her child. That soothed him as nothing else could. She was safe. Now it was time to save the youth.

He saw immediately what had happened. The youth wasn't dead, thank God. He had taken bullet wounds to the shoulder and arm. The bear needed to become boy, but that wasn't always easy for kids. Especially not in high stress situations. Like after getting shot. The bear was coming back to consciousness, thrashing in his pain. Carl kept an eye on Becca to make sure she didn't get too close.

"You have to be human, Theo," Carl said, his voice taking the sharp bark of command. "Turn back into you."

When had he shifted into a man? Once again, the change had been seamless. This form was easiest for communication, so he became a man. The other form was no longer expedient.

"Stay back, Becca," he ordered. "The last thing we need is another patient."

"He's been shot," she said, a near hysterical edge to her voice. She had to get that under control now, so he looked at her calmly.

"He'll be fine if he turns human. The shots will fade." Well, the arm one would. He wasn't so sure about the shoulder. But a human boy would be easier to control and certainly easier to haul into the nearest ER.

Becca nodded, then pulled herself upright. "Theodore Weitz, you turn human this instant!"

A good try, as the youth's eyes shifted, focusing on Becca. It's possible the rational was gaining control, but it was hard to tell. All they could do was keep talking and hope that they reached the human mind underneath the immediate pain.

"Remember what it's like to be a boy, Theo," he ordered. "Eating cheeseburgers and skateboarding."

"Video games," Becca chimed in. "Playing Warcraft with Tom and Willy."

"Come on, Theo!" Carl barked. "We've got pie at home. Picture yourself sitting and eating it. With ice cream. Think of the cold, wet sweetness of it all." Food had always been a great way for him to mentally shift back to human. At least when he was that age. And where the mind went, the body usually followed.

"That's not the way to do it," a female voice said from behind them. Tonya's voice was dry as she stepped past the sprawled bodies and waved Carl aside.

"Tonya," he said. "He's been shot. We need medical—"

"Theo!" she interrupted. "Look at me! Look at me *right now*!"

Theo did. His grizzly eyes swerved and then focused on her. Carl watched the young bear's eyes widen and his ears go back. And then suddenly, the snout started shrinking and the fur started receding. Becca gasped and murmured, "Thank God," but that was all she managed. No one wanted to interrupt the shift back to human.

A moment later, Carl heard two dull pings as the bullets slid from the grizzly onto the floor. Soon afterward, there was only a naked adolescent boy cringing at a seeping wound in his shoulder.

"I've got you," Becca said as she rushed forward. "You're safe now."

He was, though damned if he knew how Tonya had done it. He turned to ask and only then realized she was smirking. Well, he realized she was *naked* and smirking.

"You have to give him a real reason to be human," she said. Then she gestured to her body. "This is what motivates teenage boys."

He couldn't argue with her there. He also knew that Tonya was absolutely, completely *not* the woman for him, because his only thought was for Becca. He barely even noticed Tonya's nudity.

"Let's get out of here," he said. "Who knows how many others might still be hanging around?"

"We can't leave Caleb," Theo said, looking down at the cage he'd been sprawling on. Inside was the unconscious werewolf boy.

"Police are on their way," Tonya said. "We can hole up here until they arrive." Then she glanced at Carl. "I'll get your clothes."

"Get yours, too."

"You sure?"

"Yes," answered all three of them at once. Which is the exact moment that he finally caught Becca's eye. She was pale and shaky, but he saw strength in her as she tried not to fuss over her boy.

"You okay?" she asked him.

"Only if you are."

"Yup."

"Then I'm fine."

"How many times did you get shot?"

He frowned and tried to take stock. Now that he focused, he could feel the raw burn of pain across one thigh and another high in his belly. Oh, hell. That was going to suck. The thing with shifting back to human is that sometimes the wound healed with the bullet inside. Fortunately, they knew a surgeon who was clued in to the whole shifter world. He'd take care of it.

"I'll be fine."

"That's not what I asked."

He grinned. He loved it when she used that snippy tone. "I'll be in the bed right next to Theo. I promise. So long as you're on my other side." He still wasn't sure she was okay. There might be hidden injuries.

"All he did was take blood from me."

"He might have done something else—"

She raised her hand to stop him. "I promise to get checked out anyway."

"Good."

She smiled. "Good."

Then Theo grumbled at them both. "When were you going to tell me you two are dating?"

"Um...," began Becca.

"Oh, look," Carl said, his voice a little too cheerful. "Here comes Tonya with my clothes."

"Don't rush on my account," murmured Becca. He looked at her, startled by her frankly appreciative gaze. Then he felt himself flush hot red, but that was nothing compared to the color she turned when Theo groaned.

"Gross, Aunt Becca! Don't put images in my head!"

CHAPTER 23

Five days! Five days until they could assemble the surgical team to pull the bullets out of Carl. Becca was fuming at the wait, but right here was one of the problems with maintaining shifter secrecy. It didn't matter that Carl had three bullets hanging out in his torso. He wasn't dying—not quickly—so they had to wait until a shifter team could be assembled to dig them out without asking awkward questions. That meant coordinating a surgeon from Ann Arbor, an anesthesiologist from Detroit, and two nurses from Grand Rapids.

Infuriating. But at least she could use the time to learn more about the Gladwin community with Theo. What she discovered was not at all what she expected.

First, she learned that gossip ran fast through shifters. Tight-knit communities meant that word spread like lightning about Carl's heroics in saving her. Within a day, Carl's home was bursting with cards and gifts of specialty honey as each member of the Gladwin clan pledged loyalty in one way or another. Many promised new clan gifts, goods and services that needed to be organized in a complicated bartering system. Alan was overwhelmed just responding to the communications, so Becca stepped in to maintain the filing. It was the only thing that kept her from constantly touching Theo just to reassure herself he was alive.

That was the second thing she realized. Theo loved being a bear shifter. What boy wouldn't love eating everything in sight and having an entirely new group of rumble, tumble boys to bond with? Turned out there was a whole welcoming process after a First Change. As the two new shifters this season, Theo and Justin spent almost all their time together, talking shifter stories with the other teens, playing Halo to all hours, and eating whatever they wanted. School and homework would loom soon, but Becca decided this was more important, and her decision seemed justified as her boy grew stronger and happier with every passing second.

The third thing she noticed was that Carl was avoiding her. At first, it was just the business of being the alpha that kept him away. That and the fact that he slept for nearly three days. He'd told her that bears couldn't shift more than once in twenty-four hours. She'd assumed that meant they could change once a day without ill effects. Turns out she was dead wrong.

Most grizzlies couldn't shift more than once a week. Carl had done it three times in four days, fought in a challenge to the death, and gotten shot with bullets and tranquilizing darts. No wonder the Gladwins suddenly thought he was powerful enough to face down the Detroit gangs. And no wonder that when the doctor knocked him unconscious, he stayed under for three days.

But once he woke up, there was a backlog of work. He called other alphas, studied the police reports, organized the search for the missing Crazy Einstein and his cat-eyed companion, plus welcomed two new shifters into the Gladwin fold. That was the other part of the welcome process: a week closeted with the alpha as the newly changed learned what it meant to be a Gladwin grizzly. Becca asked Theo what they talked about and was told that it was shifter stuff and not for her.

Ouch.

And that was another thing she learned. No matter how much the locals welcomed her as Theo's parent, no matter how much her own fame had built as the woman who kept the boys alive until Carl could rescue them, she was still fully human and therefore not quite one of the Gladwins. It didn't bother her. She didn't need to get long nosed and hairy to feel whole. She knew her own value and couldn't care less what the others thought of her. So long as Theo was healthy and happy, all was right with her world.

Except that she could tell it bothered Carl. He overheard Theo's comment about it being "shifter stuff" and gave her son such a lecture that even Becca's ears felt blistered. Anyone who even looked askance at her was treated to an icy stare, so people started treating her like royalty. It was weird and had to stop. But every time she went to talk to him, he was busy. And since she'd never been one to force herself on someone who didn't want her, she let him be. But she sure as hell felt lonely when he slept in the dormitory with Theo and the other kids.

Conclusion: their romance had been a crisis management thing and not a real love affair. At least on Carl's side.

So Becca began to make plans to return to her life in Kalamazoo. She meant to help past Carl's convalescence, but Theo's schoolwork hit its own crisis. He'd missed so much that he really needed to get back. She'd wondered if they should leave earlier, but then Carl took the decision away from her. He arranged for Mark to take them home right after the surgery.

And so it was. Becca, Theo, and Alan watched from the viewing platform as they pulled bullets out of Carl. She was with him when he woke from the anesthetic, his shifter metabolism sealing things up nice and tight. He might not even have a scar after his next shift. She wanted to stay, feeling like events were running away from her, but Mark was waiting, Theo had to get to school, and Carl gave her no reason to stay. In fact, the last thing he said to her was that he'd miss her and that she wasn't pregnant. Apparently, he could smell a pregnancy and she hadn't conceived. So that was it. A second later, he'd turned to Alan, asking for an update on the cat shifter research.

So she left. His words had been the death knell to all her romantic thoughts of the two of them living happily ever after.

Once home, it was unnerving how quickly she and Theo picked up the rhythm of their days. He had to study his ass off to catch up, and she had to decorate cakes night and day for a week. Thanks to Stacy, she still had a bakery to come back to, and for that, she made the woman partner as soon as Stacy got the buy-in cash together. In fact, everything was exactly like it had been before this all began. Except Theo was ten times happier and she was a hundred times more furious.

How dare Carl just toss her away like she meant nothing to him? What they'd shared had been real. And he needed her, damn it! Who was going to help him express all those bottled-up emotions, if not her? And how was she going to face her boring, mundane life without the magic of him and his world? Every time she thought about what he was throwing away, the more pissed off she got.

But what exactly was she going to do about it?

Two weeks later, she figured out an answer. She set it in motion the very next day, but it would take weeks if not months to come to fruition. Plus, Theo was just getting his feet under him again academically. Becca couldn't make major changes until the school year ended. But oh, the wait burned. As did the increasing silence from the Stupid Beast formerly known as Carl. The guy hadn't even emailed her! Though in his defense, she didn't email him either. What would she say? You're an idiot? Why don't you love me? None of those would work, so she focused on making summer plans.

Which put her right back where she was at the very beginning of this adventure: in the workroom of her bakery making cakes while silently fretting.

What was that saying? The more things changed, the more they stayed the same.

She carefully finished writing "Happy Birthday, Jenna" on a cake, then set it aside to focus on her newest cake sensation. Oddly enough, it seemed to be a favorite among boys as well as girls, so that was a plus. If only a certain grizzly someone would look at the damned thing and understand what it meant.

She heard the shop door jingle. A frequent sound these days thanks to a promotion Stacy had put into effect in Becca's absence. Who knew a single radio ad could bring in so much money? She heard Stacy greet the customer, so she focused instead on fashioning the fighting figures decorating the top of the cake in front of her. This one used Cinderella's castle as a backdrop for the main action and—added bonus—required a ton less construction.

And then her back started to prickle with awareness. She froze, her mind scrambling to prepare for who she hoped she see if she just turned around.

"Um, hello, Becca. Do you, uh...do you have a minute?"

Carl. Finally.

She slowly straightened and turned to look. How many times had she imagined this moment? In her mind's eye, she'd pictured him looking everything from completely haggard because he missed her so much to dressed to the nines in a tuxedo and carrying a dozen roses. But she hadn't pictured him in an ill-fitting suit and carrying a briefcase. He looked almost lawyerlike.

"Carl," she said, hating that her voice came out

almost as a purr. Even rumpled and awkward, he still rang all her bells. "Or should I call you Mr. Max?"

His eyes widened and then narrowed in consternation. "You can call me anything you want, Becca." Then he hesitated a moment. "Unless you'd prefer Ms. Weitz?"

"Becca is fine." She leaned back against her worktable, taking the time to study him closely. He seemed tired and wary, but otherwise fine. As far as she could tell, he moved smoothly and, aside from appearing nervous, he looked healthy enough. But she still had to ask. "How are you feeling? Is everything okay?"

"Fully recovered and, yes, everything's fine. Better than ever, actually, though we haven't found..." He swallowed, clearly wondering if he should mention the whole ordeal or not.

"The bad guys," she supplied.

"Right. The bad guys." He tugged at his beard. "How's Theo doing? I heard he got an A on his geometry test."

"Amy still keeping an eye on him for you?"

He flushed. "No, I haven't talked to her in weeks. Theo emailed me. He's excited about the scholarship we've got set up for Gladwins who get into college. Wants me to know he's getting top grades."

"He is. And I'm grateful for the extra incentive."

"Anything to help." Then he stood there in the doorway, hunched and uncomfortable. An evil part of her wanted to make him stand there longer, punishment for how tortured she'd felt earlier. But a larger part wanted him in her life, so she was quick to pull out a stool for him.

"Come on in, Carl. Take a load off. I heard you've been shot a few dozen times. Probably takes its toll and you could use a rest."

"I'm not decrepit yet," he shot back. But he did take a few steps into her workroom and then carefully settled down on a stool.

"Touchy, touchy alpha," she teased, hoping they could recover their earlier sense of banter. More than anything else, she missed their easy communication.

He snorted. "You have no idea. Since everyone is suddenly convinced of my grizzly power, I've had nursing from women throughout the state. They just show up to 'help me get back on my feet.' Like I'm in a wheelchair or something."

Was that why he hadn't contacted her? Because more eligible shifter women were claiming his attention? The idea made her hands clench as she imagined tossing each hussy across the border. The United States/Mexico border.

"I've been shoving them at Alan, hoping he'll look at someone other than Tonya."

Well, that thought brightened her mood considerably. "Is it working?"

Carl shrugged. "Not that I can see. I think he's given up on the shifter community altogether. He probably wants a nice human girl to warm him at night."

Oh. Didn't that just draw the line clear and dark between shifters and humans? All her hopes started to wither inside her. With a sigh, she looked back at her half-finished cake but didn't move to start working again. "Is there something you wanted, Carl?"

Given the briefcase, there could be all sorts of police, legal, or other crap to deal with, none of it remotely interesting to her.

"Y-yeah. There is."

She looked up. Stammering wasn't his usual style. A bolt of alarm shot through her and the words tumbled out of her before she could stop and think. "Is Theo in danger? Are they coming back? What aren't you telling me?"

He reached out, his large palm stroking her forearm in a gentle press. "Theo's fine. I've got people nearby if needed, but honestly he's learning to use his shifter senses. He won't be taken easily ever again."

She nodded. That's what she told herself every night when she woke up sweating with terror. "I'd still feel better if we were closer to the main fold," she grumbled.

He jolted, his hand squeezing then lifting off her to hover uncertainly an inch above her arm. "You'd consider that?"

"Of course I'd consider that," she snapped, annoyed at him for being so thick-headed. "Theo has to learn about his father's family," she said. "Sure, he's already planning on spending the entire summer up there, but I'd be crazy not to consider moving to Gladwin permanently. He says he feels the draw even now and wants to roam around in a forest. As a bear. That isn't exactly safe in Kalamazoo. So of course I'm thinking about moving. You've got to have a sane way of doing that up there."

"We did. My mom used to organize monthly bear

parties. Kind of like big picnics that are managed for everyone's safety. We ought to do those again."

She looked at him. That almost sounded like fun. "Yeah, you should."

"I will. And you and Theo would be welcome. Only a small percentage shift. It's a time for the whole community to get together. And I'd really like it if you were there."

She studied his face. He appeared earnest. More than that, she thought she saw a quiet yearning in his eyes. An echo of the desperation she'd once seen in his bear's eyes. Lonely hunger held back for her sake.

It was the "held back" that pissed her off. Damn it, she was done with sitting on tenterhooks. She was tired of waiting for him to get off his ass. He'd shown her that she could handle herself in front of motorcycle-riding killers and mad scientists. She'd be damned if she let one stupid bear alpha make her insane.

"Damn it, Carl, I wish you'd just get to the point. Why are you here?"

His eyes widened and he fumbled on his stool. Not surprising, given that his seat was narrow and half covered in flour. But she hadn't expected her frustrated question to have him falling onto the floor.

Her first thought was that he was having a spasm. Some sort of carryover from the surgery or maybe lead poisoning from the bullet that had been hanging out inside him. But while she was scrambling for her phone to call 911, he grabbed hold of her wrist and held her in place.

"Becca—" he began, but she talked right over him.

"Take deep breaths. I'm right here with you. You'll be fine. Stacy, call an ambulance!"

"Don't call, Stacy. I'm fine!" he shouted as he re-arranged himself on the floor. He ended up on one knee while he pulled something out of his suit jacket with one hand. His other hand was firmly gripped around her wrist.

"Where does it hurt?" she asked. "Are they sure they got all the bullets out? Maybe they missed one."

"I'm fine! Damn it, Becca, shut up!"

She pulled back, but he didn't let her move far. "What's going on?"

"I'm trying to tell you why I'm here."

"But you fell down!"

"I went onto one knee! I'm trying to propose!"

It took her three replays in her brain before the words finally shifted into meaning. It helped that he flipped open a ring box to show her a diamond ring fashioned in an odd setting. It was like a Claddagh, but instead of two hands gripping a heart, one clawed paw and one human hand clasped a heart-shaped diamond beneath a crown of gold.

"Oh my God," she whispered.

"This ring has been worn by all Maximas for generations."

"It's beautiful," she murmured.

He stretched it closer to her. "Becca Weitz, I can't live without you. I love you. Will you marry me and live in Gladwin with me forever? I know it's a lot to ask. That's why I took so long. I wanted you to remember your life here, to know what you'd have to give up. I could stop being Max if you want, but

I'd rather not. Not if you think you might be able to stand it out in the country. Or at least give it a try. I want you with me there. I want to wake up beside you every morning. I want our children raised next to the forest I love. I want to be with you when I really am decrepit and have to hand over the leadership to someone I trust. Will you give it a try, Becca? Will you marry me?"

She stared at him, her eyes misting with tears. Of all the things she'd expected from him, this wasn't it. A proposal? After he'd been silent for weeks?

"Is that really why you came here today?"

"Yes!"

"So why the suit and briefcase?"

"What?" He blinked and looked down at the case. "Oh. I had to meet with the Kalamazoo police about Theo's disappearance. And I've got papers for Theo to see. It's a copy of Isaac's will. He's rewritten it to include Theo as his grandchild. Plus some other stuff about his father, if he wants to see it."

Becca blinked, struggling to sort out the ramifications of his words. Mostly she decided she didn't care, though she managed a simple, "Oh. Okay."

Carl nodded. "Great. So, um, that's good. But what about the other thing? The marriage thing?"

The marriage thing? Wow, talk about being bad at proposing.

She leaned forward, touching his face with one hand. "Carl, would you please look around you at the cakes I've made?"

He frowned. "What?"

She gently pushed his face to the side so he could see the row of finished confections. "A month ago, all I did was build castles to surround a princess. Big walls, towers of defense against the world of hard knocks. I needed a prince to tear down those walls. I needed someone to drag me out into the world and show me that I could be out there. I could make a difference."

"Um, okay." Clearly the man wasn't getting the message.

"What do you see now?"

"I see Beauty and the Beast outside the castle kicking ass. And let me tell you, Beauty looks pretty hot there with your eyes and hair, not to mention the leather ninja gear."

"Leather ninja...Oh, right. That's Donny's cake."

"Donny's got good taste."

She grinned and gently pulled his gaze back to hers. "You tore down my walls, Carl. You showed me that I could not only kick ass out there, but do it safely by your side. I don't need a castle anymore. I just need you."

"You do?"

"I do. I love you. And if you hadn't proposed to me, I was planning to drive up next weekend, drag you out of your cave, and make you propose."

"You were?"

"I was."

"Damn. I wish I'd waited. That would have been fun."

"Shut up. I still haven't answered you."

He sobered immediately.

"Mr. Max—Carl Carman—it would be my greatest honor and pleasure to marry you—"

She would have said more. She would have told

him how much she loved him, but she didn't get the chance. He was kissing her and she was wrapping herself around him. Later, she'd tell him about the property she was in the process of buying. The store-front perfect for a new bakery right on the main street of downtown Gladwin. She'd explain that Stacy was going to take over the Kalamazoo place while she and Theo relocated up north with him. She'd already checked out the school system and set up a schedule for moving her life north. She just hadn't expected that she would be moving into his home rather than an apartment nearby.

She'd tell him all those things later. Right now, all she wanted to do was kiss him. And a whole lot more. For the rest of their lives.

"You can't know how very much I love you," Carl said when they separated enough to breathe. "I've been going crazy trying to figure out a way to force you into my life."

"All you had to do was ask."

He winced. "I'm such an idiot."

She laughed and pressed her mouth to his again. "That's okay," she said a few thousand kisses later. "I love you all the more for it."

"Not nearly as much as I love you."

BEAR MEETS GIRL...

Julie Simon returns to Saginaw, Michigan, to find her ailing father's missing research on local shapeshifter lore. Unlucky for her, the only person who can help her is the darkly sexy Mark Robertson, the guy who spent an entire summer giving her the cold shoulder—and one white-hot night of pleasure...

Mark is a hair's breadth away from going feral. Soon, his grizzly side will destroy everything that makes him a man. And after years of fighting, Mark is ready to give in to the beast. Then Julie—the gorgeous, curvy book nerd who awakened his most primal desires as a young man—shows up at his door. Now, he's fighting an insatiable longing to claim her as his mate. But Julie isn't the only one after her father's research. Someone—or something—evil is tracking Julie's every move...

Don't miss the next book in the
Grizzlies Gone Wild series

LICENSE TO SHIFT

Available now

ABOUT THE AUTHOR

Kathy Lyons is the wild, adventurous half of *USA Today* bestselling author Jade Lee. A lover of all things fantastical, Kathy spent much of her childhood in Narnia, Middle Earth, Amber, and Earthsea, just to name a few. There is nothing she adores more than turning an ordinary day into something magical, which is what happens all the time in her books. Winner of several industry awards, including the Prism Best of the Best Award, a *Romantic Times* Reviewers' Choice Award, and Fresh Fiction's Steamiest Read, Kathy has published more than fifty romance novels, and she's just getting started.

Check out her latest news at:
    KathyLyons.com
    Facebook.com/KathyLyonsBooks
    Twitter: @KathyLyonsAuth

Looking for more romantic suspense?
Forever brings the action with these alpha males!

DREAM MAKER
by Kristen Ashley

After years of being responsible for her family, Evan "Evie" Gardiner is pursuing her own dreams of an engineering degree. Working as a dancer seems like the perfect way to pay for tuition...until her family lands in yet another scrape—a deadly one. Since Daniel "Mag" Magnusson knows a thing or two about desperation and disappointment, he insists on offering Evie his protection. He has the skills to guard Evie's life, but as they grow closer, he'll need to come face-to-face with his demons in order to protect her heart.

Follow @ReadForeverPub on Twitter and join the conversation using #ReadForever.

FATAL DECEPTION
by April Hunt

When criminals break into Isabel Santiago's lab and steal a deadly virus, she's desperate to find the culprits before they turn her research into a weapon. But first she must put her trust in the brooding security expert who sees danger around every corner. As she and Roman race to track down the culprits, these two unlikely partners find there's more at stake for them than they ever imagined possible—but only if they stop the enemy in time.

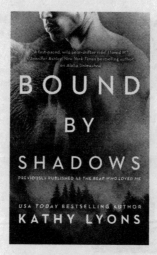

BOUND BY SHADOWS
by Kathy Lyons

As the leader of his clan, Carl Carman is surrounded by enemies. He's learned the hard way that keeping a firm leash on his inner beast is the key to survival, though his feelings for baker Becca Weitz test his legendary control. When danger stalks too close, Carl realizes he must unleash the raging, primal force within to protect everything he holds dear. But can Becca trust his grizzly side with her life—and her heart?